Somewhere
Out There

With special thanks to the following people:

Thanks as always to my family for their love and support through my writing career so far. You're always very encouraging and I'm very grateful for that.

My very good friend, Marie (Molls) thank you for your help, and especially with all of the research questions I had for you. I know I drove you demented, but that's what friends are for, right?!

Thanks to my friends old and new, who continue to encourage me and keep me sane when I spend so much time in front of a computer. I feel lucky to have such good friends both at home in Ireland and here in the UK. This one is for you.

Thanks to Sheryl Lee, Editor, who is an absolute professional from the start to the finish line. It was a pleasure working with you and thank you for your hard work.

Amy Queau, the talented woman who designed my book cover. Thank you for the beautiful cover and for your patience while I was being so fussy with the changes!

Thank you to the CreateSpace Team for helping me with the finishing touches. It's always a pleasure working with you.

To my lovely friend, Aziza Azul, a talented photographer and designer, who provided me with the portrait for the book. Thank you!

Finally, thank you to all of my readers. If it wasn't for all of you, I wouldn't have written my second novel. You drive me to continue doing what I love doing, with your encouraging comments. Thank you so much!!

I hope you enjoy Somewhere Out There.

Happy reading...

1

I stare at Laura, gobsmacked at what she has just said.

"You're kidding, right? He's 5'5"! He's too small. Nah! Look I'm done with it all now I think," I say calmly.

I place my dessert spoon in the bowl as I finish the last bite of apple pie. I look around the restaurant, noticing that everyone seems too busy chatting to have heard any of our conversation. Laura sighs and takes a sip of her wine. She brushes some imaginary crumbs off the tablecloth and pushes her plate to one side.

"You're done? You haven't even tried starting, what's wrong with you? There are five hundred men queuing up to go out with you!" Laura shouts. "Are you crazy?"

"Well now that you mention it, maybe I am and that's why I can't find anyone," I say with a smile.

"Don't start now, I'm warning you," Laura replies grinning.

"Look, you know as well as I know there's no one in this big city for me. It's full of gobshites who are all the same. I've had a few dates and I'm not going there again. They are all a bunch of muppets."

Laura giggles. "You do make me laugh," she says. "It's true, I guess they are, but there has to be one good one left for you. Maybe you're just not ready to meet him yet, darling."

"Oh I don't know. I really do give up. Look I have to get back to work, as my boss will hunt me down if I don't have a report ready by the three pm meeting."

"Alright, off you go, but don't give up. I'll be very disappointed in you if you do," Laura says to me as I brush my clothes free of the crumbs that have fallen into my lap.

"You and every other female friend I have, my dear," I say with a smile. "See you soon," I add as I kiss her on the cheek and walk through the restaurant.

Sure, the men are gawping at me like they've never seen a female before, and that's exactly what I hate. It's like they don't care that I can see them stare like primates at me. Someday, I know one of them will start making monkey or gorilla mating call noises and that's the day I'll lock myself in my office and never come out again.

I stroll back to work and it's a very pleasant day in terms of October weather. It's not raining for a change, nor is it windy. I still carry my umbrella and sunglasses in my bag all year around though, just in case.

— —

"Hey Katie, have you that report ready, please? I wouldn't mind reading it over before the meeting," Joe says.

"Joe, I'm just in the door from my lunch, can I at least get to my office, maybe make a cup of coffee, and I'll have the report to you for the three pm meeting, as requested?" I ask.

I don't leave him away with anything. I've taken too much crap from people in the past so they are afraid of me now as I always stand up to them. Joe is actually quite a sweetie in terms of bosses. He's a gentle giant and I can tell he's afraid of me at times. It's just the way to have him. A no messing, no nonsense woman is exactly what they need in this office.

Working in the finance sector was never what I wanted. When I left school I wanted to be a psychologist, but didn't get enough points to get into the course in University. Instead, I made the bad decision to take the accounting option. Sure, I've earned buckets of money, but the lack of humour in most of my colleagues just kills me.

I glance over to the office across the way. I spy Paul Douglas, who is the most boring fecker you'll ever meet. He laughs constantly at his own jokes, and by the time he finishes them, they aren't funny anymore. His wife is just as dull and boring. In fact, they make a great couple. They have two kids, who from what I've seen, never smile. I expect it's due to having to listen to their father's jokes. They are probably on the brink of running away from home, or worse.

I jump as my phone rings.

"Hi, it's me again," Laura says.

"Laura, I can tell you're excited. It's not another blind date I hope. I have work to do here and haven't got time for this."

"Look, it is, but he's lovely. He's a colleague of David's - tall, well built, quite Darcy-esque, and I know how much you fancy a bit of Mr. Darcy," she says with a peal of laughter.

"Yes, I admit that. Perhaps this time you've got my attention, and if you get it right I'll owe you." I say, trying not to get too excited.

"Ha ha, I knew that would work! Seriously, this guy is very cute Katie, hot even. You'll definitely like him."

"Oh go on then, I'm in. When are you trying to arrange this one for?" I ask.

"I think the sooner the better, so are you free tomorrow?"

"What? He'll think I'm desperate if you arrange it that soon." I exclaim.

"No, he won't, come on Katie, don't go all shy and start freaking out before a date, like you normally do, please? He's just a person, a lovely person."

I sigh, "Ok, ok, the things I do to keep you happy."

"You won't regret this," she says with a squeal of joy. "Stop hanging about now, you've got a report to finish, remember?"

"Aye aye, Captain! Bossy bitch!" I say with a snigger.

"Ha ha ha, bye.'

"Bye, bye, bye, bye, bye."

"Ha ha, I do love when you say goodbye five or six times, such an Irish thing and so cute," she says.

"Yeah, yeah, go before I start swearing at you," I say.

"Ok I'm gone, I'll call you later once I have details of the date," she says with an air of excitement.

I hang up. Funny how all of my friends seem far more excited about the dates I go on than I do.

Right! Back to the report before boss man has a hissy fit, especially if I only give it to him at the beginning of the meeting. I need to have it ready beforehand to be some bit fair to him.

Thankfully everything goes without a hitch and as home time approaches I feel more than ready to make my way via Tower Bridge towards the South Bank. A little detour for exercise is always nice, and I get to soak up the atmosphere. My phone rings.

"Darling, it's me again, we've had an even better idea. As I know you'll get all sweaty and freaked out over it being a date, I've decided we'll have a dinner party on Saturday night and we'll invite a few people so as not to make it look like we are trying to set you up. How does that sound to you? You can bring one of the girls with you too, just in case you get bored with the company as some of David's friends can be quite mind-numbing at times. They talk a great deal of politics and I know you're not too interested in spending the night talking shite, as you say."

"Ha ha! How well you know me. Yes indeed, Laura, I do hate talking shite. I much prefer to talk about shoes and nice fun girlie things and not all these bad news stories or politics. It's just not me. This sounds like a better plan, just please don't put me sitting next to some old git who's going to start a conversation about the stock exchange. I don't do work convos at the weekend."

"Ok, I'll make sure to let the old git know, and of course I'll put you sitting next to him," she trails off into laughter. "Great, got to go again darling, do let me know who's going to attend with you, I'll be putting name places on the table."

Oh for feck sake! It's not a wedding I'm attending.

"Will do, Laura, thanks for the invite. Talk soon."

Ok, who can I bring? Who won't cry with boredom? Maybe Sarah, she's always a good bet and can keep any conversation going even at a boring dinner party.

Rather than putting my phone away, I decide to call Sarah and see if she'd be on for one of Laura's extravagant dinner parties.

Sarah answers promptly, and is curious about the invitation. "Laura, have I met her? Is she the one who sounds like she's got something stuck up her arse which makes her voice sound like she's in pain?"

"Erm, yep, that would be the one. Ah, Sarah, she's lovely, and you only met her briefly that time, you didn't even get to talk to her. Give her a chance and don't be so judgemental of her."

"Ok, but if there's no talent there and it's full of old posh farts, I'm out the gap."

"Ok, ok. It's Saturday night. I'll call to you on the way and we can take the tube together. We can take a walk in along the South Bank and leave from London Bridge, how does that sound?" I ask.

"Sure, where is it we are going exactly?"

"St. John's Wood."

"Oh, lovely area Ah yeah, she sounded fairly posh to me alright."

"She's not really yeah she has money and sounds posh, but honestly she's very down to earth. I think you'll like her and I'm hoping there might be a bit of talent there. Right, I'm going, talk soon."

"Yep catch you later, thanks for the invite."

I'm definitely not telling you she's trying to set me up with someone. I know you'd tell everyone, including the guy she's trying to set me up with, the minute you enter the house.

Saturday:

I push the doorbell and Sarah opens the door.

"Hello, hello. Wow, you look very pretty. Is there someone special going tonight that I don't know about?" Sarah asks.

"I've no idea, I always get this dolled up for Laura's parties. You look pretty hot yourself there, lady, maybe you know more than I do?"

"Ha, no I don't, I think you know I don't earn enough money to mix in those circles," she says.

"Ah come on, it's not about the money, honestly I wouldn't ask you along if I thought you'd feel uncomfortable. I'll be there, and look, any party I've ever gone to with you, you're always a massive hit so you've nothing to worry about. Now, come on grab that bag and let's get going."

We totter down the street in our heels towards the South Bank. It might have been a good idea maybe to bring a pair of flat shoes in my handbag, but I wasn't alert enough when leaving the house.

"What's the latest with you? Any man on the scene?" I ask.

"Nah, ah you know, going on the usual few dates here and there, but nothing serious. I'm not sure I want to meet a man right now, to be honest with you," she says, which is unusual for Sarah.

"Really? I thought you wanted to find your Mr. Perfect, settle down and get married?" I ask.

"One day, yes, but right now I'm kind of enjoying having a bit of fun. Besides, most of the guys out there are only looking for fun, it seems," Sarah says with an air of frustration.

"Yes, tell me about it. It's all very frustrating really I think. I've borderline hung up the dating shoes, to be honest," I say as we reach the tube station and leave the beautiful night behind us, to hopefully get a seat on the tube.

Saturday is always ridiculous and you'd rarely get a seat. This Saturday was no exception.

"Oh Jesus, I'm allergic to this. Still, once we get to Green Park and Bond Street it should ease a bit."

"Great, we'll only have two stops after that," Sarah says with a giggle.

"Look on the bright side, at least there's a bit of talent swinging from the poles."

We both giggle, as we know we wouldn't go near any of the drunken gobshites who are screaming out some tunes which sound vaguely familiar.

We reach St. John's Wood and Laura's house isn't too far. We turn the corner and I spy a shop.

"Hang on, we need to take wine or something with us, forgot all about that today," I mention.

"I'm good. I bought one already today. I'll wait here for you." Sarah mutters as she checks her phone.

You look really good tonight girl, that green dress shows your legs off nicely and it matches your eyes. I've never seen you curl that long brown hair of yours either. Damn! I hope I haven't chosen to bring the wrong person and that you'll create serious competition for me.

I grab the most expensive bottle in the shop (which is ridiculously expensive) as I know Laura enjoys her wine and has acquired a palate for wine over the years. Sarah is right to a certain extent. She is quite posh, and quintessentially English, but great fun. In fact, probably the last person anyone would expect me to be friendly with as I really couldn't be further from posh. However, our friendship works, and I would never question it in any way, shape or form as she is a very loyal and trustworthy friend to have. Admittedly, I do get a little pissed off with her over her obsession with trying to set me up with some of her male friends, but she's just looking out for me.

We reach the house within two minutes.

"Should I brace myself?" Sarah asks with a giggle.

"Stop, don't have me laughing into her face when she opens the door," I say.

The door is opened by a tall, quite statuesque man. His rugged good looks are enough to turn any woman's head while walking down the street. Laura is a lucky lady.

"David, how are you?" I ask.

"Oh, Katie, do come in darling, how wonderful to see you. It's been a while since you've been here, Laura and her matchmaking skills being the reason I'm sure."

I try to fob him off so Sarah won't get suspicious.

"Ha! No, not at all, it's just we've all been very busy really haven't we. Great to see you David, have you lost weight?"

"Good Lord no, if anything I've put a bit of pudding on, need to shed it fast. I'm planning on running in the next marathon so after to-night I need to get strict, lose the pudding and get fit again. And who's this? My apologies, I'm David. I got lost in conversation there. Do come in, ladies."

"I'm Sarah. Nice to meet you."

"Oh no! I forgot to let Laura know for the place setting. She'll mangle me."

"It's ok, I've heard the name and it's on the place setting now, there was no way I could have Sarah sitting with 'blank' as her name. I did ask you to tell me," Laura shouts from the dining room.

"I know, I'm sorry, I completely forgot. Am I in the bad books now?" I ask.

"No, I'll forgive you. Sarah, please come in and let me take your coat. Welcome, and please make yourself at home," she says as she leads Sarah along the hallway.

"Sorry, Laura, can I use the bathroom please?" Sarah asks. "It's just I've been holding it since just after I left home and really do need to pee."

I giggle, Sarah will say anything to anyone. In fact, I'm surprised she didn't tell David.

"Of course, darling, here you go, the bathroom is just here to the left."

Once Sarah goes to the bathroom Laura approaches me. "Well, have you spotted anyone you fancy?"

"Yeah, the old balding git," I say with a smirk.

"Be careful as he's got an eye for the ladies," she says.

"I'll bet he does. Well, let's be honest, there's only one statuesque, Darcy-esque man in this room. Oh apart from David of course, but I'd never fancy him. As in not that he's not attractive, but he's your husband and I just wouldn't fancy your husband," I say feeling more awkward as I keep talking.

"Oh, Katie, I know what you mean, you don't need to explain yourself. Let me introduce you, come on," Laura says as she drags me behind her.

She grabs my hand and takes me through to the adjoining kitchen where said Darcy-esque is standing. *I certainly wouldn't kick you out of the bed for eating a bag of Tayto crisps! Just my type! Laura, I think you might have got it right this time.*

"Jarvis, darling, let me introduce you to Katie."

Jarvis...did she say his name was Jarvis? Oh Jesus, he's going to be far too posh for me I'll bet. Katie and Jarvis, Jarvis and Katie, hmmm not sure that sounds right.

"Oh hello there, quite charmed to meet you, Katie," he says with an outstretched perfectly manicured hand. Perfect in every way, tanned, soft skin and lovely long, but not too long fingers, and very well looked after nails.

I reach my hand out and shake his. "Pleasure to meet you, Jarvis," I say awkwardly. I stifle a giggle as I imagine myself shouting through the house calling him. I just can't see myself roaring "Jarvis darling, the dinner is ready," — at least not in my lovely dulcet Cork tones.

"So, Katie, where in Ireland are you from then, with such a beautiful Irish accent?"

"That would be Cork, Jarvis," I say, and each time I say his name it just sounds all wrong - but I fancy him so much, even if he does sound like he should be living in the Palace.

"What's happening, girl?" I hear behind me.

"Ah, Sarah, this is Jarvis," I say and again it sounds all wrong to me, and I hope she doesn't laugh.

"Hello, Jarvis how are you? Is that really your name?"

Oh fuck!

"Eh yes, Jarvis is my name."

"Bloody cool name. Same as that guy from ahhh what's that group? Pulp! Yeah he's Jarvis isn't he?" she asks.

"Ha ha indeed, indeed he is," Jarvis says with a laugh. "Should I take it you're also from Cork, Sarah?"

"Yep, born and bred as they say. So what do you do, Jarvis?"

"I'm an architect, and you, Sarah, what do you do?"

Hmmmm, they seem to be hitting it off. Damn! I really fancy him. Still, I can't stand in the way of things if he's not interested in me.

I slowly inch my way back towards the kitchen and feel disappointment set in as they don't even seem to notice me sliding away.

"Katie, what are you doing?" Laura asks.

"Oh, well Darcy-esque seems a little more interested in Sarah," I say trying not to sound disappointed. "Never mind, bring on the next one," I say with a smile. I feel like crying.

"I'm sure he's just being friendly to her. Here, it's early, don't give up yet," Laura says as she rubs my shoulder gently. "Time to eat! Come on, it'll all work out the way it's meant to, I'm sure."

"You haven't put me next to the old balding git have you?" I ask.

She laughs. "Please don't hate me. I did it as a joke. Don't worry, as I have Jarvis at the other side of you."

"And Sarah?"

"Erm, the other side of Jarvis. Sorry, I didn't think this was going to happen, and I haven't got time to change the names around now. They'll see if I do. Besides, let's see what happens when we all sit down. He may turn his attention to you at the table," Laura says in her usual positive manner.

"Ok," I say with a smile. It's a fake smile. I know he's interested in Sarah only and there's not much I can do about it.

I take a seat and I'm followed by Jarvis.

"Are you ok, Katie? You disappeared very suddenly earlier?" he asks.

"Oh, yeah, I'm grand. Sorry, I just had to have a word with Laura, and you were mid conversation with Sarah, so thought I'd leave you to it," I say with a smile.

He noticed. That's something I suppose.

As everyone gets seated, the conversation is general at first, but unfortunately for me, it then turns to those sitting next to each other, and Jarvis chooses Sarah.

"Hello darling, and what's a beauty like you doing on her own at this party?" says the old balding git. I wouldn't mind, he seems sweet, but I'm getting a sense of something dodgy about him.

"Lovely legs, I spotted them across the room earlier," he says with a chuckle.

Dirty eejit. Think, think, think! You need to get out of here, what was Laura thinking putting me sitting next to him?

I take a deep breath and hope he doesn't try to snog me or something. *You're after a few too many glasses of wine already, so who knows what you're capable of?* I take a spoonful of soup and nibble on the homemade bread (not home-made by Laura, of course, the nails...not a chance). As I do, I feel my napkin move slightly, and when I look down, I see the old guy's hand on my knee. I slap it away good and hard so that he won't try it again. He's lucky I didn't scream at him, but I know I need to keep my cool, as I don't want to upset Laura. She'd freak out if she knew what he just did.

As the night drags on, Jarvis manages to say all of probably two sentences to me. *So long, Mr. Darcy.* I can't help but feel a little jealous of Sarah. He seems to be really enjoying her company. Yet, I'm annoyed as she was the one who just informed me that she didn't want to meet anyone, and here she is, taking my prospective only hope of a husband from me. Not her fault, though, I suppose I'm just not attractive enough for him.

Finally, we aim for the front door.

"I hope that wasn't too painful for you. Next time don't bring a friend," Laura says as she takes me to one side. "He was a bit all over her really. I was quite surprised as you'd be more Jarvis's kind of woman from what I can tell. Very surprised he's gone for Sarah. No offence to her, she's a pretty girl. But you're far more ladylike, demure and just more suitable a match, in my opinion. Anyway, sorry, I shouldn't have said that. I'm just a bit disappointed in him I guess, more than anything."

"Nothing can stand in the way of true love Laura, you of all people, being matchmaker extraordinaire, should know that."

"True, I suppose, about the true love thing. However, I certainly don't think I'm matchmaker extraordinaire. Good grief, if my father heard you, he'd disinherit me as he takes everything literally. He would think that's my job title!"

"Ha ha, well he's not here so you've nothing to worry about. Thanks so much for a lovely dinner."

"Lovely dinner, just not company, is what you really want to say? I hope he behaved himself. I thought it funny at the start of the night to place him next to you, but I recall what a dirty old fart he can be. He didn't try anything did he?"

"Hah! Now that would be telling and I don't tell my man secrets to anyone," I say with a laugh. I could tell her, but bless him he's obviously not getting it from anywhere, so probably does his best to try it on with every female he comes in contact with. "No harm done. Goodnight, and thanks again."

I walk towards the tube, alone. Sarah has left with Darcy. I'm a bit disgusted at both of them actually. He didn't strike me as the one night stand kind of guy, and it seems it's all Sarah is interested in right now... or so she said. I'm sure I'll get the gory details tomorrow, though.

2

*I*t's Sunday morning and I'm feeling sorry for myself.

"Hey hey, well how did last night go?" Siobhan asks with great gusto.

"It didn't. I took Sarah. Darcy likes Sarah. In fact, Darcy took a major shine to Sarah from the word 'hello', so I really didn't get a look in."

"Oh no! But Darcy was meant for you! Did she not know that?"

"No, I didn't tell her Laura was trying to set me up. You know Sarah, she's got a bit of a mouth on her at times? I know she'd unintentionally tell everyone there including him that I was being set up with him."

"Hmmm, very true, she has got a bit of a gob on her. Still, maybe you should have mentioned something as you saw her muscling in?"

"My friend, do you not know me by now? You know I wouldn't stand in the way of someone else's happiness, even if it means I'm the one upset and hurt. What purpose would there be to that? Everyone would end up unhappy and I'd end up with one friend less. Friendship means more to me than some guy who I might not have even got on with. Especially Jarvis," I say with a smile.

"Are you serious? His name is Jarvis? As in like yer man from Pulp?"

"Yes, that's exactly what his name is."

"Wow!"

Siobhan stays silent, and just smiles. It takes a few minutes, but she bursts out laughing. "I can't see Sarah with a guy called Jarvis. Is he very posh-boy? Like was he wearing jodhpurs and rode in on a horse asking for Ms. Bennett, proper Darcy like?"

"Hah! Well yeah, he is really posh, but nice posh from what I can see. I thought there was some hope there at one point because he turned to me at the start of dinner mentioning how I had slipped away. For one split second I thought he was getting bored with Sarah, but I think he just felt bad that he had given her all of his attention and I had been left on my own. Still, it doesn't matter, although I have to say Laura got it spot on in terms of me fancying him. I really did, the minute I saw him."

"Aww Katie. This is so unfair. You're the one single person I know who deserves to be with someone. You're just unlucky that you keep meeting the wrong ones. You are incredibly low-maintenance, and so pretty. I reckon he'll come to you soon and Christmas is coming after all," Siobhan says with a massive smile. "You're sure to get a man then."

I wish I could be that optimistic.

"You say that like you'll wrap one up in a box for me, and Christmas is a couple of months away yet I might add," I say with a cheeky grin.

"Maybe I will, a naked one, how does that sound? You can't go wrong with a wrapped naked man."

"Hmmm true, but remember a man is for life, not just for Christmas, at least that's what I'm looking for. No, all I want for Christmas is a big feed of turkey, ham and decent spuds. I'll be happy then."

"Oh Katie, you are funny, but you know what, you could just have a man for Christmas too?"

"Oh stop, I'm done with that fun business, allergic, allergic, allergic!! I just want to meet someone who might take me seriously for a change. I don't want to meet any more of these gobshites who are immature and don't know what they want. I just want a man, not a boy, because that's all I seem to meet...boys in men's bodies."

"I know. I think it must be pretty vicious out there. I feel very lucky to be married — sometimes."

I start laughing as I like her pause between the words 'married' and 'sometimes'. I know she's happy, though. Siobhan has always been a pillar of sense, but she got married very young and sometimes when I look at her I wonder if she regrets it. Her eldest daughter is nearly fourteen and I know she's having hard times with her at the moment. That is something I'm definitely not jealous of and at times like this, I sometimes thank my lucky stars that I'm a singleton.

"Now, I have to go again, to collect Daisy from her friend's birthday party," Siobhan says as she struggles with the sleeve of her coat. "Weird weather we're having at the moment isn't it? I feel like the Michelin man in this coat especially when the sun comes out."

"I know, don't know what to wear these days. I know how you feel, look at the state of me," I say with a peal of laughter.

"Hmmmm, yes I don't think it's really cold enough yet for that jacket with hat, scarf and gloves, not today anyway," she says with a grin. "Right, I have to go or her friend's mother will be at the gate waiting with Daisy. She'll be cursing me if I'm not there on time. She's an awful woman, I couldn't even believe she was going to throw a party for her child as she's so incredibly stingy." She grins. "I'd imagine they probably got the smallest and cheapest bar of chocolate between twenty of them or something. I wouldn't mind but she has money to burn."

I leave a hearty laugh out of me. "She sounds like someone everybody wants to be best friends with! Ok, you go."

"Byeeeeee," she says as she waves frantically at me while leaving the coffee shop.

What should I do? Should I ring Sarah and find out if she and Jarvis are going to be an item or was it just a one nighter? I hope it was just a one night stand. Why am I feeling so hurt about it all? This isn't me...what is wrong with me these days? Hmmmm, maybe I do need a man after all. I pull my phone from my pocket and dial her number.

"Hey, Katie, how are you?"

Great, she sounds very chirpy. It's not a one nighter then.

"Hi, Sarah, so how did last night go? That was a surprise!"

"I know, I can't believe I ended up with him, he's gorgeous and not at all what I'd normally go for."

"Yeah, I thought that was what you would say as he's a bit posh and you normally shun them away like there's something wrong with them."

"True, but Jarvis is super sexy and wow. I won't go into detail, but wow says it all!"

Thanks, really needed to know that! My own fault, I shouldn't have rung.

"Ok, spare me those details, thanks. So are you seeing him again or was it just a one nighter? You did mention before that you didn't want to meet anyone right now," I say, feeling hopeful.

"I know, but isn't it always the way that you meet someone when you don't want to. No, this is good, we are going to see each other again....in fact, I just popped home to change and now and I'm heading back to his again. We're going to go for a pub lunch near where he lives. You should see his house!! Oh, Katie, I'm hanging onto this one, he's got loads of money, that could be a good thing!"

Yes, well, that was always the difference between you and me. You go for money and not love, and I go for love, not money. And I'm the one who always seems to lose out.

"Sounds great. Ok, I'll let you head off as I don't want you to be late," I say, trying to sound chirpy when I feel like my heart has been smashed into smithereens on the inside.

"Ok, I'll tell you in more detail when I see you, bye, bye, bye, bye."

Don't, please.

"Ok have fun, bye, bye, bye, bye."

I'm glad that conversation is over. Hmmmm, need chocolate or a big brownie or something now.

I leave the café and head in the direction of home. I could meet up with some of the others for lunch, but I feel down and don't want them asking what's wrong. It would just annoy me, to say the least, to have to bring the whole episode up in conversation again. As I make my way home I stop off at the corner shop.

"Alright, love? Haven't seen you in here for a while, have you been away?"

"No, sorry. I should have just popped in to say hi anyway, Edith. I'm just trying my best to avoid chocolate and general things that might be considered bad for me right now."

"Oh love, I know what you mean, it's torture for me, but the doctor told me that if I don't shift weight off me soon I'll be six foot under before I know it. Of course, that didn't make sense to me 'cos how would I know when I'm six foot under? Silly man! Anyway, love, what can I get ya?"

I can't help but smile. Edith is the nosy neighbour type, the curtain twitcher and I'm surprised she doesn't know where I've been and what I've been up to. She's harmless, though, and I like her a lot. Her husband I like even more. He's the type of man who'd bend over backwards to help out no matter what time of day or night. Makes me laugh as his name is Eddie and he's like the male version of her only probably that bit more soft and loving. Edith can be hard as nails when she wants to be.

"Edith, I need a big bar of chocolate today I think."

"Oh, love, man trouble? I can smell it in the air. Who is he and what's he done?"

I smile. "No, it's fine, it will be fine. It's just me getting over excited about someone who unfortunately fancies my friend rather than me. I just need a bit of chocolate and I'll be fine again."

"That's it love, chocolate, every woman's problem solver, why can't we just marry chocolate? Wouldn't it make life far easier for us? The way some men whinge about us" — she nods her head in the direction of the back of the shop where Eddie is pricing items with the pricing gun — "you'd swear it's they'd need to marry the chocolate. Oh, I don't know love, I'd stay single for the rest of my life, if I were you. They are just not worth it at all. Nine out of ten mornin's I wake up with a banging headache from his bloody snoring. But, saying that, I do love him. He's a lazy old sod at times, but a cuddly one and he'd do anything for me. So, I really shouldn't complain should I?"

I laugh. "Definitely not. Eddie is lovely and a gentleman. If I could meet someone my age who acts like him, I'd be so happy. But for now, Edith, I think you might be right, I might be better off staying single. Yes, in fact, I'm going to take my chocolate and go home, stuff my face and stay single for the rest of my life, buy some cats and live in a big pile of cat poo."

"Well, love you don't have to take it that far, leave the cats out of it I'd say as you know we like to live in hope and if you stink of cat poo there's no hope for ya." She screeches with laughter at her own joke.

God, your laugh is dire. I've never heard such a loud and draining laugh in my life. You are lovely, but I do feel for poor Eddie at times.

"So, have you been up to anything nice this weekend?" I ask in order to change the subject, I'm sick of my love life being the topic of conversation for most of late.

"Not this weekend love," Eddie shouts from the back as he starts walking towards me. "We're off back up to Manchester next weekend, though. May have to shut up shop, love, so if you're looking for anything, you might have to come before and buy it."

"Oh, is there not someone who can take care of it for you?" I ask.

"No love, everyone we know has families so it's just easier to shut up for a few days."

"Well, I'm at a loose end next weekend, I could look after it for you if you'd like? I can't promise I'll open it for full days, but even if I did half a day for you each day. I'd hate to see you losing business because you're going for a two day break home to Manchester," I say.

"Are you mad, giving up your weekend to look after the shop for us?" Edith asks.

"Maybe I am, but I'm willing to do it if you want me to. As I said, I have no plans and I'd doubt anything that major will crop up between now and then, the social life isn't too hectic of late."

"Well, you know what lass, you're like a little angel in disguise. Thank you, if you can do that we'll be best pleased with you. We will, of course, pay you," Eddie adds.

"Oh Eddie, I don't want money, I'm just happy to see you two get away for a bit without any worries. Now, I must pay you for this as I'm dying to get stuck into it," I say with a smile.

"Oh no you won't pay for anything lady, off you go now put your money in your pocket, it's no good here," Eddie says as he tries to shuffle me out of the shop, but in fact, it's more like he's pushing me.

"Ok, I get the message. Thanks for the chocolate, I'll call over some evening during the week and you can show me how things work."

"We will love, we will. Thanks so much, you're such a good lass," Edith says with a grin.

As I walk out of the doorway I can hear her chat to Eddie inside. "Oh what a sweet girl, she is. I always knew there was something special about her. She'll find him one day, when she least expects it."

Oh for fuck sake, how many more times are people going to say that to me, or about me?!!! I'm sick of hearing it. Maybe I should have bought a few bars of chocolate for this evening. I've a feeling I might need more than one.

3

The weekend approaches a little too quickly and I'm starting to regret having said I'll look after the shop. At least they're not leaving until tomorrow morning which gives me time to digest the fact I'll be stuck in the shop. What I was thinking, I'll never know. Anyway, it's all set now, and I can't let them down. Who knows, I may actually enjoy it?!

It's Saturday morning and I turn the corner to see the car being loaded up by Eddie.

"Eddie! How long are you going for, a month?"

"Oh, don't talk to me love, she's always the same when we go away. 'We have to take this just in case, we have to take that'," he says, mimicking Edith's voice.

"To be fair, I think the majority of women have a problem with packing when going away somewhere, it's all just in case," I say with a smile.

"Oh, I'm not gonna win this argument then, am I lovey?"

"Aww, poor Eddie. Do you want a hand with something there or will I go on in and make myself at home?" I ask.

"You go ahead love. You're a great lass for doing this, we really appreciate it."

"I know you do, it's no problem," I say as I stroll to the shop entrance.

The thing is I know they appreciate it and it's when I hear that, I realise what good people they are and that I'm doing the right thing making this little sacrifice, to give them the break they need.

"Morning lovely locks, how are you today?" Edith asks.

"Lovely locks? That's a new one! I'm good thanks. I can tell you're excited!"

"Well you have lovely locks, just like that Cheryl girl, the singer. You know who I'm talking about? Beautiful girl she is, you've got beautiful hair like hers."

I laugh. "My hair is nothing like hers. Mine is long wavy fuzz right now that I can't do anything with. I wish I had hair like hers for sure," I say with a smile. "Thanks for the compliment." I don't try to argue with her as she'll win. When her mind is set on something, it's set.

"Edith, love, come on get a move on or we'll be up when we'll have to come back down again."

"Alright, alright I'm coming. Oh I swear, men!" she says as she rolls her eyes.

I just smile. I wish I knew what she meant!! As the car starts to creep off, I wave goodbye. They seem so excited about it all and I know it's been some time since they've managed to get away for a break. I walk back inside the shop and perch myself on the stool behind the counter. Part of me is hoping it'll be a slow day, the other part hopes it won't as I can imagine it will drag if no one comes into the shop.

"Alright love," says a deep sexy voice as a man walks past the counter and down the aisles. "Nice day out there today, you stuck here all day?" he asks.

Show me your face. You sound lovely, let me see your face!!

"Tis lovely out there alright. Yeah, I'll close up for lunch, but I'll be stuck here all day. I'm just helping out for today and tomorrow."

He's got his back to me now and I can't help being a bit of a perv by checking out his broad shoulders and his arse. *Not bad, seven maybe eight out of ten. Stop perving!!*

"Ah yeah, they said they were going away for a few days and some pretty Irish girl was looking after the shop," he mutters.

Ah, for feck sake, not another set up. I'm done. I stop checking him out immediately. I want no part to do with a set up again.

"Ah right," I say, acknowledging him but not his compliment. But then he turns towards me, and he's a God, a greater God than Jarvis. He has piercing blue eyes and a rugged, very handsome look about him. I'm starting to reconsider the set up thing.

"So, you're from around here are you?" I ask.

"Yeah, see that new build, I'm in there."

"Where, the ones just around the corner?"

"Yep, that's where I'm talking about."

"But, I live there. I've never seen you around before."

"I work odd hours. It doesn't always coincide with people who do nine to five jobs so I generally don't see anyone for long periods of time. My body clock is a bit messed up from it all, innit?"

Oh God no! He said 'innit'. Is that something I'll get over? I'm not sure.

"But, my darlin', I've seen you around from time to time," he says.

Hmmm, have you now. Ok, how do I work this, be nonchalant towards him or be polite and keep chatting. I wonder now is he a player, like all the other muppets?

"Oh, and when would that have been? As I work a nine to six job, surely that wouldn't coincide with your body clock events?" I ask.

Oh no, what have I just said? It wasn't meant to sound like that!

"Ehuh ehuh ehuh," he responds, sounding like what I can only describe as a donkey. "Oh, darlin' that's funny innit? So, no, my body clock events wouldn't be at those hours exactly, but I'm sure if I was given the opportunity to show you, I could make them coincide with your home time."

I scrunch my nose up in disgust. "Is that all you're buying?" I ask.

"Yeah, so what do you say darlin'? You and me, at my place, tonight? I'll show ya a good time," he says with a cheeky grin.

He's quite a cheeky chappy which I like, but that was just too much for me and while I don't doubt he could show me a good time, his whole proposition is turning my stomach.

"Ah, that's one pound fifty please?" I say, holding out my hand.

"And as I gazed into her Irish eyes, her face flushing, I took her hand and placed a kiss upon it, in the hope she would take me up on my offer," he says.

If you were anyone else I'd probably enjoy that, but knowing what you're really like already, I'll definitely be skipping on that.

"Spare me will ya? Willy Shakespeare you're definitely not," I say and stifle a laugh.

"Here you go, one pound fifty darlin'. Oh, you'll be mine yet," he says as he turns, winks and swaggers out of the shop.

Great! This should be a fun weekend!

4

"Have you thought about it yet?" says the voice at the entrance to the shop.

"Oh, will you ever just piss off and stop annoying me?" I ask.

"I haven't even started yet, you're unlucky that today is Saturday and I'm off all day."

"Oh great. So are you telling me you're going to call around here every two hours to annoy me?" I ask.

"No, I'm just gonna stay here now innit? Come on love, it's just a bit of fun. Ok, I want to get to know you. What's your name?"

I'm reluctant to tell him my real name, but he lives in the same block of flats as me and I know that he can quite easily find out what flat I live in and see my name from the letter box.

"Ok, I'm Katie, and you are?"

"Guess," he says with that stupid donkey laugh again and a smirk.

"Dick?" I ask.

"Haw, very funny, aren't we? No, it's Pete."

"Close enough, they both mean the same thing don't they?" I quiz.

"Eh, come on love, I'm just bein' friendly, we're neighbours after all. Give me a break?"

"Ok, sorry, but you were out of order earlier."

"I'll admit I came on a bit strong, so are we good?"

Was that an apology??

"Hmmm, yes. So, Pete. what do you do to say you work odd hours?"

"Stripper, ain't I," he says quite proudly.

My face drops. "Really?"

"No, but it was worth saying it to see your face drop. I'm an aircraft engineer, I fix them planes that go soaring through the sky."

Ohhh! He's intelligent!! "I think it's fair to say I know what an aircraft engineer is. So how many that you've worked on have crashed?"

"Oh, now, you're getting very smart all of a sudden aren't you? I think I've met me match."

No, no, that's one thing you have not done! Get that horrible thought out of your head right now. "You think one thing, I think another," I say with a smirk.

I've silenced him and now I'm feeling awkward. He actually looks, dare I say it, upset.

I like this side of you! "Sorry, I shouldn't have said that. I've taken it too far now. If necessary you can kiss my hand, I'll allow you to do that," I say with a smirk.

He looks straight into my eyes and says, "No thanks, I wanted to do that earlier, but no, it's too late now. You've cast me aside like a shit-ridden shoe and I no longer wish to kiss your fair Irish hand." He turns and heads for the door. I can't figure out if he's really upset or messing about.

"Pete, are you ok? Are you serious?"

"You'll find out in two hours darlin' won't ya?" he says with a cheeky grin and walks away.

I can't help but smile and dare I admit it to myself, I think I might have some odd attraction to him. He's certainly brightened my day so far, even if in an over the top way.

An hour passes, and I'm starting to hope that Pete might change his two hour recurring visit to one hour and surprise me. Although, then I think back to what he said earlier in the day and how his mind works, and I wonder if I really want to know him. Next thing I know he'll be asking for my phone number so he can start sending me dodgy pictures and the like. Thanks, but no thanks, I don't want to see any man member on my phone. He strikes me as the kind of guy who might be like that, though. I put my thoughts of him to the back of my mind, and as I go to price some items and shelve them a customer walks in.

"Well, fancy seeing you here? I thought you work in the finance sector?" Jarvis asks.

I can feel my face is burning. "I, I do. I'm just helping out here. The owners have gone for a mini break and I offered to look after the shop for them."

"That's rather sweet of you that you would do something like that for them," he says.

"Oh, I will admit I kind of regretted it after I had offered, as it ties me a bit during the day time hours over the weekend. They're sweet though and deserve a break without worrying about the shop, so I don't mind.

"So, what brings you to this area?" I ask.

"Well, Sarah actually," he says with a smile.

Which would explain why I haven't heard a peep from her, all week.

"Alright darlin', you been missing me?"

Ahhh, such timing, Pete!

"I have greatly," I say sarcastically.

"I hope you ain't chattin' up my bird, mate?" he says.

"Pete, I'm not your...."

"No, mate, I'm not. And who are you?" Jarvis asks.

"Oh Jarvis, I'm sorry, this is Pete, who I met here in the shop roughly four hours ago."

"How cute, you've been countin' the hours. See mate, she loves me, you better give up," he says with an air of confidence.

"Oh, don't worry Pete. I'm seeing Katie's friend, Sarah, you've nothing to worry about," Jarvis says.

That's the moment when he ripped my heart out, stood on it, danced on it and fed it to the lions. I now stand without a heart. I am emotionless, and I don't feel anything anymore.

"Sarah? No way mate! Ohh, you need to be careful there, shark she is, she'll take all of your money mate. See, if you was quick off the mark, you'd be dating Katie here, but I've got there before ya now so looks like I've lucked out in this situation," Pete says.

Jarvis looks perplexed.

What was that all about and where did it come from? Pete has no idea who Sarah is, or does he?

"Erm, right, I'd better be on my way, I just popped in for a bottle of wine and some chocolates. What do I owe you, Katie?"

"That's eighteen pounds, ninety eight please, Jarvis. Sorry about Pete. He seems to make a grand entrance every time he enters the shop," I say.

"Oh don't worry, however I'm curious as to how he knows Sarah and why he called her a shark," Jarvis says with concern.

"Ignore him, he's most likely made it up I'm sure. I can't imagine Sarah knows him," I whisper, knowing that even though he's at the back of the shop, he'll probably still hear us.

"Right. I'll go then, thanks very much. It's good to see you, Katie," Jarvis says.

"Yeah, likewise Jarvis, you take care now," I say, trying not to still look upset by his previous comment.

"Bye, Jarvey mate, good luck with the shark," Pete says with a laugh.

"What the hell was that all about?" I demand.

"It was me knight in shining armour routine of course. Is he your ex? I could see you was upset with what he said, so I just said I'd jump in and help you out."

"No, he's not my ex and thanks for stepping in, but really there was no need," I say defensively.

"Course there was, we're friends now right? We've met more than three times, to me that means we're friends."

I can't help but smile and it feels weird, but all he's managed to do all day is make me smile.

"Yeah, ok, we're friends. Thanks for coming to my rescue. That's actually kind of sweet," I say with a smile.

"I knew I'd melt your heart if I tried for long enough, persistence pays. I never give up, never," he says, and winks at me.

"I can see. Ok, so tell me more about yourself then," I insist.

"I will, but first, you need to tell me what the story is with ex lover there, as I don't want to be crushing anyone's toes with me big size fifteen feet," he says.

"Size fifteen?" I say with shock.

"Yeah darlin', London's finest size fifteen feet, and you know what that means don't ya?"

"Pete, stop referring the conversation back to your member, please," I say and realise I probably sounded like his mother.

"Ehuh ehuh ehuh," he laughs.

Not sure I'll ever be able to handle that laugh.

"Sorry, I'll stop now. I don't actually laugh like that either. I just thought it would add to my delightfully funny character, but I can see it's annoying you by your wonderful facial expressions," he says with a smile. "So come on, tell me," he says.

"Ok, for starters he's not my lover, and never has been. I met him for the first time last weekend at a dinner party. Admittedly, it was a dinner party which was kind of arranged so we could meet, and hopefully get together. However, Sarah came with me and he took more of a shine to her. Odd thing is he's completely what I'd go for, and not at all what she'd fancy normally."

"Is that your way of telling me I don't stand a chance? Maybe you should be brave like Sarah and go out there into the storm and tackle what's thrown at you. I might not be what you normally go for, but at least I'm more fun than serious Jarvey there. Come on, you know we could have a good time together. We're having fun now, so why not give me a try?" he asks.

"I didn't say I wouldn't." The words are expelled before I realise what I've said. *Shit!*

"Ya love me doncha? You do, I can tell. I knew we was meant for each other darlin'. I wouldn't pursue you like this otherwise."

I give up. Ask me out you clown because if you're a player like the rest of them, I might throw you and your size fifteen shoes into the river.

"So, Jarvey ran off with your mate, and you're left heartbroken? Am I reading this right?'

"I would hardly say heartbroken. I don't even really know him. I just feel let down, but it's nobody's fault as neither of them knew I liked him."

"Right, so would I be a rebound case then, if I was to ask you out?"

"No, you wouldn't!" I say in a very matter of fact manner. "No! Definitely not - ask me out and you'll see," I say.

"Oh you're changing your tune now, well you might have to wait another two hours because my time here is up and I don't want to over-run the clock."

"The shop will be closed before then," I say with a smirk.

"I'll just have to come a little earlier then and help you, won't I?" he says as he again exits the shop.

Why do I attract so many odd or weird men? I just don't understand it. Is there anyone normal out there for me? At least Pete is quite sexy, and he is witty. Maybe I do need to give him a chance.

"Oh, by the way, I know you're thinking of me now," he says as he backs back into the shop and up to the counter.

I blush. *Grrrr, yes, I am thinking about you. Now go because I can feel my face getting redder by the second.* "No, I wasn't, and if you don't want to buy anything can you leave now, please?" I say, smiling.

"Cute, you blush. I love a girl who blushes, it's very sexy, just like you," he says as he thrusts his body over the counter to plant a kiss on my lips.

Feck!

"Aw, did I take you by surprise darlin'? Hope you enjoyed as plenty more where that came from. See ya soon," he says as he winks and walks out of the shop.

He really is something.

5

It's closing time and before I know it I hear the now familiar tones of Pete approaching.

"Alright mate, haven't seen ya in a while, you put on a bit of pudding since I last saw ya!" he shouts to the man across the street.

"Piss off mate, you can talk, got a bit of a gut going on there!" he says with a laugh.

"Hi sexy, you ready for a night on the town with your new sexy man?" Pete asks.

"Seriously, Pete, take a step back slightly now or you'll have me running," I say.

"Oh, come on. You know I'm joking around with you. So, what d'ya fancy doing?" .

"Erm, I was planning on going home, but I could go for a coffee with you, if you want?" I say.

"Coffee? Are you serious?" he asks.

"I'm serious. Don't you drink coffee?"

"I do, but in the morning maybe, not at 6:30 pm! It's fun and liveliness we need this evening darling, we ain't sleeping. It's off to the pub we go for a fun night out. Come on," he says. "I might even stretch to buying you a bag of chips on the way home or as a big treat we can go to McDonalds," he says with a huge smirk across his face.

"You charmer, I feel so lucky. Well, I don't have any plans tonight, so we could go for a couple of drinks I suppose."

"Oh, Sarah blown you out for Prince Jarvey?" Pete asks.

I roll my eyes. "I had no plans in general tonight and hadn't arranged anything with Sarah. Seriously, don't piss me off now Pete or I won't go anywhere with you," I say.

"Ok, ok, keep your shirt on, although I'd prefer to see you with it off," he says with a laugh. I give him a withering look. "Sorry, I'm sorry, I won't say anything like that again, I promise."

We walk in silence for a few minutes.

"So, do you think we'll end up holding hands on the way home then?" he says and winks at me. I can't help but smile as he breaks the silence.

"I don't know, maybe," I say with a grin. "Tell me something about you Pete. Have you family around here? Parents still alive?"

"Yeah, I have an older brother, I'm the youngest. Parents are both angels now sadly. I miss them a lot, but always feel they are around me when I need someone to be there," he says as he smiles at me.

Cute smile there Pete and you come across so well when you're having a normal conversation. Keep it like that for a while, please. Actually, keep it like that always.

"Are you close to your brother?" I ask.

"Not really. I only get to see him every once in a while, as he lives in Italy. We aren't particularly close, but we do enjoy seeing each other, when we do. How about you, you got family?"

"Just me, my story is similar to yours. I do have ten aunts and uncles who worry about me now, though," I say.

"Spoilt then?" he asks.

"No I wouldn't say that, but I'm close to some of them and we talk on the phone regularly."

"Regularly, as in every day? What could you possibly have to say every day? It's like trying to draw blood from a stone talking to you," he says with a smile.

"Thanks, I think you're great too," I say with an air of sarcasm. "Not every day, and it's not always about what you have to say, it's about hearing the person's voice," I say in a defensive tone.

"True, I'm sorry. I've upset you now. It must be difficult living away from home and away from your family and friends. I've always lived in London so I wouldn't know what it's like, but I know I do miss my folks a great deal and while I'm not that close to my brother, I sometimes wish he lived closer to me. I suppose that's something I as a Londoner never think about and I just assume that everyone is everywhere when you need them to be. You're a brave lady. So, what made you move away from home? What part of Oireland are you from anyway?"

"That's the saddest Irish accent I've ever heard," I say laughing.

"I know it's crap, I'm not the best at accents. I can't even speak proper English so how can I expect to do any kind of accents?"

I laugh. "I'm from Cork to answer your last question. What made me move here? Well, I needed a change. I was tired of life. You know when you've stayed in one place forever and never seen beyond it? It's a big world out there and I decided I wanted to travel. However, I only managed to get as far as London," I say with a smile.

"So some London bloke captured your heart and you stayed?" he asked.

"Hmmmm, sort of, more like some London bloke broke my heart. I arrived here four years ago and within two weeks of arriving here, I met someone. The one I thought I'd marry, but as it turns out, he was already… leading a double life. He had a wife and two babies – twins to be precise - aged three. I have no idea how he managed to get away with seeing me as he used to stay with me four nights a week almost. I was heartbroken when I found out."

"Fuckin' hell! I'm sorry to hear that, that explains why you're so cold towards me and probably men in general," he says.

"You don't hold back, do you? You say whatever you like whenever you like?" I say.

"Sorry, I've upset you again. I didn't mean for it to sound mean. It's just an observation that maybe I should have..." he trails off and whispers, "kept to myself. I'm really messing up here ain't I?" he asks.

"No, you're not, actually. It's nice that you're showing an interest and asking me questions about myself. Of late all I meet is guys who want to talk about themselves and they never actually want to know anything about me. It's like they are after one thing and when there's no sign of getting it, they disappear into the sunset."

"On a fucking horse that gets lost I hope?" he asks.

I start laughing hysterically. "Well, it must be on a horse that gets lost and the same one each time, if so! I'm not sure, but there could be a big bunch of arseholes gathered somewhere in the metropolis who are totally lost," I say, laughing.

He sniggers. "Well, I've no intentions of getting on that horse darlin'. I want to know more about you, lots more, so keep talking. I really like listening to your accent, it's so soft and, I don't know, poetic."

"Are you schmoozing now again? You don't have to, I actually feel at ease talking to you, it's weird," I say.

"Good, so getting back to the subject, if you don't mind, but I'm at a loss as to how this idiot managed to get away with his double life especially having two little babies. How could he do that? Have you seen his wife? Is she a munter or something?"

I laugh out loud. "I have seen her, and she's beautiful. I have no idea how he managed it. Once I found out I didn't want to know anymore. He did explain to me, that he told her he had to go to London on business. He lived in Manchester so it worked for him, until she followed him to London one of the days and ended up knocking on my door."

"That's pretty serious. Was it all guns blazing, duelling pistols out, hair extensions on the floor?" he asks, trying to make light of it.

"Hah! No, of course not! I'm not like that and thankfully neither is she. I have no idea what she did to him afterwards, but she didn't say a great deal to me. I think she saw the look of confusion on my face when she introduced herself as his wife. She was very dignified actually, as was

I. I never saw her after that. I just got the brief lowdown of, 'I'm guessing you didn't know he was married with two babies, twins to be precise, three years of age?' That was enough to silence me."

"And I assume he at least phoned you to apologise?" Pete asks.

"Of course he didn't, because he is an asshole! He disappeared behind her, and didn't even look back. Obviously it's for my own good that happened, because I'd never want to end up with someone like that... ever!"

"So, you think the wife kept him?"

"I really couldn't tell you, I hope not for her sake! Waste of space, time and effort, that's what he was," I say matter-of-factly.

"English bastard," he says with a smirk.

I laugh. "Yeah, you'd know all about that," I say joking.

"I'm sorry that happened to you darlin', it's not a nice experience to arrive somewhere and be treated like that. I'm surprised you stayed, you must have some good friends here, apart from Sarah that is?"

"Ah, Sarah is lovely, I just got carried away in my own mind I guess with that situation and hoped for the best. I can't go around thinking I'll be happy with someone who I don't even know, particularly if they don't fancy me. Yeah, I'm surprised I stayed too, but as you said, my friends were great. But one thing I vowed was to never go near an English man again after that," I say looking at the ground with a smile on my face.

"You are kidding, ain't ya? You can't tar us all with one brush love. Hang on, let me get the door," he says as we reach the pub and he enters before me so he can hold the door ajar for me. *Impressive, there's more to you than that rugged laddish way of yours would suggest.*

"Thanks, such a gent," I say with a grin.

"I can be, I can be a real gent for the right girl," he says.

"You are funny. You do realise you only just met me. I could be a nutter or a psychopath, and you are being totally over the top acting like we are together already."

"If you was a nutter or a psychopath, they would've arrested you long ago and you wouldn't be me neighbour living in that expensive block of flats. Besides, who's to say I'm not a nutter or psychopath? You don't just meet them in cyberspace you know, they can exist in the real world too."

I shiver at the thought of it. *What if you are a psycho?*

"It's alright darlin', I'm not!" he says with a laugh. "The look on your face just now said it all. Nah, I'm just normal Pete from across the block. I think you can sense you're pretty safe with me, by now? Now what can the gent buy the lady to drink?" he says with a grin.

I smile, "While I don't really know you that well yet, I still get a good feeling from you so yeah, I feel safe with you," I reply with a smile. "Hmmmm. Gin and tonic please," I say.

"I shall be back in a moment good lady," he says and smiles as he walks away.

Why do I fall for guys so easily? This guy is so charming and my God, he really does look after his body. I can get a clear view of him from all angles now and after walking next to him, I feel reasonably small as he must be about six foot two or thereabouts. Let me work this out, I'm five foot seven so with my three or four inch heels I'll be five foot ten or eleven. Perfect, he'll still be taller than me. I feel a smile creep across my face.

"Here you go, what's that little smile about?" he asks.

"What smile?" I ask.

"You was grinning like a Cheshire cat when I came over with the drink, just wondering why?"

"Was I? I didn't realise it. I don't know why. So tell me more about you," I say trying to change the subject.

"Yeah, you was. You're havin' fun ain't ya?" he asks.

"Hmmm, maybe," I say, trying not to give anything away.

"See now, can you imagine what a dull and boring night you'd be having if it was Jarvey you was out with? Seriously, I could smell the boring side of him from afar. I think I'd fall asleep if he spoke for longer than two minutes. Terrible ain't it, how people can be that boring and not be able to entertain a conversation?" he smiles.

"Well we don't know how boring he is as to be honest, I've not really spoken to him except for a few words earlier today and you don't know him at all, so we really shouldn't judge him. But I have to say, yeah I'm having fun with you, you're good company," I say, deciding it's time maybe to lower my guard slightly. "So, stop changing the subject now, more about you? What's your love life situation then? Been in a relationship before I take it?" I ask.

"Ah yeah, my story isn't the best. I was with a girl for five years and she died in a road accident." He hangs his head, "And that's it really."

"Pete, my God, that's terrible. You must have been distraught after that. So, you haven't met anyone since?"

"Well, I've met girls, but nothing serious. I don't know, nice girls are hard to come by you know?" he says.

"Yeah but, and don't take this the wrong way, are you comparing them to the girl you lost?" I ask.

"No! At least I don't think so. I never looked at it like that. No, I'm good, I've moved on and feel ready to meet someone, but I want her to be the one," he says.

"You seem pretty set on what you want. Are you trying to scare me off now?" I ask jokingly so as to make the conversation a little lighter.

"Ha! No. I know I act a bit full on, but I do really like you. I've seen you around before, I think you're really pretty and it's taken me a while to work up the courage to talk to you. I might as well tell you seeing as we are being so honest and I've gone all serious all of a sudden," he says sheepishly.

"Wow, where has that come from? I like serious you, it's nice to see this side of your personality. And I feel flattered that you're being so straight up and honest with me, and complimenting me so much. I'm just not good with compliments. I suppose I find it hard to trust after Dillon, that was his name - that married fool."

"I'm not surprised. Well, for you, my lady, I'd be willing to take things really slow until you feel you're at that trusting point with me. That is, of course, only if you're willing to give me a chance."

I smile. "You're a really nice guy."

"But?" he says.

"You know what, but nothing, I like you. In the past, I've fallen for guys too quickly, but you seem far more genuine than most and I feel good around you. You make me smile."

"Good, I'm pleased to hear that. So, can I kiss you now?" he asks.

"Erm, bit soon? I mean we got to the pub all of twenty minutes ago and now you want to kiss me after about forty minutes of conversation and you're not really meant to just blurt it out."

"It's me. It's who I am, I'm a cheeky chappy, you know that already. Besides, I already kissed you earlier in the day when you was behind the counter. I took you by surprise too didn't I?! I like surprising people, so, if you like surprises I'm your man," he says with a big grin on his face.

I can only imagine what his kind of 'surprise' would be. He'd probably be that naked man in the box that Siobhan was talking about. He is sweet, though.

"Save the kissing for later, I'm enjoying us chatting for now," I say with a smile.

"As the lady wishes, but you do realise you've just given me permission to kiss you later. You can't back down now or I might have to arrest you and you know where that leads don't you?"

"Ha ha, I'm not going to say no, but I can guess. You never stop do you?"

"Me and my size fifteen feet never stop, never. Have you ever gone out with a man with size fifteen feet before?"

"No, I have to say I haven't," I say.

"Yeah, it's difficult to get shoes to fit, I've to get them made sometimes. Used to get mocked a lot when I was in school, the usual you know 'clown feet, don't trip on the pavement etc.', used to really piss me off. That's bullying that is! These days you'd be expelled for that."

"Did you not stand up to them?" I ask.

"No, I was a quiet guy. I guess I was always a bit self conscious of my height and shoe size and just about everything when I was in school. I was six foot tall when I was fourteen, you know the slagging you get at that age. It dented my self confidence a lot. It wasn't until I was eighteen that the guys who mocked me realised they were always going to be smaller than me, most likely forever. Then I realised I could probably kick the crap out of all of them, but I wouldn't. It's not in me you know. I'm just not a violent person, never have been, never will be. How was school for you? Must be a bit different in Ireland?"

"Yeah, it was fun. I never had any problems really. I don't think bullying was as prevalent in Ireland back in those days. People just got on with things and life was much simpler wasn't it? Thinking about it though, London is a big city so you're going to have more characters and mean bullyish people around as they probably feel they have to be 'hard', or 'ard' as you'd say, to survive. But where I'm from it's smaller, and today I know it's changed a lot, and not completely for the better, but that's a sign of the times I guess," I say.

"Yeah, look at us getting all philosophical. We also sound like two old farts who need a holiday out of this place. That's it, let's go on holiday together," he says.

"Seriously, we haven't even got to kissing yet and now you want to go on holiday?" I ask.

"Well, I can kiss you on holiday, that'll give you time to find out if you like me or not," he says with a grin.

"And what if I don't?" I ask.

"Right, same again?" he asks.

I laugh and wink at him. "My round," I say.

"Oh! A lady who offers to buy the gent a drink? It's some time since I have had the pleasure of such a wondrous occasion," he says.

"I always get my round in I'll have you know, sir," I say with a smile.

"Really? Is that an Irish thing then as I always see that with Irish lads too? It's nice, you're generous people," he says.

"Yeah we are, very! Now what's that you're drinking?" I ask.

"Oh, it's a JD and coke please darlin', thanks."

I make my way to the bar, and I can't help but smile to myself. *I like this guy, he's got a bit of a mouth on him, but he's so sweet and is a softy under all of that bravado. I believe he's quite genuine. I can't lose the run of myself now though as I don't know him very well yet, so best to keep a level head on me for now...until the drink sets in at least.*

"Here you go me darlin'," I say with a cheeky grin.

"Oh calling me darlin' now, you'd better watch yourself, that could be misconstrued for flirting darlin'," he says and winks.

"Maybe it was me flirting, after all, you don't know me very well do you?" I ask.

"No I don't, but I know you like me, and I know you're beautiful. Even though I've only spent a short time with you yet, I really like you," he whispers.

Shivers. I take a sip of my drink and can feel it dribbling down my chin as I miss my mouth slightly.

"Ha ha ha ha, am I making you dribble? Oh, that's a first for me, I'm liking that," he says laughing hysterically.

Oh for feck sake! This is a nightmare. Why did that have to happen just as he whispered to me? Still, it is funny and you're laughing and what a beautiful smile you have. I love that little dimple on your cheek.

"Your eyes are glistening," I say. *Idiot!! You weren't meant to say that out loud!*

"Are they? Looking into my eyes now are you?" he says.

"No, not like staring into them, I erm, I just noticed that when you smiled they were glistening."

"Is that a compliment the kind lady is bequeathing upon me?" he asks.

I smile. "Hmmm, maybe. Why, is that a rare thing for you to get compliments?"

"No, I get them all the time, just never from the girls I want. But, I want you, so I'm chuffed now," he says rubbing his hands together.

Right now I actually want him to kiss me. His eyes are so blue and sexy and I really want him.

"Kiss me, just fecking kiss me will ya?" I say. *Aghhhhhhhhhhhhhhhh what the hell am I doing?*

"Ha ha ha you're feisty ain't ya? Oh, I like this side of ya, dirty little thing," he says, trying to contain his laughter.

"Sorry, I don't know where that came from, I normally would never say anything like that," I protest.

"It's alright, I liked it. Do you want me to kiss you then?" he asks.

"I, I... I don't know," I say with a slight laugh. "I can't believe I just came out with that, it's just not me at all. Seriously, totally out of character for me, but yeah, sod it, kiss me Pete. I'm attracted to you so kiss me."

I close my eyes and wait for him to lean forward and kiss me. Instead, I hear him laugh out loud.

"I'm sorry, I'm not gonna do it now. It's too forced, not the right time," he says.

Cringe! Don't do that to me!!

"No, don't worry and don't look so sad, I will, but just not now. I'll wait until later when it'll be more romantic and it'll just occur naturally," he says.

"I feel like a gobshite now. I hope you know that!" I say.

"Don't, no need to, it's only me. Look I know you don't know me that well and that, but I'm a nice guy, trust me, I'm not going to take the piss out of you or anything like that. I feel really flattered that you want me to kiss you. And I do want to, so just relax for now. I know I was messing about earlier and I do want to, but I was going to wait until the end of the night. I'm sorry I probably shouldn't joke around so much. Have I offended you now?"

"Not offended me, but made me feel a bit stupid maybe? You know I have feelings too. It seems you put on this big bravado act, and you're a really sensitive soul underneath it all. But I don't put that act on, I wear my heart on my sleeve and I don't need someone like you making me feel stupid when I'm so cautious already of getting my heart bruised again," I say defensively.

He puts his arm around me. "Listen, I'm so sorry. I know I can be a knob at times when I kid around and yeah you are right, I'm not confident, it's all an act really and it's stupid of me to treat you the way I just did. I apologise and I hope that you can forgive me because if I've messed up here I'll never forgive myself," he says with a serious face and a look of real concern.

"I feel like we are having our first argument and we've just met. Is that normal?" I ask.

"Probably not, but then again I don't do normal. Normal is boring, this is fun and it might be an indication that we'll have a feisty, but romantic and sexy relationship."

"Ok, relationship…. we are on our first date, let's not jump the gun maybe?"

"Oh is this a date? Even better, I thought we was just two friends going for a drink," he says and winks.

"I give up! I can't cope anymore," I say laughing.

"Am I forgiven then? I do think this will lead to more by the way. You might not believe it yet, but it will! Another drink?"

"Ok, forgiven. I like that you are so confident about it all. Yeah, let's have another drink, thanks."

"I'm not confident at all but I know me gut instinct and it never lets me down. You're in 'ere now," he says as he beats his heart with his fist. "Always trust your gut instinct," he says and turns to head to the bar.

Oh God, I wish my heart would stop pounding so much. It's too much for me, this guy is just so charming and easy to fall for. I'm sure it's not just me thinking this. Others must fall for his charms as easily as I am. Oh cop on woman, cop on!!

He returns with two drinks.

"Thanks for the drink. Listen, I'd better go after this as I need to be up early tomorrow to open the shop again and I don't want to let them down," I say.

"Oh, ok, I thought you was enjoying my company?" he says, looking hurt.

"I am, but I'm also trying to be realistic here. I know you all of what… three hours now? And we are talking about relationships. Next it'll be babies and marriage and we don't even know each other well enough yet. And I'm not used to someone trying or getting so close to me. It's difficult for me to be able to trust that easily. I fancy you, I fancy you like crazy. You've been incredibly honest with me about everything from your past and how you've been bullied. The fact you've told me it's all a façade, well that was very open and honest of you. I really like this side of you. The crazy side is very, very charming indeed, but I like the honest side of you even more. This is what scares me, I am afraid the same thing that just happened with 'Jarvey' as you call him, will happen with you. I can't trust myself that's the problem. I can't trust myself to just see you as a friend starting off and then let it lead to something else. I fall too quickly and I'm worried this could be something that would just crack my heart in two again," I say.

"That's incredible," he says.

"What is?"

"You've just given me more information about how you feel about me now in twenty seconds than what you have all evening. I mean what I say. I don't want to hurt you and I don't want to get hurt either. Remember, I've fancied you from afar for quite some time and it's taken me a long time to get that courage up to ask you out. Admittedly, it was a bit forward, but it took a lot of me practising what I'd say to you in the mirror before I did all that theatrical stuff. I kid you not."

"You practised it in the mirror?" I say with a smile.

"Yeah! I know I sound pathetic probably, but I always do that. If I'm going on a date, I try to think of things to talk about and practise them in the mirror beforehand. It has to be done, what if I mess up a really funny line?"

"Did you ever hear of going with the flow?" I ask.

"Yeah, but that doesn't always work darlin'."

"So this whole thing was a set up then, that you've practised in the mirror and you've hoped I'd answer your questions the way you want me to?"

"No, no, no! How can I word this to sound right? Ok, I have wanted to ask you out now for probably six months or so. And to do that, I had to pluck up the courage. I had to practise in the mirror and pretend that it was all going smoothly and that you wanted me greatly, so that I could get to that stage of asking you out. I had to mentally prepare myself to think positively and that this was how you would react. Otherwise, I'd never have got to this stage and I wouldn't have ever had the balls to ask you out."

I smile. He's cute. I like him, a lot.

"Ok, I get what you are saying. Walk me home and we can talk more on the way," I say.

"You drank that back fast," he says.

"I know, I was nervous I suppose, I'm not sure why I did actually, as I don't drink a great deal in general. Come on," I say. I stretch my hand out. "You did ask earlier if we'd hold hands walking home," I say with a smile.

He takes my hand and squeezes it tight. "Ok, so I get to hold the hand, would I be pushing my luck now if I try to kiss you when we get to the flats?" he asks, biting his lip.

"Let's walk and when we get there, we'll find out," I say.

"How about a cheeky arm around you to keep you warm, it's chilly out tonight, innit?"

"Go on then, I'll allow that, for now," I say with a smile.

We walk up the road and I love the feeling of his arm around me. He is keeping me very warm and I feel safe with him, even if I don't know him that well. We don't say much en route, but we catch each other's eye a few times and smile. A smile and a glance that tells me that we most certainly will have that goodnight kiss.

As we reach the flats, Pete opens the gate and lets me enter.

"So, I'll walk you to yours. Or would you like to come to my flat for a quick drink before you go home to bed? I know how exhausting it is for an old lady like you, having to get up tomorrow morning for work," he sniggers.

I playfully punch his arm. "Stop! You know I'll be hungover if I drink anymore and it could be a very long day. However, I will go for one drink," I say hoping he won't think me to be a party pooper.

We reach his door and he fumbles for his keys for a moment. "I need to get this light fixed," he says as he points to the blown bulb above his doorway. "Although maybe I shouldn't as this is quite romantic, just standing here with you. In fact, wouldn't this be a nice little setting for our first kiss," he says with a smile and winks at me.

"It might be," I respond feeling slightly shy.

Again, he smiles and I can feel my heart beating faster as he bends down to place his lips against mine. I feel a tingle rush through me as I never imagined his kiss to make me feel so good. He embraces me in his arms and right now I don't want this moment to ever end.

He pulls away from me and looks into my eyes, smiling. He turns the key in the door and says, "Come on darling, let's not get cold out here. We can snuggle up on the couch," as he leads me by the hand into his flat.

6

 t's Sunday morning and my head feels fuzzy. *Oh crap!* I turn quick-ly in the bed as a feeling of horror sweeps over me. *Please tell me I didn't. Oh thank God, I didn't.* I breathe a sigh of relief as I realise that Pete isn't next to me, and I didn't lose the run of myself the night before. *Hmmm, what did happen? I remember that amazing kiss we shared. I really shouldn't have had those extra drinks.* I drag myself from the bed, make my way to the kitchen and throw a few slices of bread into the toaster. I check the date on the paper covering the bread. *Ah, jaysus, was there mould on that?* I quickly pop the toaster again and check, but it looks ok, and I decide to just go with it as there is no visible mould. *I must remember to put food in the bin as it reaches its sell by date.* I hear a knock on the door and go to see who it is. I look through the peephole and start to giggle.

"'Ello cutie, you gonna let me in? I brought breakfast for you."

Oh, how sweet you are. Ok don't lose the run of yourself lady, you need to act cool. Leave him in, but act cool. I open the door. "Oh Pete, that's just lovely, how thoughtful of you."

"Well, after the few extra drinks you had at mine last night and all that snogging, I thought you might need something to eat before you go to the shop."

"Oh no!"

"You forgot, didn't you? About the shop? I hope you haven't forgotten last night?" he asks.

"Last night, what do you mean? Well, nothing happened," I say.

He's smiling like a Cheshire cat. *I didn't sleep with him there and make my way home did I?*

"Pete, why are you smiling at me like that?"

"Uha hua ha, sorry, I couldn't resist. No, nothing happened except a very long passionate kiss and speaking of which, you haven't even given me a peck on the lips this morning," he says, sounding hurt.

"Oh sorry, I do remember that kiss by the way," I say and lean forward and peck him on the lips. "There, is that better?" I ask.

"Much better, thank you darlin'. Now, we have a choice. You've got eggs, you've got muffins, croissants and crumpets. What would the lady care to eat?" he asks.

"You know how to impress, don't you? Crumpets would go down well, thank you. Where did you get all of this on a Sunday? It's freshly baked or at least looks like it!"

"Well, that's my secret weapon for the girls, I made them all. I love to cook and bake in my spare time. Not too unheard of in this day and age for a fine young man like myself."

"Less of the young... you're in your thirties darlin'," I say with a smile.

"Still young, I'm not ninety, am I?" he asks.

"Fair point! I won't argue with that. Just so you know, I'm incredibly impressed with you right now," I say.

"Why, thank you angelic creature that's been sent from above to me, so I could bake crumpets for you and whisk you off to idyllic places far and wide throughout the universe," he says with a grin.

"Bit of a poet, are we?" I ask.

"I like to dabble from time to time," he says.

"Nice," I say with a smile and say nothing more.

We eat our breakfast and while nothing more than a kiss happened the night before, I feel very close to him. I like this guy, he's different, very different from what I normally go for, and he's incredibly attractive.

"What time do you need to be at the shop for?" he asks.

"Oh, it doesn't matter, maybe ten. They asked me to do a few hours, but I'll do the day as I like helping them out."

"Ok. Should I bother calling to see you today then? I don't want to bombard you with my presence or it might turn you off me. It might make you run off into the sunset, and leave me forever."

"I won't do that. No, I'd like you to visit me today, maybe make it every hour rather than two today, what do you say?" I ask with a smile.

"Is the lady telling me she likes me by asking me that?" he says.

"Hmmm, maybe," I say with a flirtatious smile as I slide from the kitchen stool and make my way to the hallway.

"I need to go for a shower, are you happy to wait for me to continue our conversation, or do you need to go?" I ask.

"Oh I'm happy as long as you are my lovely. Here, you can't just leave me and not kiss me goodbye " he says.

"I'm only going to the shower, I'll be back in ten minutes," I say, laughing.

"But what if you decide to go via the back door and leave me here all alone like some lovelorn fool?" he asks.

I walk back towards him. "I wouldn't do that to you, Pete," I whisper in his ear and then press my lips to his. "Besides, there's no back door," I say with a smile.

"Ohhh, saucy, I like that side of you, more of that please," he says.

I giggle. "I really do have to get ready. I won't be long, you can walk me over to the shop if you want and if you have the time to hang around?" I ask.

"Course, I'd love to, and you might get to see me every half hour today. Am I scaring you now?" he asks.

"Nope, dare I say it, I might enjoy that!" I say with a smile as I turn my back and walk to the hallway.

This guy could be a keeper.

7

"Bloody 'ell, you must be the first woman I've ever met who is ready in ten minutes when she says ten minutes," he says as I walk into the living room.

"I like to surprise," I say. "But if truth be known, I'm never on time for anything and I was only ten minutes this time because I'm conscious of the fact I need to be at the shop. Under normal circumstances, you'd be waiting a lot longer."

"Oh, so I'm not just a special guy then? I was getting excited there, thinking you were just dying to see my beautiful shiny locks and shining eyes and smile."

I smile and grab his hand. "Come on you, let's go."

As we walk up the street he lets my hand go free and decides to pull me closer instead by sliding his hand around my waist. I like it and instead of asking him to remove it, like I normally do when playing hard to get, I decide to leave it there and I slide my arm around him.

"Oh, we like being held tight, don't we?" he says with a playful smile.

"Maybe, you do have a good firm grip bless ya," I say with a snigger. "What the hell? Guys, what are ye doing back so early? I was just opening up," I say with surprise.

"Oh! We always arrive back early on the Sunday. We like to rest a bit before Monday. It's normal for us, Katie love," Edith says. "And would you look, eh Eddie, looks like our plan worked. Oh, Pete, you've had a right fancy of Katie for some time, delighted you two got to spend time together and looks like a budding romance," she says clapping her hands together like a child who's been given sweeties.

"I have, haven't I?! And she almost blew me out can you believe? If it wasn't for old Jarvey popping into the shop I think she would've ignored my advances, and I'd have been driven to the depths of despair because the one I have fallen for had cast me aside," he says with a laugh.

"Oh such a romantic boy you are Pete," she says. "Who's old Jarvey?" she quizzes.

"Well, he's me new mate now. Jarvey is the one who ignores the girl next door pretty, sexy types and goes for the sharks," he says with a smile. "Much to my advantage, I might add."

"Oh Pete, stop it," I say. *Did you have to bring Jarvis into the damn conversation?*

"Oh look, Eddie, they're arguing like a couple should be already," she says.

"I like that idea!" Pete says. "Come on, let's go do something fun today Katie. Let's go to the cinema or go for a nice walk down the Southbank. Oh, I love the Southbank I do," he says with a dreamy look on his face.

"So do I," I reply with a grin. "Let's do that, we can go for a nice lunch and just people watch," I say excitedly.

"Now you're talking. Ok, thank you so much for coming back early. I'd like to offer you my beautiful girl's services for the afternoon still, but I'm sure you'll forgive me if I whisk her off on a white horse to take in the wondrous sights of London and the Southbank," Pete says.

"Pete, they might need my help still?" I say quizzically, looking in their direction.

"Don't you even think about it, my love, you get your young selves off out there and enjoy what this sunny Sunday has to offer you," Eddie says.

Edith nods in agreement. "You know we never leave the shop for more than a night. Pete, you'll assure her won't you?"

"Course I will. It's true and for as long as I've lived around these parts, which is about seven years now, I've never ever seen this shop closed on a Sunday. Absolute bloody workaholics they are," he says and winks at them.

"Well, it could be worse," Edith says. "Now, love, pop the kettle on. I'm dying for a brew," she says to her husband. "You two be off or I'll have to get angry!"

Oh bless you, you couldn't get angry...I just can't picture that for a moment. "We're going," I say with a smile. "Thank you."

"No, my love, thank you for your help and I'm glad you two have got it together finally. I've always thought you'd make a cute couple. It was so difficult trying to see if you fancied Pete though without dropping him in it. I was like a spy for months. I'm so glad I don't have to pretend I don't know anything anymore," she giggles. "Bye now and have a fun day," she says as she makes her way into the shop.

"Treat her like a lady Pete, she's a good 'un," her husband roars from the back of the shop.

"I will sir, and if she misbehaves I'll sell her for something more worthwhile in Borough Market," he says with a cheeky grin.

"You're some cheeky fecker," I say as I playfully punch his arm.

"Oh, you know me now," he says as he breaks into song. "I got the hots for you."

"Spare me, Pete, spare me!"

He winks.

You're definitely very cheeky, maybe a little too cheeky, but you're sort of, hmm I don't know, special also.

8

We stroll down to the South Bank. I love it so much, the buzz and vibe around is amazing, no matter what day of the week. I particularly love it around London Bridge. On weekdays, you get a mixture of well clad men and women who are bustling about in and out of their offices, mingling between the tourists and on weekends you see them relaxed and casual. The atmosphere around here is wonderful as people stroll up and down the river side, frequenting the shops and coffee bars, with the bars and restaurants intertwined between all of the attractions. Today, however, I feel like a visit to Borough Market. There's always so much choice for food and the ambiance is always very lively. Pete and I stroll along hand in hand, with not many words passed between us. It's oddly like a very comfortable silence for both of us it seems.

"I'm afraid to break the silence," he whispers in my ear.

I smile. "If you feel the need to then do," I reply.

"I have to, because we're coming up to the best food stand in Borough Market and I'm going to treat you," he says with a smile.

"Ohhhh you are spoiling me today, first making me breakfast and now treating me to lunch?"

"Yeah, you're worth it. Besides, it's only going to cost me around a fiver. I wouldn't bother if it was more than that!" he says with a peal of laughter.

"Oh ha ha, you're hilarious Peter."

"That's serious, you're calling me Peter." He frowns. "People only call me that when they are angry with me or are looking for my attention somehow. I'm a bit scared now."

I snigger. "I thought it might grab your attention. Ok, so what should we do, sit here, relax and get to know each other or walk while we eat?" I ask.

"Well there's not really anywhere for us to sit, this is kind of a street food thing so we might have to just stand, wolf it down and then go for a drink somewhere. How's that sound?" he asks.

"Yeah, ok, very romantic," I say, not too impressed. *I thought you'd put a bit more effort in. At least take me for a nice sit down lunch or something.*

"I know you sound disappointed, but this will sum me up for you today. If you don't fall madly in love with what I'm about to feed you," he stops and sniggers.

"Pete!!!"

"What? I'm taking you to a food stall to feed you, what the hell did you think I meant?" he says, as if completely innocent, with a smug grin on his face. "Honestly, you have a mind that is just fit for a gutter. You might turn me off you now, you know? I'm looking for a lady," he says with a wink.

"Well you'd have to be dragged to the gutter with me then!" I say.

"I wouldn't have to be dragged, I'd be there waiting with open arms for you. Oh, here we are and as I thought, a queue to the back of the market. As I said, you'll fall in love with this food today, and with me, I'm the added bonus," he says.

The queue is into the back arse of nowhere and I'm starving. "So, what is this food? It looks like some sort of hot dog stand or something?" I ask.

"Yes, but they aren't hot dogs. They are the best sausages you'll get anywhere! I tell you, it's simple, but really delicious and you will not want food for hours after it," he says with a smile.

"Do you want to move on somewhere else? I suggest. The queue is fierce long isn't it?" *Hot dogs, posh hot dogs is what you want me to eat! I'll be starving in no time again. Still, I suppose I can't expect too much for a second date. He'd better step it up some bit for the next one.*

"Oh tis, fierce, fierce tis " he says with a giggle. I'll never understand why people try so hard to take the piss out of the Irish accent because they only make bigger gobshites out of themselves when they try. They should just leave well enough alone.

"Yet another pathetic attempt. I am hoping there will be a time when you give up on trying to achieve the perfect Irish accent. It won't work, not with your cockney one."

"I know. I suppose I have to some day before we grow old in each other's arms. You know I only do it to annoy you don't you?" he says with a grin.

"Yes I was guessing that but if you like me so much why would you want to annoy me?"

"Because I do like you so much, because it's my way of playing with you, showing how much I like you. Letting you know I want more," he says as he plants a kiss on my lips. "There, now that made you smile," he says.

It's true it has. I can't help but smile at him. He's cheeky, funny and incredibly handsome all rolled into one. *What the hell is wrong with him, though? There has to be something, he can't be perfect surely!!*

"Pete, can I ask you something?"

"Sure you can, what is it?"

"Well, I'm afraid as this seems to be moving along a bit quickly. You know what I mean, like we only met yesterday and I feel like I've known you for years. I'm worried you'll get rid of me as fast as you found me. Do you have a long history of girls?"

He cups my face in his hands and looks into my eyes.

"Katie darlin', I'm the type of guy who just gives it his all. I've had relationships which have ended with me being the one who's upset, not the other way around. I'm probably too soft, I admit I get attached so easily. I try not to, but when I truly like a girl, I have to go with it. I have seen you for months, walking in and out of our block of flats. I've wanted to ask you out for months, I told you that yesterday, but I just couldn't get the courage because... oh crap, I shouldn't say this as you'll think I'm weak or something. But I was terrified you'd knock me back if I asked you out. I was telling them in the shop day in day out, I'm gonna ask her today. They always smiled and said it would happen when the time was right. I started to believe that Katie. For the past few months I've spent a lot of time finding myself, who I really am, meditating, and just doing things by myself to find out what I like and who I actually am. I'm in a good place now and I believe because I am, this was why the time was right to ask you out. I'm not going anywhere, unless you want me to. I will respect you and if you aren't interested in me, I'll walk away, just tell me. I don't want to cause any problems for anyone."

"Wow, Pete, I wasn't expecting that from you," I say in shock. "I don't know what to say, that was so open and honest. I've never had someone look me in the eye and say something like that to me before."

"Well, I mean what I say. Katie, I really like you, and I'm just hoping you'll give me that chance to see if you like me too. That's all I want, for you to give me a real chance."

"It's ok, I know that's what you want, but I already know that I like you, a lot," I say with a smile.

He's still cupping my face in his hands as he smiles and lowers his lips to mine. "We can take this slow, it's up to you. I just know I'm going to enjoy spending every minute with you," he says as he kisses me again.

I feel ill, not like stomach churning illness because he's so lovey dovey, no I feel ill because I'm so damn excited about him.

"Here we go darlin', get this into you," Pete says as hands me the food. I reach out and take it from him and giggle as I taste it. Pete is staring at me waiting for my reaction and he looks so excited, it's actually cute. I take a massive mouth full and as the flavour erupts, I smile and nod my head. *Hmmmm you know your good food, don't you? Maybe I got you all wrong. This might actually be a really good choice of venue for a second date.*

"Good, innit?' he asks with a smile. "I know what I'm doing. I wouldn't take you to some shoddy spot."

"I have to admit, I'm very impressed," I respond with a grin.

I feel a buzzing sensation in my pocket. I take a quick peek at my phone and put it back in my pocket. *Such timing.* It's Sarah, I choose to ignore it. After all, she's hardly been knocking down my door asking me to go for drinks or a catch up since Jarvis arrived on the scene. Well, I have my own guy now, and dare I say it, he's far better than any Jarvis and I've a feeling this man might just be the one for me.

9

*I*t's Monday morning and I'm allergic — not just because it's Monday, but because I have to face into that job that just bores me to death so much. The only reason I stay there is the money and Ted, my gay best friend there, who keeps me sane. I can't even be bothered to make an effort today. I haul myself from the bed, hop in the shower quickly and grab the first thing I see to wear. It's unfortunate that I didn't turn the lights on while getting dressed and chose to get dressed in the dim light of the sunrise instead. I'm now sporting an orange/red skirt with green tights (which I thought were black), and I resemble someone who might be going to play a game of football or suchlike with the garish colours, rather than going to work. However, I don't care. I might even brighten up the office a little bit.

As I push the office doors open, I can see people looking at me and feel them boring holes in my back as I walk passed them. The sniggers are almost unbearable and I feel like I'm going to snap at any second.

"What date is today?" Ian asks Ted.

"Well it's October twenty fifth mate, I believe," Ted replies.

"Really? I thought it might have been St. Patrick's Day," Ian replies with a laugh.

"Oh, shut it Ian," I say, stifling a laugh. I can see why he would think it, the white shirt I'm wearing with my ensemble just sets it off to perfection - I am sporting my country's colours — unintentionally. "Look, it was more or less dark when I was getting dressed this morning and I thought the tights were black, ok?" I am laughing at this point because I can see the funny side of it. I should know better, as there was no way on this earth I was going to avoid getting ridiculed over my dress sense today.

"Sorry, Katie. It's a good look, though, very leprechaun-esque, but you've spoiled your St. Patrick's Day outfit now, you'll have to re-think it all," he says.

I never get offended at what these guys say, they are only joking and I know they both love me to bits. Thankfully, I have a sense of humour and don't get offended easily. "Be careful," I say, giving him the death stare. "Don't make me silence you, you know I can with one foul swoop of my sarcasm."

"Don't I know it. Ok, I'll be quiet now, not a peep out of me for the rest of the day," he says.

"Good, and for the trouble you're causing, you can buy me a few drinks in the pub later in the week as an apology," I say with a grin. "And don't think I'll forget, I won't!"

"Ok, ok, well I know you won't forget, but I can't promise anything Katie, especially if you turn up dressed like a flag again," he sniggers as he walks off.

Little fecker. I wouldn't mind but I could probably dance a jig on his head he's so small. A small man with a big gob. As much as I like him, I think he suffers from SMS sometimes (Small Man Syndrome).

— —

I spend the day thinking about Pete, and wonder if I should drop him a little WhatsApp message to say hi. Although I worry then I'll look too keen. Such a difficult situation, I never know what to do at the start of what could be a relationship. It's the awkward moment where you don't want to look like a stalker, but you don't want to look like you don't care either. I bite the bullet at 5 pm and decide to text him.

Peter, are ya well? How's your day gone, I hope you're not
working too hard? x

*One kiss, two kisses? No kisses? Ahhh, this is difficult. Put one, you did spend two days snog-
ging the face off of him so why not? One it is. Casual, but shows I care. Right. Send!!*
I keep my phone in my hand in the hope he will reply soon. *Oh for
God's sake, put the phone away. He's a male and most likely will play games and won't
answer for hours on end, if at all. You've shown you're too keen now, he'll take the piss
and run.*
My heart skips a beat as the phone vibrates in my hand. *Message from Peter.*

Hello darlin', I didn't have work today. I work shifts so
won't be working again until Wednesday. How was your
day? Want to meet up tonight or is three days in a row too
much for you? xx

Ohhh two kisses and he wants to see me tonight.
"Hey! Fuck sake love, watch where you're going," some random
stranger roars at me as she runs past. Admittedly I was doing that annoying thing that people do on the street, checking my phone while
walking, but part of me thinks she was to blame too with the speed she
was running at. I was lucky I didn't drop the phone and break it.
"Ah, feck off and watch where you're going yourself," I roar after her.
Rude bitch.
I turn my attention back to the text message. I don't want to leave it
too long before I reply as he may want to make other plans if I don't meet
him.
*Hmmmm what'll I say? I want to see him, but don't want to be overly keen. I'm over ana-
lysing this, just say yes if you want to see him.*

Ok yes let's meet up tonight, I'm on my way home, should
I meet you here in the city centre or back at mine, or
yours? x, I text back. *Yes, keep it to one kiss... for now.*

Great, make your way home I'll cook for you at mine, just so you can refresh your memory of what my place looks like. xxx

Woah, you're keen! Oh, funny man is back to play I see. It's nice that he wants to cook for me. though.

Ok I'll be home in about twenty minutes; I'll walk as a nice evening. I'll bring the wine, red or white? x

Stick to one kiss, I notice he's sending one extra each message he sends, is he playing?

Great, I'll surprise you with my culinary delights tonight my darlin'. I enjoy a nice red, and because I'm making you the finest steak you'll ever taste, it might be better to have red. Unless of course you prefer a nice white? Thank you darling and see you soon. Xxxx PS Am I too over the top with the kisses?

I smile to myself as I reply.

Maybe a little, but have to admit I kind of like it. See you soon. x

I have a massive grin on my face for the entire journey home.

What did he mean about his culinary delights? I hope he did just mean food and nothing else... it's too soon for me, far too soon. I'm sure he did just mean his cooking ski'ls... oh, Jesus... stop! You're doing it again. You'll turn into a crazy woman from all the analysing.

I then realise I might have to take a detour to my flat on the way, especially when I remember what I'm wearing and how over the top Irish and eccentric I look today. I'm so proud of my Irish roots, but I don't make it my daily business to intentionally go out looking like the flag of my wonderful country. I reach the street which the flats are on within twenty minutes, and call to the shop to buy some wine.

"Oh, 'ello love, how are you today? Oh is it St. Patrick's Day today? You're looking very festive," Edith says with a smile.

I know that this is innocent though and she's not being smart so I laugh. "No, no, just me deciding to get dressed in the dark this morning and somehow came up with this concoction which has opened me up to many smart comments today," I say with a giggle.

"Oh love, I wasn't being smart, sorry. How was your big date yesterday? He's a good lad that Pete, he's helped us out with fixing shelves and the like in the shop when Eddie's back was bad. A good lad he is. Had his heart broken a while back you know? We want the best for him, but we know you're a good girl too and you look good together," Edith says with a giant grin on her face.

"Hi, thanks and it's early days," I say with a smile. "He is lovely, though, I have to admit. I really do fancy him, even if I only know him three days now, well, two really as I haven't seen him yet today," I say.

"I like the use of that 'yet' word," she says with a giggle.

"Well, I am on my way there now to see him. I need to buy some wine. He's cooking me what he claims will be the best steak I'll ever taste."

"Oh my, isn't that nice he can cook. I do all the cooking 'ere love, most loverboy down the back of the shop can cook is beans on toast if I'm lucky. But you know what, I wouldn't change him for the world and from time to time I don't mind him making that for me tea, if it means havin' a break and I know it's made with plenty of love, which is what makes it even better," she says.

"Oh, that's so sweet. You see, that's what true love is and too many people today think it's all about money. That's exactly what I'm looking for and I know I don't know Pete all that well yet, but he's not money obsessed and he's romantic. He has that element of chivalry in him which seems to be gone in most of the guys these days. He holds my hand, and he opens doors for me. These are all the things that matter to me! I don't care about money. I never have and never will. All I want is for someone to love me the way that Eddie loves you. Keep your fingers crossed. I have a feeling he is a good one, but I'm scared I'll end up with a broken heart," I admit to Edith.

"Oh my love, if he broke your heart, as much as I adore him, I'd be hunting him out the door of this shop and chasing him up the street with me mop. I won't hear of him doing that to you. I know him well enough though, and he won't do that, no he definitely won't. He's a good lad," she says with a smile. 'And here you go, two bottles of red wine on the house."

"No! I'm paying you for this."

"Your money is no good in my shop, you helped us out greatly at the weekend, let me thank you in this way as you wouldn't take payment. At least you can sit down and enjoy this with your meal tonight."

"Thank you," I say as I take the bag reluctantly.

I feel guilty taking this, it's too much and I was happy to help them out, they needed a break.

"Now off you go, do let me know how things are going in a few days won't you? Don't forget us old gossipy couples who need a bit of excitement in their lives," she says with a grin.

"I'll let you know and thanks again," I say as I leave the shop.

I make my way towards the flats. *What'll I do, will I go home or go straight to him? I don't know if I can take any more of this mockery of me looking like a flag. Oh, sod it, I'll brave it and go straight to him.*

I open the gate with my key and make my way to number ten. I press the bell.

"Pete's love den and steak house," booms the voice over the speaker.

"Hi there, my name is Katie, I've come to sample the goods," I say with a giggle. *I might as well play along.*

"Oh well, you better come on up then. I will warn you, we have naked chefs in this establishment, I hope you're ok with that?"

Oh God! I can't go in now, Talk about putting me under pressure. How can I excuse myself now?

"Ha ha ha Katie, I'm joking about, I'm not naked, come on up. I loved that silence, was you trying to think of how to get out of coming up to my flat?"

"Oh, just let me in!" I demand.

I make my way up to the second floor flat. He's in the three bedroom flats, mine has two, but I'm more than happy with that, it's plenty big enough for me. I'm just about to knock on the door when it swings opened.

"Hello darlin'," he cups my face in his hands and plants a lovely soft kiss on my lips. He looks into my eyes and smiles. "How was your day? What the fuck? Is today St. Patrick's Day?" he asks.

I erupt into laughter. "Ahh, too many questions! I was expecting that from you. I've put up with so much ridicule today, due to my wonderful dress sense," I say as I blush.

"So, what happened to make you choose this very authentic Irish look today, my little leprechaun?" he asks.

I smile. "Well, I've had to explain this to so many people today. I woke up, allergic, didn't want to go to work as is the normal on a Monday for me and so decided to just get dressed in the faint light of the sunrise. I know, even if they aren't in the correct order I resemble my national flag. Now, forget what I'm wearing and talk about something else, please?" I ask.

"Oh, how lovely, well if you feel uncomfortable you can take your clothes off," Pete says with a grin.

"Ha ha funny man, you know I'm not here for that reason so I hope you don't have any great expectations tonight."

"Oh, I know you're not, don't worry, I jest my darlin'. You know me now, and I did tell you already, it only goes to that stage when we both feel it's right. Tonight we are still getting to know one another. You can tell me some dirty stories of when you were in your twenties instead, that will keep me happy," he says as he tries to muffle a laugh.

My face drops. "Would you like me to leave now?" I ask.

"Oh come on, you know I can't resist. Please, let the lady sit and I shall pour her a nice glass of... Blimey! That's expensive wine," he says as he pours it into the very nice crystal glass that sits in front of me on the table.

"Well, expensive wine for the expensive glass it sits in," I say. "Don't worry, it was free, and I really didn't want it to be. I called to the shop on the way here to buy it and they wouldn't accept any money from me. I wasn't even going to go for this particular wine. I just kind of mentioned that you were cooking me a nice steak for dinner and you know how Edith gets excited? Before I knew it she had two bottles in a bag and wouldn't take any money. She said it was payment for me looking after the shop and she just seems so thrilled that we're hitting it off."

"Blimey, that is expensive. Oh, we can do something nice for them some day soon to thank them, I'll not let that slip by," Pete says.

"I know, they are sweet." I take a deep breath and inhale the smell of the red liquid in the glass. "I'm no wine expert, but it smells like blackcurrants and a hint of blueberries," I say with a giggle. I hold the glass up and clink it against Pete's and we take a sip.

"Oh you got that one right love, you're definitely no wine expert," he says with a wink and a smile.

10

*I*t's a Saturday morning. It's a beautiful day out, but very cold, and the clear blue sky is making me want to go for a nice long walk. I look at my phone and it's only 7:30 am. I decide for a change that I'll get up early and make my lovely new man breakfast. It's been twelve weeks since he first stayed over and he's hardly left since, even though his flat is just across the courtyard. I'm not complaining. I love his company and to wake up in his arms, when he's not after falling out of the bed that is.

I'm in the kitchen cutting some fresh fruit, might as well give him something healthy before the bad fry up.

"'Ello 'ello, beautiful," I hear from behind me as a hand slips around my waist.

"Aww, I wanted to surprise you for a change with breakfast in bed," I say with a smile as I kiss him gently on the lips.

"That's sweet of ya. Shall I go back to bed then?" he asks.

"You can and I'll bring it in once it's ready," I say.

"Oh, don't worry darlin' I'm up now I can't go back to bed at this stage. You know me, I'm an early bird. I'll sit here and admire your derriere through those nice silky arse clinging pyjamas you're wearing, instead," he says.

I throw a strawberry at him, but of course as always he's on the ball and catches it with his mouth. "You shhhould know behhter," he mutters as he chomps on the strawberry.

"I know, I know. I'll learn some day," I say.

"So what's the plan of action today? Are we doing our own thing or you want to do something with me, or what's your plan?" he asks.

I like this about him, he's not too clingy and knows I like to spend time with my friends also and not just with him.

"I'm meeting Sarah today. I haven't seen her in ages and well, I felt a bit guilty when she rang when we were out that Sunday and I didn't answer. I think maybe she's feeling guilty too as she's spent so much time with Jarvey, as you like to call him, of late. I think she's finally realised she's forgotten her friends."

"Well you were right not to answer that day, what does she expect when she ignored you for the past few weeks just because she was loved up. I'll never understand you girls. You forget your mates so easily."

"Well, I haven't. I was just peed off at her and didn't contact her as she was making no effort when I did call her. I didn't forget her just because you came on the scene though, aren't I meeting her today?" I say defensively.

"Calm it, calm it. I'm not suggesting you have. I'm happy you chose to spend time with your friends still, it's far healthier for both of us, and I get to spend time with my mates too. I don't want us to get to a stage where we are with each other twenty-four-seven. I know it seems like we are lately probably, but we still have breathing space. It's just not healthy to spend all of our time together even if we are in what they call the honeymoon phase... and the shenanigans are great," he says with a big cheeky grin.

I can't help but smile, he's right, the shenanigans are bloody great and I want to hop on him every time I see him, even right now. "You're right," I say. "We are being a bit more mature about this I suppose. Yeah, mature is a good word to describe our relationship... well to a certain extent. I'm the mature one and you're the child who's learning how to become mature," I say with a smirk.

"Oh well, for that comment, I'll have to be a bit naughty with you now. You know that don't you?" he says with a big dirty grin across his face, as he starts to gently kiss my neck while brushing my hair to one side.

"I'll burn the rashers," I say with a giggle.

"Oh, we'll just turn them off," he says as he reaches over my shoulder and turns the gas off. "I'm far more important than rashers darlin'," he says as he winks at me and grabs my hand. We head for the bedroom.

"I'll decide that, thank you very much," I giggle. I just can't resist him for even one second. *I'm one lucky lady.*

— —

I wake suddenly and check my watch. "I don't believe it!" I scream.

"What's wrong darlin'? What happened?" Pete sits upright in the bed with fright.

"It's 1:30! I'm meant to meet Sarah in forty-five minutes. I'll never be ready in time," I shriek.

"Oh you will, you look gorgeous babe, you have that after-glow. Put your hair up and stick some clothes on, you'll be there in twenty minutes."

"I need to shower. I can't go out smelling!" I say.

"I don't think she'll be that close to you will she?" he asks.

I laugh. "No, but I'd just feel a bit fresher if I shower. I won't wash my hair. Tis all your fault," I say as I grin at him over my shoulder as I head for the shower.

"Oh, blame the boy, always blame the boy," he says with a pleased look on his face. "I tell ya darlin', it was worth it though wasn't it?" he shouts out.

I pretend not to hear him. But it was. Pete is like no other I've met. He is just amazing and from the first night we started going out together, I can't stop thinking about him.

I rush in and out of the shower as quickly as possible. My brown hair now looks a little greasy so I do what Pete suggested and just pin it up. *There, that looks ten times better and he's right, I do have a certain glow. I won't bother with makeup.*

"Ok, I'm off," I say as I plant a kiss on his lips. "Help yourself to whatever you want here, will you be here later or will we have a night off?" I ask.

"I don't mind, I was gonna hook up with the boys and see what's happening. I don't want to rush you either so let's see what happens later, I'll text you," he says as he purses his lips together again for one final smooch before I go.

"You do know if anyone saw our display we'd probably make them vomit, we're so lovey dovey," I say.

"I don't care, I'm a sensitive, loving man and if I want to show my beautiful lady affection whether it be in the great outdoors or in her bed, I shall do so and no one shall stop me," he says in an action hero voice.

I smile and blow a kiss at him. "Talk or text later, have fun with the lads."

"I will thanks, and you too with Sarah. I hope she ain't bringing that Jarvey fool with her!" he says as I close the door.

"Thanks, no I'd doubt it!" I roar.

11

"Hello my love, how are ya?" Sarah asks with open arms to give me a hug.

"Hey you, I hardly remember what you look like," I say playfully. "What's been going on with you?" I ask.

"Oh I'm sorry Katie, I've been a terrible friend, I know, I'm so sorry. I just got swept up in the fact that someone as gorgeous as Jarvis would fancy someone as normal as me— oh I just love saying his name now, it's so posh and I never thought I'd end up with someone called Jarvis. I know I've neglected you and I'm sorry."

Woah, jumping the gun a little? End up with, are you getting married to him already or what?

"Ah that's ok, I've been pretty busy myself," I say with a smile. *I wonder will you ask why there's a big smile on my face or have you even noticed?*

"Oh good, oh I just have to tell you all about Jarvis, he's just amazing Katie. Last week he...."

Oh great. I can see this will be a great day.

I listen as best I can, but my mind is elsewhere. I can still smell Pete on my skin after this morning and it makes me smile so much. He's the best thing that's ever happened in my life so far, and I'm determined to keep it that way.

"Katie, Katie, are you listening?" Sarah says.

"Oh sorry, I am sorry Sarah. I just remembered something I need to do, so got a bit side tracked, carry on," I say.

"No, no, sorry I'm probably boring you. Tell me all of your news as I'm sure you don't want me banging on about my lovely new man when you're still single," she says with a smile.

Damn girl, was that a dig? You used never be like this, what has happened to you lately? "Oh no you carry on, I've got news of my own I can share with you later.... whenever you finish," I say sarcastically. I know she'll get that little dig. *Don't ever try to outdo me in the sarcasm stakes Sarah, ever!!*

"Well, no, it's ok, you can tell me all about your news, I want to hear it," she says with an air of hurt pride. I know that she's feeling guilty, though, what she just said was quite hurtful and she knows I'd never retaliate with a sarcastic comment like that to her unless it was really necessary.

"Ok, well, remember that weekend you met Jarvey... ahem, I mean Jarvis?" I say trying to hold back the giggle.

"I do yes," she says with a smile.

Thankfully that worked, just the mention of his name and she's grinning like a Cheshire cat. "Well, I was working in the local shop, looking after it for the couple who own it, and to cut a long story short, I met Pete. Pete is my neighbour actually. Anyway, it seems he's had a thing for me for the past six months or more and he asked me out while I was in the shop. We've been seeing each other since. He's lovely, he's fit, got this great six pack...oh just to die for, he's just lush. Absolutely lush, delicious, delightful and delicate too as a very sensitive caring type of guy."

"Oh, you sound like you're in love already and how long do you know him?" she asks.

DIG!! Says the one talking. You've had verbal diarrohea in relation to Jarvey since the moment I saw you today. "I wouldn't say in love as it's a bit soon for that maybe, but in very deep like. He's right up my street, literally as he lives across the courtyard," I say with a giggle. "Oh, that's..." "And he's so tall and just handsome," I finish while interrupting her at the same time.

"Fantastic, girl. So, maybe we can all meet up sometime?"

Oh no, what do I say to this? I can't introduce Pete to Jarvey again as last time he wasn't very polite and he also referred to you as a shark. Think fast now before you put your foot in it and you end up knee deep in shit.

"Yeah well, let's see how it all goes, it's early days for both of us yet," I say.

"Are you saying you don't think Jarvis and I will last?" she asks.

"No, of course not, I'm talking about myself and Pete," I manage to shout out with great haste as I realise it's the only way of getting out of what I just said. It seems everything I'll say today will be misconstrued so I'll just need to think carefully before I open my mouth.

"You're not sure about him so, are you?" Sarah asks.

"Ah shur you know yourself, you just never know what way it'll go when it's so early. Honeymoon period and all that, fantastic as it is and I'm loving every second of it, but you know what I mean. I'm just being careful. I prefer to know that I'll definitely be with the person long term before I start introducing friends."

"Yeah, I get you. So what else is going on, how's work in the Financial District? Are they still boring you to death?" she asks.

"Erm, that would be a yes. Ah they're ok, nice people, but they get so into their work sometimes. Every conversation revolves around work you know? Like one day recently one of the girls asked if we saw Celebrity Big Brother and I had just happened to see it the night before so said yes, I had seen it. Then one of the lads roars out, "Well they make some money out of that and I'd love to see the profit the TV producers make." I mean really, why not take a time out and just discuss what happened on the show rather than think about the money aspect of it? It's all about the money! Jesus!"

"I'd die in there. I'd just die in my seat I'd say. Sitting at my desk looking at the computer and plonk, head onto computer, dead," Sarah says with a laugh.

"You probably would. I wouldn't be surprised if that's how I go, although I hope maybe to change jobs soon before anything like that happens. Let's hop in here," I say, pointing to the Mudlark pub.

It's a hidden gem under London Bridge and near Borough Market. "Strategic planning let's have a few drinks and then we go to the market for some food?" I ask.

"Good thinking lady," Sarah says with glee. She seems like her old self again all of a sudden and I'm definitely not complaining.

It's 6:30 pm and we're both nicely merry. I feel my phone vibrate in my pocket. I take it out when Sarah goes to the toilet as I hate using my phone when in others company, it's just rude.

Awww a text message from Pete.

Hello Darlin', how's your day going? I'm after a few pints and feeling frisky as hell, fancy coming home early? xx

Hello Darling, day going well, no sign of Jarvey either you'll be glad to know. I'm a bit merry myself, but no plans to come home just yet. We are having a good day. I'm sure I won't be back too late. Will you be at home? xx

Yes, ring my bell when you get here, hahaha xx

I'm smiling to myself when Sarah returns.

"Oh, lover boy texting?" she asks.

"Yeah, he's asking if I'll be home soon. I told him not a while as I'm having fun. Unless of course, you want to go, or are meeting himself?" I say.

"No, no I'm happy out for a while. Although I am a bit more tipsy than you, I think. I'll slow down on the drink now. What do you fancy doing?" Sarah asks.

"Let's go to that Karaoke club down the road, it's always a good laugh there."

"Great thinking and it's been so long, let's do it. Hang on, I think Laura and a few of the others will be there tonight too, it's her friend's birthday. Actually, have you been onto Laura lately?" she asks.

"Erm, no, I haven't seen her since that dinner party, the one where you met Jarvis," I say.

"That's a bit unusual, did you fall out as you are normally very close? I've just seen her a bit more lately as I've been out and about a lot with Jarvis and his friends," Sarah says.

"Yeah you know how it is, when people are busy you lose touch for a little while and then you see each other and it's like you only saw each other yesterday," I say.

I can't tell you I'm avoiding Laura as I know she's pissed off over the whole Jarvis thing, and I didn't want her to feel any more awkward. Still, I'll have to bump into her at some point I guess. It might as well be tonight when I'm hammered.

"Well let's go so, I'll text her on the way and we can have a good auld night out all together. Would you mind if Jarvis comes along later?" she slurs.

Yes, I do mind!!

"No, no that's just fine," I say with a smile... a fake one.

We make our way to the Karaoke bar, and one of my favourite songs is on the list so I can't resist putting my name down to sing.

"Katie! Katie! Oh how fantastic to see you," Laura drags me to one side. "Oh Katie, I'm so sorry I haven't been in touch, I still feel so dreadful after what happened that night with you know who! No names mentioned just in case," she whispers.

"Seriously Laura, it's fine and besides, he'll be here later so let's not pretend it had any weird effect on anyone. I've moved on anyway since then," I say with a grin.

"What? Who? Tell me all. Oh are you going to sing tonight?" she quizzes.

"Yes, lady, I'm going to sing 'Don't You Want Me Baby' by The Human League. Great auld song and I'm merry enough to sing now...probably out of tune, but that's what makes it fun," I shout as the music gets louder.

"Well I'm going to join you!" she giggles. "Let's go."

As my name is called out we head to the stage. Sarah is laughing when she sees us both go. She's happy, Jarvis has arrived and she's clinging to him for dear life.

I can hear I'm totally off key, but Laura isn't helping as she's tone deaf anyway. At least when I'm sober I can normally hold a tune. She's just drastic anyway and would make a dog cover its ears. Bad as we are, we end to rapturous applause. I'm pretty certain it was the booty wiggling that Laura displayed was probably what got us that reception. She drops the posh side every now and then if she's after a few drinks, and sometimes exaggerates it. I know she has been out for most of the day also, just like us.

"Oh Katie that was so funny, you girls are hilarious together." Sarah says. "And, I never knew Laura was one to loosen up like that," she whispers.

"Oh, Laura's a wild one when she lets her hair down," I say with a smile.

As I look up Jarvis is staring at me, with a look of what I can only describe as longing, like he wants me. *Too late mate, you missed the bus a few weeks back.*

I smile, "Jarvis how are you?" I ask.

"Ah Jarvis, you remember my friend Katie from the dinner party don't you?" Sarah asks, clinging to him again as if he is going to run off and leave her.

The way he's looking at me, I wouldn't be surprised if that's exactly what he has on his mind. However, he won't be leaving her for me, that's for sure. As much as I still find him attractive, I would never, ever do that to a friend. I do feel sorry for her, though.

"Of course I remember Katie," he says with a smile and bends down to kiss me on both cheeks. 'How are you, Katie? That was a magnificent display up on stage."

"Oh, thanks, Jarvis, nice to see you again. That's not something I'd normally do, only when hammered," I say with an air of pride, in the hope that he will stop looking at me with sexy eyes. *Surely, if I let you think I drink copious amounts of alcohol on a regular basis that will turn you off? All lies, but you won't know that.*

"I didn't know ladies like you got hammered?"

"All of the time Jarvis, twenty-four-seven, can't you tell?" *Is this working?*

He smiles. "I keep telling Sarah she should let her hair down more, go out with the girls more and get hammered, as you say. She just doesn't seem interested though or if she does, she gets very quiet. I like that you get fired up and full of spirit after a few drinks, you're full of personality aren't you?" he asks.

"Erm, well thanks, but you know everyone is different and I know Sarah has had the same amount as me today, but yeah I suppose it just affects people differently. She gets quiet, I get wild," I say with a smile. "So, how's life in general with you, Jarvey...eh, Jarvis?"

"Yes well, life is good thanks. Work is more fun lately, interesting workload. I've been out a lot with Sarah, probably a bit too much if I'm honest. You know yourself, feeling a bit crowded now," he says with a smile.

I clearly had a lucky escape from you, you insensitive pig. "Ah, I don't think I'm the one you should be saying that to. If you're feeling crowded then you need to explain it to Sarah and don't treat her like crap or tell her friends with the expectation they might deliver the message for you," I say as I give him the death stare. *Asshole!!*

"Ok, sorry, maybe that was a bit insensitive of me. I like her a lot, but she is getting a little too clingy, I might have to say goodbye to her soon. I can't handle clingy people. They just drive me to drink. Anyway, what I'm getting to is, should I finish this thing with Sarah, would you be on for, you know, meeting up going for dinner and see if we'd have any interest in each other?"

Close your mouth Katie...close your mouth!! I can't believe you've just asked me that. Had this been different circumstances, had you not been with my friend for all this time, yes I'd consider this, but wow, you're some piece of work!!!

"Go Fuck Yourself," I whisper in his ear and smile at him. I stand back and wait for a response. "You heard that didn't you?" I ask.

"Ahem, yes I did and you surprise me," he says. "I thought you were keen on me."

"Well, there was a time when I was, but you chose Sarah over me. And now I'm choosing Sarah over you," I say, feeling very pleased with myself for coming up with that line.

"Right, well, we better be off then," he says as he turns his attention to where Sarah is standing with Laura.

"Sarah, you're looking tired, shall we go home?" he asks.

"Oh yes, I could do with my bed now, I'm feeling drained as we've been drinking all day," she says.

"Yes, your lovely drunken friend there has just informed me," he says.

I say my goodbyes to Sarah and once her back is turned and he looks at me, I give him the finger. Something I never do, but he has made me so infuriated, it's like a reflex action.

Did I just do that? I feel ill at the thought of him now, what on earth was he thinking? Sarah in the same room as us and he comes onto me, as if I'd jump on him and declare my undying love for him. I feel so sorry for Sarah. How do I broach this subject with her? Do I stay out of it and wait for him to break up with her? Oh, I'm just not able!!! I need to go home. I can't handle anymore tonight.

"Laura, I'm heading home. I'm absolutely wrecked."

"Oh you were in flying form five minutes ago, what happened?" she asks.

"Nothing, I suppose it's just hit me suddenly," I say in a carefree tone, even though it's far from carefree I feel.

"Ok darling, you head off, we'll speak soon and arrange a lunch or something. Oh that's a shame. I was having such fun with you. It's so good to see you and I'm sorry again, I just did feel awkward with the whole Jarvis situation. On that note, was there any awkwardness there tonight? I hope not?" she asks.

"Hmmm no, none, all good. We'll definitely hook up for lunch soon," I say trying to sound a bit more enthusiastic.

I manage to escape after air kissing Laura and her friends. I make my way out into the fresh air and the cold breeze hits me immediately once I step outside. I wrap my scarf around my neck and look at my watch. It's 8:30, still early. I'll call to Pete on my way home.

I reach the apartment block and let myself in via the security locked gate. I ring Pete's door bell.

"'Ello?"

"Hey you, can I come up?"

"Oh helllooooo baby. Of course you can, I'm delighted you called."

I smile to myself as I push the door opened. I'm looking forward to seeing Pete tonight. He's one person I always feel very happy to see. I reach his door, and before I can knock he opens it.

"Mmmmmm, I've been thinking about you all evening," he says as he pulls me close and puts both hands around my waist. "I just want to kiss you all night," he says as he looks into my eyes and smiles.

Oh, you're so romantic! I hope though you're not like Jarvis behind my back!! I try to cast that thought aside as I don't want to let that idiot ruin my romantic night in with Pete.

— —

The following morning, I wake quite early again. I look at the clock, annoyed to see that it's 8:30. Why can't I sleep longer at the weekend lately?

"Mmmmm, is my beautiful Irish queen awake early again today?" he turns in the bed to face me.

I smile. "Seems I am," I say.

"What's wrong? I can see it in your eyes there's something bothering you," he says.

"Yeah there is, really bothering me actually. Oh God! Hold on, I think I'm going to be sick," I say.

"Oh, charming! You turn to me and I make you want to puke, that's the nicest compliment any woman has ever given me," he shouts with a snigger as I run to the bathroom. I reach the toilet just in time.

Where the hell did that come from? I felt fine a moment ago.

When I look at my reflection in the mirror, I look pale. I wipe the beads of sweat from my forehead and as I go to leave the bathroom, I can feel it coming on again. I lift the toilet seat again and sit on the floor, it seems like it's never ending, yet there's nothing left to vomit. I feel vile.

Pete sticks his head around the door, "Love, are you ok? That was sudden!"

He called me love, he's said that before, but this was with concern. Oh, I wonder if it means he loves me. Ok, one thing at a time, you've your head down a toilet bowl at the moment, you can think about that later. Try to figure out how to get rid of this bug you caught, or is it a very bad hangover?

"Bad hangover or a bug? I don't know what this is, but I feel awful. It'll be a day in bed for me I think."

"That's alright, you stay here, you've got the TV in me bedroom and I'll look after you darlin'. I wouldn't mind just a duvet day with you today, cuddling up. I'll make you feel better," he says.

"Pete, I'm sick, I won't be on for any fun or frolics today," I say.

"No, I know, that's not what I meant. I meant I just want to cuddle you and look after you, give you a bit of TLC that you deserve. You're me lady, me girlfriend, I just want to treat you right and take care of you when you need taking care of. Give you hugs when you need them and today is one of those days. That's all, I didn't mean I wanted to have me wicked way with you. I'm not some freak! You have got your head down a toilet bowl puking," he says with a giggle.

"Sorry, I misunderstood," I say. I'm not sure how to take anything today, I'm just so out of it. "Duvet day with you it is, and I'll look forward to those hugs and cuddles as I really feel I need them."

I head back to the bed with Pete helping me and tucking me in like I'm some old lady, but it's sweet, and I like that. He's adorable and I do hope he's going to stay this way.

"So, how you feeling, you was gonna tell me what was bothering you earlier, until the sight of my face made you puke," he says with a smirk.

I touch his face, it's just so beautiful, there is no way that could ever make me feel ill in any way. To me, he's perfection. "I'm not sure it's something you'll want to hear to be honest, but I will tell you. Last night when I was out with Sarah, we went onto the Karaoke club in London Bridge. We met Laura there, you know Laura is the one who originally tried to set me up with who you call Jarvey?"

"Ah yeah, good old Jarvey, yeah. I remember you mentioning Laura before," Pete says.

"So, had a great laugh and did a very dodgy, but crowd pleasing rendition of 'Don't You Want Me Baby', with Laura. Which as it happens turned out to be a very appropriate song. While we were performing, Jarvis arrived. He was keeping Sarah company, and was chatting to the others also."

"Firstly, great song! However, I'm not too pleased that Jarvey is the cause of the puking! I should have known! Go on, sorry!" he says with a smile.

"So, when we got down from the stage, we returned to where Sarah was standing. I felt a bit awkward as I was worried in case Jarvis would say something about you calling Sarah a shark."

"Heahaheehahhh I'd forgotten about that, oh dear, he didn't say anything, did he?"

I giggle, "No he didn't, but he did come onto me."

"What? He came onto you? Well, you are gorgeous, but does he know we're together? Surely he got the hint that day? I know it was a while back and he might have thought you'd never go near me, but bloody cheek, trying to steal me girlfriend. What about Sarah, where was she? What a knob he is!"

"Yes, my sentiments exactly. She was chatting to Laura at the time. He was insinuating that he'd be finishing with Sarah, and if we wanted to give it a go he'd be delighted to try." I paused as I remembered the scene, then continued as I saw Pete waiting. "He said he loved how fun and spirited I get after a few drinks as Sarah tends to wind down. I was disgusted."

"What did you say to him?" Pete asks.

"I whispered in his ear. I said 'Go Fuck Yourself,' which seemed to take him very much by surprise. I was annoyed. I'd never say that to anyone normally, but he drove me to it, stupid idiot," I say.

Pete erupts into laughter, "I'd have given anything to be there, above all to hear you say that to him. He must have been totally shocked. I would be, as that's not you at all!"

"I know and then as he left he gave me this look as if to say 'your loss' so I gave him the finger. Obviously, it was the drink of course, as I'd never do that either normally."

Pete can't control his laughter and I can't control the rumbling and gurgling of my stomach as I run for the bathroom again. *This is definitely the worst hangover I've ever had.*

12

It's Monday morning and I still look and feel like crap. However, I make my way to work for what I expect will be a long week. I haven't heard from Sarah since Saturday so I decide to drop her a WhatsApp message.

> Hey you, how was the head yesterday? I was sick as a dog, still not feeling great. Hope you weren't in the same state?

I put the phone back in my pocket as I don't expect a reply for a while, if not a day or two. Thankfully the day goes by quickly and I rush home as I want to spend some time with Pete. I loved how he cuddled up to me yesterday when I was ill. I just wanted more of that. I ring his doorbell, but there's no reply. *Hmmmm, I wonder where you are, it's not like you to not be home before me.* I cross the courtyard and make my way up the stairwell to my flat. I feel like I haven't been here in ages as I ended up at Pete's for the entire weekend. I throw my bag on the sofa and put my glasses on the shelf. My eyes are tired having spent the day looking at spreadsheets on the computer. I check my phone to see if Sarah has replied. Nothing. However, there is a message from Pete.

Hi my darling, I got good news today so I've gone out with the boys to celebrate. Will tell you all later if I'm home early enough. x

Hmmmm, I wonder what he's celebrating that he can't tell me about before the boys? Am I less important than them now? Well, feck it anyway, it's my own fault for getting too attached too soon. Of course he doesn't have to tell me things first, but why do I feel like he should have?

I put my phone on the table and grab the remote control, switch the TV on and lie on the couch. I end up nodding off while watching the music channel.

DING DONG! *Oh God! What was that? What time is it? Where am I?*

It takes a few minutes for me to realise that I'm in my living room and that I had actually fallen asleep on the couch.

"You there, darlin'?" I hear the voice shout through the letter box.

I drag myself up from the couch and make my way to the front door. "Hey you, how are you?" I ask.

"I'm great thanks," Pete slurs. "I had the besht day ever, but now I need sleep and I want to talk to you and cuddle you," he says. "How was your day? Are you better?"

"Hmmm not really, still not feeling the best at all, that was some mother of a hangover. I'm not doing that again, ever," I say.

"Famous last words darlin', famous last words," Pete says as he catches my hand and leads me to the bedroom. I know he's going to fall fast asleep, but I'm anxious to know what he was celebrating.

"Hey, don't you go falling asleep now you hear? I want to know what the big celebration was tonight, are you going to tell me?"

"Oh yeah! I'm moving to Italy, I'm moving to Italy!" he says with an air of excitement and he passes out on the bed.

Is he for real? He's moving to Italy? What the feck does he mean he's moving to Italy?

I'm fuming! I'm exhausted and still feeling sick. It's 11:30 and I know I won't get any sense out of him now if I wake him, but he better be joking or he'll be out that door in the morning and won't be getting back in.

— ~

It's 6:30 am and I haven't had a wink of sleep. My stomach is still in bits and I really feel like calling in sick. My eyes are red and sore as I've spent the entire night with what feels like matchsticks keeping my eyes opened. I can't stop thinking about Pete heading to Italy and what he meant or whether it just drunken talk. I'm starting to fall hard for him and he could be leaving me. *I think I'm going to be sick.*

"Oh Jesus, my head hurts," I hear from the bed as I have my head stuck down the toilet again. "Is that you puking again? That must be some virus or something you've picked up love, come back to bed and stay here for the day. Did I mention I'm off today?" he asks.

"Yes, yes, and no," I manage to say between vomiting my food from the day before. "Oh God, I feel awful, I'll call in sick, I can't do anything right now."

"Yeah, come here and give me a cuddle, we might both feel better," he says.

"Pete, you said last night you were going to Italy. Was that the drink talking or are you going?"

"Oh yeah, remember I was telling you about that course I wanted to do to get to a higher grade? It's a two year course and they're running one in Italy. Only two of us were offered the position if we wanted to do it. I can't turn an offer like that down, I'd be mad. It's so exciting!" he says.

And me? Do I fit into your fantastic life now that you're off to sunny Italy? Are you going to ask me to go with you? "That's great, congratulations," I say as I lay there next to him trying to sound happy for him, which I am, but can't help but feel let down at the same time.

"You don't sound too pleased. Look I know we've become really close and over a short time and well, I don't want this to spoil what we have, ok? Look at me Katie, please?" he pleads.

I turn towards him and stare into his huge eyes. "I'm sorry, I am happy for you, it's your dream, and I don't want to stand in your way, you know that," I say with a smile.

"Katie, I love you! I know I probably should have said this sooner, but now feels like the right time, I love you and I don't want to let the distance come between us, ok?" he says.

Oh, you love me? You've said it! Am I supposed to say it back now? I can't! I want to, but I can't because my stupid pride is stopping me. There's not even a mention of me going to Italy with you. Surely you know this is what I'd want?!

"I, I... I can't talk to you right now. I feel really ill, Pete, and I don't think this is the right time for us to discuss this," I say. "I am happy for you," I say as I turn on my side and bite my lip in a bid to keep the tears at bay.

"Oh for fuck sake, I really don't understand women sometimes," he says as he grabs his clothes and marches out of the bedroom. I hear the front door slam a few minutes later.

Our first fight. I wasn't expecting it to be so dramatic. I hope the making up will be good, if we do make up.

I curl up in the foetal position and close my eyes. I can't really think of anything right now except maybe getting rid of this virus.

13

I've slept all day and I haven't had as much as a text from Pete. I pick up my phone.

Hey, I'm sorry, I've slept all day and feel a little better now thankfully. Can you come over? We need to talk about this? x, I text.

No reply, but there's a loud knock on the door thirty minutes later. I run to answer it.

"Hi," Pete says without even looking at me when I open the door.

"Hi, are you coming in?" I ask.

"Not sure I should. I mean, are we going to argue about this again for the night? I spent the whole day thinking about this, and I think you're being a little selfish here. You know this is my dream and it could further my career big time. I know we've become so close and I meant what I said..."

I stop him. "Pete, just come in please and we'll talk about it, where the curtain twitchers won't be in sight or in earshot," I say.

"Oh yeah, sorry." He stifles a laugh and walks inside the door. He catches my hands, and looks into my eyes. "I meant what I said earlier today. I love you Katie. I've grown so close to you I just can't believe it. My heart just thumps when I see you, or hear that cute little Irish accent of yours on the phone. It's going to kill me to leave you. I mean it's too early for me to ask you to come with me. I'd love you to, but what if it doesn't work then and you'll have given up everything here. I think we can still work like this for now. I can come home for weekends, you can come over to visit, and then maybe later on, we can talk about you coming over to live with me, if things get even stronger between us. What do you think?" he asks.

Well, that's an improvement on this morning. At least he's suggesting me going at some point now, and he won't just be off on a jolly jaunt with his colleague to find loads of women.

I smile, "Pete, I've fallen so madly in love with you and this is crushing me. You're the guy I'd normally never go for, but I went out with you and now you mean so much to me. I just feel that this was my one chance of happiness and now it's being carted off to Italy. It's not fair. But, I know it's your dream and I'd never stand in the way of that," I sigh. "If the only way around this is what you're suggesting, and yes thinking about it, it does make more sense for me not to give everything up, then let's do that. Let's keep it long distance and see what happens."

"Great, now give me a kiss, because I haven't kissed you yet after telling you how much I love you and I'm sure it'll be spectacular after us having a fight," he says with a smile, and places his lips on mine. I tingle all over, it does feel different, it feels like we've just been brought even closer together. He pulls away.

"How are you feeling? That sickness gone yet?" he asks. "Eh, I hope you ain't preggers," he says with a smirk.

My face drops, "I didn't even think of that," I shriek.

"Hey, darlin', come on, I was joking. You couldn't be, we was safe and stuff. It's just a virus, loads of people have it at the moment. Oh God, you won't sleep tonight now either thinking about that," he says with a nervous laugh.

I slap him playfully. "I know I'm not pregnant, the entire office staff are coughing and spluttering and have bugs at the moment. It was inevitable that I'd catch it, just bad luck it was on a weekend where I was on the tear as they probably all thought I was hungover yesterday."

"Here, come on, let's go to bed and snuggle up. I was drunk and cold towards you last night and you didn't deserve that. I'm sorry. I promise to hold you tight all night tonight to make up for it."

"Oh, go on then," I say as we make our way to the bedroom.

The next morning, thankfully, I feel bright as a button, no sickness and I feel relieved as that must mean I'm not pregnant! *Phew!*

I set off for work and feel in high spirits as I realise that maybe every few weekends in Italy might suit, and it could all work out for the best.

I start planning during my lunch break which weekends would be good for me to go to Italy for a visit. If I have any meetings on Mondays I have to avoid going those weekends. It's looking good though and I actually feel excited about telling Pete. *Am I jumping the gun a little here? Oh, sod it! I'm excited now about this.*

My phone rings.

"Sarah, Sarah, Sarah, how are you? Don't tell me you're only recovered from Saturday now?" I ask with a giggle.

She starts sobbing, "He fecking dumped me the big bollocks."

Act surprised Katie, otherwise she'll be suspicious that you knew it was coming.

"Oh God Sarah, I'm so sorry. When did all of this happen?" I ask, feeling guilty as I'm guessing it was Saturday night.

"Sunday night. That stupid fecker spent Saturday night in my bed with me and all day Sunday and to top it all off, he called me Katie while we were in the middle of the bloody act," she roars.

What do I say to that? "Ah, I'm sure he didn't, maybe he called you matey? Yeah maybe that's a new nickname he has for you or something and you misheard?" *That was pretty lame, like she's going to fall for that. Jesus, he must have it bad for me.* For a split second I feel really happy that someone was thinking of me, and then I just feel weird. *Shivers.*

"For fuck sake Katie, I know what he said, he roared your name. Is there something going on with you two? Tell me the truth, do not lie to me!" she shouts even louder.

"Ok, calm down now for a second there. I would never go near any guy you've fancied or have been with, you know that. NO! There is not anything going on between myself and Jarvis, nor will there ever be! My God, it turns my stomach to even think about it now," I say.

"Oh, so sorry, my taste in men isn't good enough is that what you're saying?" she asks.

"No, I'm saying that the idea of me having an affair with one of my friend's boyfriends turns my stomach. It's not something I'd ever do and you bloody know it too, so back off fast. I have no idea what goes on in Jarvis's head while he's in the midst of passion with you, but I do know that there is a line which I would never ever even come close to crossing. I am a bit disappointed, to say the least, that you would accuse me of such a thing," I say.

"Ok, sorry, I'm just upset now. I thought we were going so well. But Katie, did you know or has he ever said anything to you that would suggest he fancies you?"

"Look, he did kind of come onto me in the pub the other night while you were talking to Laura. I don't want to lie to you about that," I say.

"He did? Well that cheating, lying little…. she takes a breath. What happened?"

"Look, it doesn't matter, he suggested something and I told him to go fuck himself."

She giggles. "Did you actually say those words?" she asks.

"Yes Sarah, I wanted to tell you, but it's an awkward situation to be in and I didn't know what to say. It's difficult you know, you're one of my best friends and for me to come up and say 'oh your man came onto me last night,' it looks like I'm jealous of you and I'm trying to break you both up. Clearly, as he managed to do that himself, I can be honest and upfront with you now. You're better off knowing what he's really like. I thought he was a really nice guy, a gent and he always came across as that, but I suppose you never really know someone that well do you, until they show their true colours?" I say.

"No, you're right, that's very true. I suppose it's better I found out sooner rather than later isn't it?" she says sounding a bit more relieved.

"Look, let's meet during the week as I got a bit of bad news myself too over the weekend. I've been sick as a dog for the past couple of days by the way. I thought it was a hangover, but discovered it was a bug after it went on for a bit longer."

"I had a terrible hangover, which Jarvis told me a bit of action would cure. All that did was give me a bigger headache. Anyway, I won't go on anymore. I'm heartbroken, but I'm sure I'll be fine in a few days. I hope you feel a bit better?"

"Yeah, I'm good today thanks. Ok, I better go here, chat later yeah?

"Yep, chat later," Sarah says.

I hang up. *That creep! That's just gross now the more I think about it. I feel sick again at the thought of him.*

My phone rings again as I'm about to put it back in my bag. It's lover boy.

"Hey you, how's your day?" I ask.

"Hi darlin', day is fine thanks, how's yours?" he says.

Hmmm what's up with him? I can sense there's something wrong, he sounds sad. Oh no, I hope they haven't decided to not offer him the place on the course after all of that, he'll be gutted. "Yeah, grand thanks, what's up? I can hear something in your tone of voice," I ask.

"I'm packing here at the moment, they're sending me off tomorrow," he says.

"What? So soon! Surely you need more notice than that?" I quiz.

"Well, ideally yes, I would like more, but it seems they messed up the dates in Italy and they have two spaces on the course commencing this week, not the one in a few weeks time. So, it's a rush job to get us there."

"So I'll only have you to myself tonight before you go? Or will I even get to see you?" I ask as my heart sinks.

"That's the worse news. I literally have to go within the next thirty minutes. They are collecting us and we're staying in a hotel near the airport tonight. We have to go to work for a couple of hours before we leave as a last minute crash course brushing up our skills, just to keep us fresh and ready for what's ahead. I'm so sorry, I feel so bad about this," he says.

You do? I want to die right now. I feel like you've just ripped my heart out again for the second time this week only this time you're dancing on it.

"Ok, I'm just going now. I can't talk on the phone. You know I'm going to start crying and I don't want to sound like a hyena in public," I say. "Just let me know you get there safely and call me! And Pete, don't forget me, please? This is just wrong, I need to see you before you go," I cry.

"Of course I won't forget you, silly. I love you, you're the love of my life and I want you out in that sunshine to see me very soon, yeah? Now I don't want to upset you anymore, this is breaking my heart too, believe me. Katie, I wish there was more time for us to say goodbye my love, but maybe it's better this way, as I don't think either of us will cope very well otherwise. I love you, Katie."

"I love you too, Pete. Safe journey. Goodnight."

I hang up. I love him, I love him so much and right now, my heart is sinking even further, because I feel like he's never going to contact me again and I've just lost him forever. I sit there on the bus, with my eyes welling up and feel completely crushed. *What is wrong with me? I had my barriers up recently as I knew when I met him that he might break my heart. When did I lower them? God, I'm such an emotional wreck lately!*

14

I reach the flat and look upwards in the hope that the light in Pete's flat will still be on. No such luck. He's gone. I just want to hug him and kiss him and say a proper goodbye. I open the door to my flat and make my way in. *How could they be so unfair, to expect us to have no time together before he leaves? It just doesn't make any sense to me.* I lie in my bed as I feel exhausted, between my work day, Sarah and the whole news of Pete upping and leaving. I look at the clock. *7:30, I suppose I should get up and make a dinner. Do I want a dinner? I still don't feel very well, maybe I should just lie here.* I slowly drift off into a very deep sleep.

I wake at 8:30 am. *Well, feck it anyway! They'll have a fit at me for the lateness today of all days.* Joe, my boss, is due to give a presentation and I'm meant to be there even earlier than usual so he can run through it with me and so I can ensure it's all set up properly. *He's going to mangle me.*

I grab my phone and call him. "Joe, I'm so sorry. I'm late, I have no idea how, but I fell asleep on the bed last night at around 7.30 and only woke now. Naturally, I didn't set the alarm at that time as I didn't think I'd nod off."

"Oh, Katie, you know what, you're lucky, as the meeting has been cancelled. The main Director called in sick and he's the one I had to impress, so they cancelled. You have nothing to worry about. Are you ok?

You've not been yourself lately, maybe you should take a few days off if you're not well. You're clearly burnt out if you're sleeping all that time."

"You know what Joe, I do feel a bit exhausted. I may just take a few days if that's ok? Maybe I'll get something from the doctor to pick me up as I feel deflated."

"No problem, take the week if you want, you know we've nothing big on this week. Quite a few of the others are on leave, but we have plenty of cover around to help out with any of your workload that might need sorting."

"Oh Joe that would be great, thank you, that's greatly appreciated. I'll call during the week to let you know when I'll be back. I might just need a day or two to get rid of this thing completely."

"It's fine, take your time. Get some rest and speak soon."

"Thanks, Joe, bye."

I hang up and feel relieved, I just want to curl up in my bed. I feel absolutely shattered and upset, it's really hitting me now that Pete, the one man I've truly fallen for in my entire life, has gone off to Italy so suddenly and I've no idea when I'll see him again.

I call Sarah. "Don't suppose you're around are you?"

"I am, I've called in sick today, I'm so pissed off I just couldn't handle looking at some of those feckers I work with. I know they'd mean well, but they'd be asking all day "are you ok? Blah blah blah. I can't be dealing with that crap now. I just want to hug the duvet for the day."

"Ok, I'm off sick too, but I genuinely do feel like there is something wrong with me so they've given me a time out. Can I call over?" I ask.

"Of course, are you ok? Oh, sorry, I sound like my co-workers now. You have been sick a lot lately, you must be burnt out," she says.

"That's what Joe said...my boss. I'll leave in ten minutes. I warn you, I'll be makeup free and I've greasy hair. I look like death warmed up so be prepared to be scared."

"Ha ha, great, I love it, we can look like crap together. I've masses of chocolate and crisps in, we can pig out and watch Bridget or something. That feels appropriate for me right now."

"Hmmm, well it's kind of appropriate for me too. See you shortly."

I hang up, and just know that Sarah is now most likely wondering what I meant by that. I'm so confused I really don't know what has happened to my life overnight. I set off and make my way through the run-down back streets until I finally reach the South Bank. As I stroll along, I breathe in the air. I won't say fresh air as it's a pretty smoggy city, but the fact that I'm near the river makes it feel like it's a little fresher. Thankfully it's a cold, but beautiful day.

There's a slight wind blowing and the sky is cloud free and very blue. I pass by some tourists who are looking in awe at the man pretending to be a golden statue. This is someone I take for granted at this stage. I pass by nearly every day on my way to work, unless I decide to take a bus. It's making me smile to see so many people enjoying themselves. I feel so lucky to live in such a vibrant city, but then I turn the corner and see the dour faces of the men in suits, clearly having a bad day at the office or are late for a meeting due to transport problems.

It reminds me of how lucky I am not to have to take the tube to work anymore. I avoid the cranky, morning people. When I first moved to London, I lived on the outskirts. It was up North and I used to take the tube to work each day and home in the evening. The one thing that annoyed me each time I had to get on the tube, was that nobody spoke unless they already knew each other. People looked agitated as if they wanted to start a fight, and some mornings it nearly did happen, between both men and women. I'm glad I don't have to suffer that anymore.

I reach Sarah thirty minutes later and when she opens the door I can see there are fresh tears on her face.

"Oh Sarah, you really fell for him didn't you?" I ask.

She sobs again and wipes her face with her sleeve whilst snivelling, "I did, and he's a bollocks for doing what he did."

I give her a huge hug and bite back the tears I have myself and hope they won't fall, at least not yet.

"Come on let's have a duvet day. I brought my PJ's and we can eat loads of chocolate, have wine and just veg out for the day," I say with a smile. *I hope that was convincing, maybe I shouldn't tell her anything right now, although I need to have a bit of a cry myself.*

We sit down on the couch and pull Sarah's duvet over us. In between sniffles she manages to get some few words out. "I mean, I thought he loved me too. He said he did, but clearly he didn't. Why would someone do that Katie, why? If you don't love someone, you shouldn't say it and then just up and leave them."

I wonder that too, for some reason I feel like that is exactly what Pete has done to me. Maybe I should keep this to myself, for now, I need to figure out exactly what has gone on between us and then I can tell Sarah. "I know love, I know. I'll never understand men, they are all a bunch of big hypocrites at the end of the day, say one thing and mean another. The part that makes me sick is when they backtrack on something they've said, and try to turn it around to make it look like your fault," I say.

"Exactly!" she screams. "Exactly! Fecking inhuman gobshites! I'm not going near one of them again for a long, long time Katie, no way. I'm done now, done."

I can't help but feel the same, but I'm starting to think I'm over-analysing the Pete situation. I mean, I'm still with him. I just didn't get to say goodbye, which would have been nice, but it's not like I won't ever see him again. *Wow, this is turning into a bit of a man bashing episode, maybe I should try to distract her and put a film on.*

"Do you have any other films we can watch? These are all break up films and I've a feeling you might need something to cheer you up, not depress you even more," I say.

"Yeah, but Bridget is there and I love her. I never get tired of laughing at the one-liners and well, it turned out good for her in the end. It's fine, I won't cry. I might scream at some points and go off on a man hating rant again, but there will be laughs too at least," Sarah says with a smile through her tears.

"Ok, Bridget it is." I press play and I have to admit, every time I watch this myself it makes me giggle a lot too. We eat the chocolate and open the bottle of wine I brought with me, even though I'm slow to eat or drink. I let Sarah to tuck into it and hope she doesn't notice I'm not eating or drinking too much. "Let's go mad later and order a takeaway," I say. *Why did I just say that?*

"Sounds good to me girl, let's do it," Sarah says, sounding far more upbeat.

I've no idea why I just suggested that. I can't even drink the wine and I'm barely touching the chocolate, not to mind the thought of eating a takeaway.

"Hey, I'm sorry I've been babbling on, what's going on with you? You said this film was quite appropriate for you now too, what did you mean by that?"

"Oh, nothing. I," *I have to tell her something or she'll be suspicious of me.* "Well ok, Pete is gone off to Italy for work," I say reluctantly.

"Ok, for a week, two weeks?" Sarah asks.

"Erm, not quite. He's been sent on a course and has to work there as part of the qualification. So he could be gone for up to two years," I say with an air of sadness.

"Hang on a second, you're completely in love with this guy and he is with you, right? And now you're telling me that he dropped this bomb on you suddenly? Because you didn't mention this on the phone yesterday so I'm guessing this was a sudden thing?"

"Well, yeah, but it's not his fault. He didn't know himself until a couple of days ago. We are still going to carry on as a couple, but it'll be a few weeks before I see him and well, if things go ok I might think about heading out to him for a bit and see what Italy is like. Obviously, I wouldn't go out straight away, as I'd be silly to give up everything here when we've only been together a short while," I say.

"But has he gone already?"

"Well yes, that's the part that has me doubting the whole thing. When I got off the phone from you the other day, he rang to tell me he was packing quickly as they messed up in the office and he was booked onto a flight this morning out to Italy. They had a refresher course to complete that evening and then they were being put up in a hotel in the airport last night to fly on the early flight this morning. I didn't even get to say goodbye," I sigh.

"What kind of animals are they to say they didn't give you both time to say your farewells and all that? That's not fair! But, he was upset, right?" Sarah asks.

"Yeah he sounded as gutted as I was, I couldn't even talk to him as knew the tears were coming so I just said goodbye and safe journey and that I loved him. He said he loved me too, but Sarah I don't know, I have a wrenching feeling in my stomach that I'll never see him again. It's like a dull pain in my heart and I don't know why. Am I over analysing and just making it bigger than what it is?"

"No of course not, you're in love and you didn't get to see him before he left. Of course it's going to have this kind of effect on you. However, I don't believe you won't see him again, I'm sure he'll want to talk to you tonight on Skype or Facetime you or something?"

"Yeah, I suppose, I can't believe I didn't even think of that. For some reason I was thinking the worst and that something would happen on his way there. I hate when I get these horrible feelings, it's just not right."

"Maybe Bridget isn't the most appropriate film for both of us today then. We should just head out and have some lunch and drinks at a pub," Sarah says.

"You know what, I know I suggested a takeaway earlier, but I don't think I can even think about food. I'm still not right after this bug and not back to proper eating yet, it's lasting ages. I hope it just buggers off soon as I want to get back to my usual self, I can't handle feeling like crap," I say.

"You're not preggers are you?"

"Oh stop, I'm not. No chance of that," I say. *Shit! At least I don't think there is! There was that one night... No. No, I'm not. I'm not pregnant, I cannot be!*

"Ok," Sarah says with a smirk, "I might be Aunty Sarah yet," she says with a giggle.

"No you won't and get that thought out of your head now, please?" I say. *Stop freaking me out, please? Oh God, no I can't be, it's not possible. I wonder what Pete would say if I was. Would it bring him back to me? Probably not. Anyway, I'm not, so get that thought out of your head now Katie girl, get that thought out, and don't let it back in.*

I sit in silence for a while as I watch the film. Sarah is busy tucking into the chocolate and is starting to get very merry on the wine. I, on the other hand, feel sick.

15

M y phone rings. I reach for it from the desktop and almost
drop it, I'm in such a rush.

"Hello?" I say.

"Hello darlin', you alright? I'm missing that lovely accent of yours so
much already," Pete says.

"Oh Pete, I miss you so much. I wish I got to say goodbye, everything
feels so up in the air without you."

"Oh darlin, it's ok, we didn't get to say goodbye because it wasn't
goodbye. Anyway, I don't do goodbyes, ever. I'll make sure to get you
over here soon, it's great weather, even for January. You'd probably get a
little tan on you if you was here now."

"Sweet you don't say goodbyes, but rubbing it in about the weather is
making me think you're less sweet," I say. I can feel myself smile.

"Good to see you haven't lost that sarcastic humour of yours, there'd
be something seriously wrong if you did! I can't stay too long my love,
we're off to do a bit of hang-gliding. Can you believe it? It'll be amazing here, I love hang-gliding, and being able to do it here in Italy. The
scenery is going to be just spectacular," he says with excitement.

My heart sinks at the idea. I hate the idea of him attempting anything of a dangerous nature and particularly something like that. Still, I

suppose he knows what he's doing, as it's been one of his favourite things to do here, for years.

"Erm, you will be with professionals doing this hang-gliding I take it?" I ask.

"Of course I will darlin'. I wouldn't be so stupid as to put myself into a position of danger if I don't know an area, We'll have pros with us. I want to be able to come back to your smiling face darlin'," he says.

"Ok," I say softly. "Just be careful and let me know how it goes. So have you started the course already today?" I ask.

"No, that's tomorrow. Going to enjoy the day first and then we work. Play hard, work hard. It's meant to be the other way around, but we're doing it all wrong as usual," he says with a laugh.

"Will you call me tonight? I just want to know you'll be safe after your hang-gliding session. I'll be sick thinking about it."

"Oh, don't worry, I'll be onto you tonight to send you off to sleep with my words my darlin'," he says.

"Great, you plan on boring me in other words?" I ask.

"Ah now that's my girl, that's the Katie I know and love so much that my heart pounds and pounds when I hear her dulcet tones," Pete says.

"Oh feck off," I say with a laugh. "You sound like the day we first met. Although I should enjoy that, it's the reason I fell for you after all. Go on my love, you go and have fun, and I look forward to hearing about it all tonight," I say.

"Right darlin', I'm off, I shall speak with you later. Until then keep that smile on your face, I can feel it coming through the phone to me. I like to know you're smiling. Talk later. I love you," he says.

"I love you too Pete, bye," I say and hang up. *Thank God! I feel so much better and I am smiling. He's right, I was smiling down the phone. That's weird how he could sense that. Right, get your arse up and head back into that living room and cheer your friend up, she's the one who's broken hearted, not you.*

I make my way back to Sarah, who I can see is shaking and curled up in a ball. *Oh no, bless are you crying again?* Once she hears me coming she looks at me, but she's shaking with laughter, not tears. "Oh, this film is the best thing since the sliced pan girl, makes you appreciate being single. I can't stop laughing, but feel so like her right now," she says with a burst of laughter.

I reach for the bag of crisps which sit in front of me. "Now I feel like eating these," I say.

"Yeah, go for it girl, eat all of them, there's loads in the cupboard," Sarah says. *Oddly enough, I feel I could eat this giant bag and more, but I'll see how I'm going.*

"Well, was that himself?" Sarah asks.

"Mmm," I say as I munch on the crisps. *Damn, these are good.* "Sorry, I'll tell you now in two minutes, I just need to eat more of these first as they're very moreish," I say.

"Katie, I don't know, it's like you're having a craving there or something, I'd go take a test if I were you."

I change the subject quickly. "So, anyway, yes that was himself. He's fine and he's there safe and sound, although I'm not keen on what he's going to do today, especially just after arriving."

"Oh, what's that?" Sarah asks.

"Hang-gliding, would you believe?" I say.

"You're kidding? I thought he had to go to his course today?"

"No, seems that doesn't actually start until tomorrow," I say.

"Living life on the edge eh? Shame I never got to meet him, he sounds like a nice and fun guy," Sarah says.

"He is, but this is one type of fun I'd prefer he wouldn't attempt while there, or anywhere really. I know he's experienced enough, but how safe can it actually be?" I ask.

"Yeah, true. He'll be fine, I'm sure. It's just a lot for you to take in right now, so you're probably worrying excessively," she says.

"You're right. He sounded like he missed me, which is a plus and he's going to call me again tonight too," I say with excitement. "Any more of these crisps in the cupboard, I've a bit of a thing for salt and vinegar crisps today," I say.

"Ha ha, girl, you seriously need to do a pregnancy test. I have one here if you want it. Well, it's not mine actually, it belongs to my flatmate. She bought it two weeks ago as she thought she was pregnant, but it turned out that she wasn't. She was pissed off to the last as she's dying to have a baby sometime soon," Sarah says.

"Really? Would she be happy to bring a baby up on her own?" I ask.

"Not happy, but she would. You know how guys are these days. A lot of them shrug the responsibility anyway, but if she could find someone who wants to be with her, then that would be her ideal situation, but she's happy to go it alone if it were to happen," she says.

"I'm not pregnant! I've just not eaten much lately and the taste of these crisps is really good and it's not making me feel ill," I say as I make my way to the kitchen. *Hmmm, what if I am? Maybe I should do that test if no one else is using it. I can replace it another time. I will, I'll do it, just to see. After all, I am over a week late. I hope I'm not, especially now that Pete is in Italy!!*

I grab the other bag of crisps and tear the top open with great gusto. "Ok, you know what, I'm starting to wonder myself now. I like crisps normally, but I'd never eat them with this much passion. It's like I'm in love with them or something. Maybe I should take that test," I mutter as I stuff my face.

"Take it. You're late, aren't you? You wouldn't even consider it otherwise," Sarah says.

"Yep! Only by a week, but I have been vomiting a great deal lately. I don't feel right, you know? I feel like there could be something growing in there. Although saying that, it could just be my belly with the amount of crisps I've eaten in thirty minutes. God Sarah, what'll I do if I am? I'm not ready for that yet!"

"Katie, you're thirty-eight years old. You're more than ready and you know you're shuffling on a bit too like. Better to have one now than later," Sarah says.

"Feck off with your shuffling on, I'm still good to go for a few years yet. I just don't know if I'm ready now, so suddenly."

"Is anyone? I wouldn't know myself, as you know. From what some of the girls say, though, none of them were ready to have a baby. However, when they did, they all took to it instinctively, like little ducks to water, girl. I guess it's up to you whether you sink or swim, but I believe you'd be great as a mother Katie. You've got that instinct. Whereas I just want to hand them back and I'm happy," she says.

"Hmmmm, I don't want these crisps now. Where's that test, I'm going to take it now. I need the loo anyway so might as well go for it now rather than later. Get it over and done with," I say nonchalantly.

I'm not pregnant at all, I couldn't be. We've been so careful, there's no chance. But what if I am? What am I going to do?

"Ok, so here you go. Do you know what to do?" Sarah asks.

"No, I've never done one of these before, I've always been very careful. That's how I know it'll be negative. What do I do?" I ask.

"Who knows? I've never had to take one either, thankfully," Sarah says and we both burst into hysterical laughter.

"Ok, I'll go to the loo and read the instructions there. I'll take a few deep breaths while I'm at it. If I'm not out in ten minutes, you know I'm crying in there and freaking out. I'll leave the door unlocked, just in case, but I know it's not going to be the case. It'll be grand, no problems at all, super duper, and I'll carry on eating my crisps with no guilt attached," I say with a nervous laugh.

I close the bathroom door and take a deep breath. Feck, *how am I supposed to go on that?* I sit there and read the instructions carefully as I don't want to void the whole thing by doing something wrong. Once finished I set the stick to one side and sort myself out. I pull the toilet lid down and sit on it, waiting patiently for an answer. *Of course, this is just one, even if this comes up positive, I'd have to do another one or two, just to be sure. There's no guarantee this is spot on, they don't get it right always. How many more minutes?* I sit there and stare at the second hand on my watch. It seems like an eternity. I take a deep breath. *Ok, that's it. Oh God, stop shaking woman, it's a pregnancy test, not something explosive.* Although I feel explosive at the moment, the mood swings and the sickness are definitely a sign. I know already what the result will be. I take the stick in my hand and drop it to the floor when I see the result.

"SARAH, SARAH," I shout as I open the door.

She rushes towards me with a smile. "Well, it's negative, is it. You wouldn't burst out like this if it was positive. I knew that would be the case. I'm just curious. Do you feel a bit disappointed now? I mean, you know how we got a bit psyched up about it there, you were nervous, but were you secretly hoping it was going to be positive? I think I would. I know that sounds like a contraction, but I reckon if I had to do one, there would be that element of surprise at the end and if it was positive, it would be kind of nice, sweet, but then I'd probably freak out afterwards," Sarah says with a smile. "Sorry, I'll stop talking, and let you get a word in," she says.

I look at her straight in the face, "I feel sick," I say.

16

"Jesus Mary and Joseph. Jesus, Mary and Joseph," Sarah says.

"Can you stop saying that, please? You sound like someone's mother." I say.

"Sorry, I just, I'm speechless. I thought with the way you were shouting at me it was negative. I'm not freaking out at you. No girl, I'll be here for you every step of the way, but I just wasn't expecting it, I suppose."

"I know, neither was I," I say. The crisps no longer look appealing. *What am I going to do? I'm all alone in London. My baby's daddy is off sunning himself in Italy for possibly two years, and I have to tell him tonight that he's going to be a baby daddy. How did this even happen?*

Sarah looks at me blankly. "I don't know what to say to you," she says.

"I know you don't. I don't know what to say myself, Sarah. When do I tell Pete?" I say.

"Hold up now one second, you need to get this confirmed before you tell anyone anything. Try another test. If that comes up positive, then tell Pete, but you'll also need to go to the doctor," she says.

"Yes, I know. I'm just in shock now. I'm going to get dressed. Where the nearest pharmacy or supermarket?" I ask.

"Two minute walk. I could suggest going in your pyjamas, but it's not really a very classy look," Sarah says.

I manage a smile of sorts, but I don't feel like smiling. "Ok, I'm off to get another test," I murmur as I quickly throw my jeans on and throw my jacket over my pyjama top. I open the door and fly down the stairs at lightning speed. *I'd better be careful in case I fall down the stairs and hurt my baby. My baby, my baby, baby, baby, baby. Aghhhhhhhhhhhhhhhhhhhh, MY BABY! I'm having a baby! Calm it, calm it, you might not be yet, let's not get ahead of ourselves.* I turn the corner and into the supermarket. I pick up the same test and head to the register.

"That will be ten ninety nine please?" the shop assistant says.

I hand her my card.

"Ahem, sorry madam, but this card won't work," she says with a smile.

I look at her, confused. "Why not?" I ask, and then see I've handed her my Oyster Card.

"Oh sorry, I'm in a bit of a confused state right now," I say and place my debit card on the contactless reader instead.

"That's ok, I was in that confused state myself not too long ago," she says with a wink. "I had a little girl."

Thanks love, that's just what I wanted to hear. Although a little girl would be lovely. I could dress her in loads of beautiful girlie things. The clothes for girls these days are just fantastic and I could call her a really pretty name.

"That's nice, congratulations," I say with a smile. I kind of feel like crying right now though. Pretty names or not, this was not my plan right now. "Thank you," I say as I take the test and run back to Sarah's flat.

"Ok, got it!" I say waving it in the air like it's a prize from a raffle. "Ah feck!! I'll have to drink a few gallons of water now to get the flow going again, I can't take it straight away," I say.

"Ok it's fine, take your time, you've all day. Katie, calm down a bit love, it's not going to be the end of the world you know?"

"I know, I know, but I'm not sure I'm ready for this just yet Sarah. It's a life changing thing you know? Although, I was thinking about if it was a girl and what I could call her. Imagine all the beautiful clothes I could get for her they have stunning stuff in the shops these days," I say.

"I know and think about what her Aunty Sarah could buy her! It would be fantastic, but just as fantastic if it's a boy. If you're pregnant that is! You're starting to sound excited by the idea now Katie."

"I do sound excited, don't I?" I say. "That's something I certainly wasn't expecting. But you're right, I need to take a step back, and look at this positively. Yes, of course I'd be happy if it were a girl or a boy, just as long as it's healthy and happy, that's all that matters. Of course, I might not be pregnant yet so I'm not going to get too excited. Or at least try not to. I sound like a psycho. I'm changing my mind every five seconds. It has to be hormones I suppose. I think I'd be kidding myself if I think this one is going to be negative," I say.

"I agree, but let's wait and see," Sarah says.

17

*H*ello?"

"Hi, did he call?"

"No! I can't believe he didn't call, and I'm waiting here like a big eejit for him," I say.

"Shit! He's probably out drinking, after his hang-gliding,' Sarah says.

"Well, that's no good to this hormonal mammy to be," I say.

"I know love, I know. Relax a while look, it's early yet, it's only 9:30. He might call yet," she says.

"I think not, it's 10:30 in Italy and he's up for his course at 5:30 in the morning. He won't call now. I'm sick. I don't even know how to tell him. This should be something I tell him in person, but I can't even fly to him now for another two months at least. I've no idea how he'll take this. What if he just dumps me?" I ask.

"Oh, he won't. Come on, he's a mature guy. From what I heard you say it sounded like he wanted a mature relationship and I believe he will stand by you no matter what. You know what? I don't want to keep you on the phone now as he might be trying to get through. I'd suggest a Facetime if you try to call him. Might be better to tell him to his face, even if there's a screen between you. At least you'll be able to tell by his reaction whether it's good or bad news," she says.

"Hmmmm, true. Ok, I'll let you know how it goes. I might try calling him now I think, as otherwise I won't sleep for the night probably. Let's hope he picks up," I say.

"Ok, love, I'm going to head to bed myself. I feel tired and that bottle of wine still has me feeling merry at this hour. Good luck!" Sarah says with a yawn.

"Thanks, Sarah. Good night, sleep well," I say, and hang up.

I look at the phone for a minute. *Should I call him now or leave it until tomorrow? What if he's asleep and I wake him up? Then if I give him the news he might have a freak attack on the phone at me because I woke him, but woke him to that news. Oh sod it! I have to call him.*

I press on my contacts and feel sick again as I press his name. I wait patiently for a monotone beeping noise, but there isn't any. Instead, I get a message, *"This person's phone is out of coverage or is switched off, please try again later."*

18

I haven't slept a wink. I'm so glad Joe has given me time off. If I had to go to work today I'd be in some dire state. I lay in the bed and look at the clock, 6:25 a.m. *Oh God, I feel like crap, I wonder now if I talk to the baby will it hear me? I mean how big can it be? Would it have ears yet? What am I thinking? I don't even know how many weeks I'm pregnant. Pregnant, I'm pregnant. . having a baby, a teeny tiny baby that's going to look like Pete, and me. How weird! I'm sure it'll be a gorgeous baby. Amazing, I have something growing inside of me, a little human. How will I tell him? Pete, you're going to be a daddy? No that's too straight up. Guess what Pete, I've a surprise for you, I'm not sure how you'll feel about it, but we're having a baby. NO!! Not we're,* **I'm** *having a baby as it's growing inside of me. No, no, it's his baby too, I'll say we're having a baby. Yeah, that sounds ok. Oh no, it sounds too rehearsed, happy families. Damn it anyway, I'll just come out with whatever I come out with, and see what his reaction is. I hope it's good.*

I pick up the phone and dial his number again. Same voice message at the other side. *Maybe his phone won't work there, no roaming or something so he has it turned off. Although, he's at his course now so that's probably why.* I lie down again and sink my head into the pillows, and drift off to sleep. It's not long before I wake again making a beeline for the toilet. *Oh God, how long does this morning sickness last for? I'm not sure how long I can hack it.*

My phone rings and I clean the sick from my mouth and stroll to the dresser to get it. It's gone before I get there. One missed call and no number. *What if it was Pete?* I frantically dial his number again but the same message remains on his phone. *Ok, so that must have been work or Laura as she's the only one I know who doesn't have caller ID showing up.*

I climb back into bed and pull the duvet over me. This time, I fall asleep very quickly and into a deep slumber. The next time I open my eyes it's 3:30 pm. *Wow! Did I sleep all that time? It's true then that you do feel exhausted and drained when having a baby.* I try to call Pete again, but still no answer. I'm starting to worry a little bit now. *Did he lie to me? Is he really in Italy? Why the hell hasn't he called?*

I get up and shower. I feel a great deal better afterwards. I ring Sarah to see if she's around, but she's at work. I call Laura then, no answer. I could ring Ellie, Siobhan, or a few of the other girls, but I know they'll all be at work. *I wonder if Dan, Pete's friend, has heard from him? Oh, stop it! You're like a stalker woman. Take a few deep breaths and if you don't hear from him later this eve, maybe call Dan. Oh, wait! You don't have Dan's number nor do you know where Dan lives. That's it. I am officially up shit creek without a paddle. He's gone and I'm never going to see him again probably.*

I leave the flat in a state of torment, but a nice long walk up the South Bank for fresh air will sort me out nicely. Sarah should be finished work in an hour and I'll see if she can meet up with me then. I take deep breaths as I walk up the embankment and try to forget my dilemma, and forget Pete for now. I have too much going on in my head and it will drive me demented if I think too much. I stroll up past Tower Bridge and down by Butler's Wharf. I'm tempted to go to All Bar One for a sneaky drink, but I can't, not when I have little junior inside trying to make him or herself look more human like than pea like. *So many things I can't do now, I feel so restricted. I really have to think about this and how I'll handle the situation. What if Pete is gone? How can I bring this child up on my own? I suppose I could, but what if it becomes a struggle financially? Oh God, what time is it? I need to talk to someone. It's 5:30. Great, Sarah should be finished work now, I'll call her.*

"Hi Sarah, how are ya? Can you meet me? I'm in a dire state. I really need to talk to someone?"

"Of course I can, where are you? I hear noise so you must be out and about?"

"I'm outside All Bar One on the Wharf."

"You're not drinking I hope? Please say you're not?"

"I'm not. It's very tempting to drink myself into oblivion right now, but no I'm not drinking. I really need the chats now though so do you want me to walk in your direction?"

"No no, I'm on my way, I'll be with you in about fifteen minutes. Is that ok?"

"Sure, thanks, Sarah. See you soon." I hang up. *Fair play to her I suppose she's walking over from St. Paul's. That's a nice walk and she loves her walking.* I take a seat and relax with a chamomile tea while I wait for her.

"Boo!" booms the voice from behind me.

"Jesus Christ!" I turn to see none other than Jarvis standing there.

"Oh seriously, you need to get out of here fast as Sarah is on her way and I don't want her thinking that you and I are up to something we shouldn't be up to, because we most definitely are not!" I say defiantly.

"Wow, there's a welcome! I thought at least I might deserve a 'Hello Jarvis, how are you?' I swear you Irish girls are a bit psychotic!" he says.

"Ah no, we're not, but in case you forgot, you've broken my best friends' heart, and not only that, but you bloody roared my name out in the middle of a passion session with her. How the hell would you respond if it was the other way around?" I ask.

"I'd be damn flattered I should say, if you were with that what's his name, the scruffy guy in the shop that day and roared my name out, I'd be very flattered indeed. And I wouldn't hang around either, I'd make a play for you if it were the case," he says with a grin.

"I swear to God, I could beat you with a stick now if I had one! For starters, that scruffy guy's name is Pete and he's my boyfriend I'll have you know. I bloody love him with all my heart, and I will not have you put him down. From what I know of you, he's far more intelligent, caring, and loyal than you'll ever be, so you can forget about me screaming your name at the height of passion, you fecking eejit. Now have a good day. Sarah is on her way and I don't want her getting upset when she sees you. Leave please."

"Bloody hell, you're a bit feisty today. Bloody women and their hormones," he says with a smirk. "I'll leave you in peace. Good day to you," he says.

"Goodbye."

Good day to you too you tool. Hormones indeed. I wonder how far along I am. I need to get to a doctor soon.

"Hi girlie, sorry I'm a few minutes late," Sarah says as she turns the corner.

"Thank God for that!"

Eek! Fool, she'll want to know what you mean now.

"Why, what's up?" she asks.

"Oh nothing, eh, just had a bit of a bonding session with the toilet bowl again," I say quickly to put her off. *I hope she believes me.*

"Ah bless ya, you poor thing. God, it must be awful, is it? So, tell me what did Pete say? Took it well I'll bet?" Sarah asks.

"Pete doesn't know yet. I can't get through to him and he never rang last night," I exclaim. "I'm worried about him, Sarah. I'm worried also, or paranoid I suppose is a better word, that he's lied about something. I mean, why wouldn't he call when he said he would? What if something happened to him and I don't know about it?" I ask.

"Ok, look, don't panic! I'm sure there's a perfectly good explanation for all of this. I know I never met him, but he sounds like such an amazing guy and he certainly doesn't sound like the type of man who would just tell you he loves you and then bugger off and never contact you again. Maybe he lost his phone or the battery is dead or something like that. It'll be a very simple explanation I'm sure," she says in a calm manner.

"I don't know, something is telling me that there is something wrong, it's not just little baby whirling around in my tummy, this is instinct kicking in."

"Do you have any of his mate's phone numbers? We could call them and find out if they know anything. Besides, surely you'd be the first to find out if anything had happened?"

"Well, that's the thing. I've only met one of his mates yet. Dan, he seems a nice guy too, but I suppose we've spent so much time on our own so far as it's only been a couple of months, and we never really got to meet up with any mates as such, except for randomly meeting Dan that night. To be honest, I don't even think they are that close."

"Right, that kind of screws that idea then. Do you know where Dan lives or anything?"

"No, I'm seriously at a loss here Sarah, what do I do? I'm in no fit state to even think now and I'm just distraught in case he's gone and I'm left to have this baby on my own."

"It's ok, love, we'll sort something out and remember what I said, I'll be here for you anyway, no matter what, ok?" she says as she places a reassuring arm on mine.

Should I tell you I met Jarvis? He might as well have come onto me again today! I hate keeping secrets from you, but I really don't want to upset you. You deserve far better than him so you need to forget about him now I think. I won't mention him.

"Let's go home. I need to come up with a plan," I say.

"I think the best plan for you now is to eat something, lady. When was the last time you ate?" she asks.

"I can't remember, to be honest. I think it was probably those crisps yesterday, but I can't keep anything in for long. I have to admit I feel a bit hungry now, though," I say as I rub my non-existent baby belly.

"That's cute, you're rubbing your belly already. Let's get dinner here and then I'll walk back with you. You might feel better after a bit of food and be able to think more clearly as you know you're starving your brain by not eating, not to mind the poor little creature growing inside of you?"

"Let's do that, I am a bit ravenous now," I say.

Later that evening we head to our respective homes. I turn on the TV to watch a bit of what I normally hate, the evening news. I find it depressing as there's never any good news on it.

This was no exception.

I feel like nodding off until the next headline grabs my attention.

"A young British man has been declared missing today, off the coast of Italy. What was meant to be a fun hang-gliding expedition turned into a disaster as he got into trouble. The accident took place yesterday and coast guards and emergency services have been combing the area, with no luck as yet. Peter Reynolds, aged thirty-seven, from South East London is an experienced hang-glider, but sadly things went very wrong for him yesterday. He is presumed missing until a body may be found. A very sad story indeed," the newsreader says.

Oh Jesus! Oh Jesus no! "I WILL NOT ALLOW THIS TO HAPPEN!! NOOOOOOO, NOOOOOOO, NOOOOOOOOOOO!! PETER YOU CANNOT BE DEAD, YOU CANNOT BE DEAD," I shout as loud as I can as the tears consume my face.

I pick up the phone. "Have you seen the news?" I ask through the tears, "have you Sarah? HAVE YOU SEEN THE NEWS?" I shout.

"Oh love, I'm so sorry. I've just switched it off. I've called Laura. We're on our way to you now, pet. Hang up and sit down, I'll be there in less than twenty minutes," she says.

I don't even reply. I just hang up.

19

Ten weeks later...

hat was that? I wake to a banging noise on my door.

I head to the door and wipe the sleep out of my eyes. "Are you ok?" Sarah asks.

"What? Yeah, why? You gave me the fright of my life banging on the door like that!"

"Sorry petal, you do know you're going to be late if you don't get a move on? I tried calling four times, but your phone is off or the battery must have died," she says.

"Really? Oh no, Oh NO!! I have my three month scan today. Sorry, I have no idea what's going on with me, baby brain?? I'd normally set my alarm, but I must have nodded off last night without setting or charging it and the battery died. Right, give me twenty minutes...have I got twenty minutes?" I ask.

"You have, go on," Sarah says as she flicks the switch on the kettle.

I rush to the shower, and once finished, I quickly throw some clothes on. "Right I look totally dishevelled, but this will do," I say as I run to the kitchen a bit flushed.

"Whoa, woman calm it, your blood pressure will be sky high. Calm down a little bit, there's no major rush, you still have ten minutes before we need to leave," she says.

"Time for a quick cuppa?"" I ask.

"Yes and some food! You need food remember, you're getting a little bump going on there now, that's cute!" she says.

It brings a smile to my face. The morning sickness has passed and I'm starting to feel much better these days which is also enabling me to eat and helping my little bump to grow. I love the look and feel of it all now.

"Ok food eaten, tea drunk, let's go," I say feeling a bit chirpier. "I'll drink the water on the way as I'll need the toilet again straight away otherwise. I wish we didn't have to drink so much water. Would modern technology ever hurry up and make it unnecessary? It's so uncomfortable having someone press into your stomach when your bladder is full," I say.

"Oh I know, it's awful. I remember I had an ultrasound once and I thought I was going to pee myself when they pressed down. I felt ill too as I couldn't eat, could only have water. Awful, just awful," Sarah says. We make our way to the hospital which is only about a ten minute walk from where I live.

"Am I waddling already?" I ask.

"Ha ha! no, you're not, you've got a bump the size of a pimple. It wouldn't cause you to waddle yet. I'm sure towards the end you'll be like a duck, though, dearest," she says.

"Thanks. Ah, it's not like a pimple is it? Should it be bigger do you think?" I ask.

"No, I'm joking. You look about right to me. I wouldn't know personally, but I'm just going on any of my other friends who've been pregnant and they looked around the same. I'd say it depends on the frame of the person too, you're quite slim so you may not show a lot until the end," she says.

We enter St. Thomas's hospital and I nervously wait to be called for my scan. "Katie Brown?" the nurse calls. I look up and leave a squeak out of me, "Yes."

Sarah sniggers, "what the hell was that?" she asks.

"I've no idea, a nervous yes, I think," I say as I smile. "Come on, come in with me, you'll probably have to put up with me through this whole process now, so you deserve to see the baby too," I say.

"Oh lady, I'm there. I'm so excited, I feel like I'm the father," she says with a stutter. "Sorry, I didn't mean that, you know what I meant," she says.

"I know, stop worrying. I've come to realise I may have to accept the fact that Pete may be gone now without a trace and never to return to me. You don't have to be careful anymore. I can do this, I can bring this baby up by myself, I'm strong enough to do it, if I have to," I say. *I really don't want to believe that Sarah, I still believe he's alive. I still believe.*

"You know you have me, too," Sarah squeaks.

I smile. "I know, and thank you. Right, the moment of truth, I'm excited!"

"Ok, Katie, let's see how this baby of yours is doing, shall we?" the sonographer says. "Right well, we have a very well formed baby here, it's doing really well. See this is the head, and its little arms are here and legs. Look it's moving its little feet, can you see?"

"I can't see anything, can you see something, Sarah?" I ask.

The sonographer laughs. "It's quite common when you don't know what you're looking at, I'll draw an outline as I'm going along, I'll just do a quick once over first and then show you what I mean," she says.

"I can see the head but that's about it," Sarah says.

"Oh look, I see what you mean now, look, Sarah, look at the little arms and legs...Oh My God! This little baby is inside of me!"

I sit back, and I start to cry as this is the first time I have seen my baby as more than just a little embryo, and it's also the first time that I really feel alone.

"Oh lovely, I know it's very overwhelming, but it's a joyous time so enjoy it. Your hormones are all over the place now too at the moment. Are you ok?" the sonographer asks.

"Yeah, I'll be fine, it is just all very overwhelming," I say with a smile.

Sarah looks at me with pity and she puts her arm around me. "It'll be fine babes, we'll stick together and I'll help you through this every single step of the way," she says.

I nod my approval because I can't talk with choking back the tears.

"Here's some tissues sweetie, you wipe those eyes now and enjoy this moment. I'll see you again when you're at thirty-six weeks, and by then you'll see some major differences. Main thing you need to know now is to eat plenty because that baby of yours is fine and healthy. We want to see it grow to be big and strong, like a big bouncy ball," she says with laughter.

"I don't want to look like a big bouncy ball, though," I say with a giggle.

"Ha ha you won't, you'll just be blooming, like you are today," she says with a smile.

I hoist myself up from the gurney and make my way out of the room with Sarah.

"Thank you," I say as I leave.

"You're welcome lovely. Remember now, eat plenty and drink loads of water, you need to keep hydrated," she says.

"I will, don't worry."

I leave feeling very happy, but that loneliness that I felt on the bed still lingers inside of me, and I still wonder where the hell Pete is.

"Oh, this deserves a bit of a celebration, let's treat ourselves to lunch on the South Bank today," Sarah says.

"Ok! But no booze for me, thank you," I say with a smile.

"Oh, I know. You're lucky you don't drink a lot anyway. I reckon it must be very difficult for someone who likes their booze as in someone who goes out a few nights a week on the tear, to have to give it up during pregnancy," Sarah says.

"I know, I can't imagine how... oops sorry!" I say as I bump into a person rounding the corner.

"Dan?" I say. *Is that him? Pete's friend that I met that night a few months back?*

"Hi, hi yes, it's Dan. I'm so sorry I've forgotten your name. You were with Pete that night I met you," he says.

"Yes, yes that's me, Katie, Katie is my name. How are you?" *Oh please tell me you know something of Pete, please?*

"I'm fine thanks, Katie. How are you? Dreadful about poor Pete isn't it?"

"I'm good thanks. Em, what about Pete?" *Oh, don't cry, do not cry. This guy obviously thinks you were just a friend of his and no more than that.*

"The accident, in Italy? I haven't seen him myself probably since that night I met you both. And I'm assuming now that you haven't either. He went to Italy to do a course with his work. The day he arrived, he went hang-gliding with some of the other blokes. Something went wrong somewhere along the line and he came down, but no one knows exactly where he landed, if he did. He still hasn't been found. They've searched high and low for him but no sign. He's presumed dead at this stage. He most likely drowned. I thought you might have seen it on the news maybe?"

"We know," Sarah butts in.

Think fast Katie, as you don't want Sarah letting him know that this is his baby.

"We know it must be a very sad time for all of you," I say in an extra loud voice cutting Sarah off.

"It is. I thought you knew him better, but clearly you don't. I'm sure this is probably a shock for you still, though?" he asks.

Quick, get in before Sarah. "Yes, yes that's right, we just knew each other through friends. I only met him randomly that night. We never hang out together normally. That is very sad," I say. "Well, we'd better be off. It's terrible news, I do hope he's found to put everyone's mind at ease," I say with a slight quiver in my voice.

"We all do. He has a brother living in Italy who hasn't stopped looking as yet. Even if they did find him at this stage it's clear something catastrophic must have happened to him as he would have contacted his brother otherwise. Unfortunately, in my opinion, I reckon he's gone, the poor bugger. He's missed greatly by all of the lads."

"That's so sad," I say, trying to choke the tears back for the second time today.

"Anyway, how are you? You look very well, happy I would say?" he says.

Will you just stop talking? I am about to burst into tears soon if you don't stop!!

"She's ecstatic now, I'd say," Sarah mutters under her breath.

"I'm good thanks. Yeah, we are just off for a bite of lunch so I'd better go. It was nice to see you again, Dan," I say, trying to sound happy.

"Yes you too, and your friend," he says with a smile and sticks his hand out to shake Sarah's. "I'm Dan, sorry, I should have introduced myself before."

"Sarah, nice to meet you."

"Sorry, my fault I should have introduced you, I'm the common denominator here after all," I say with a smile.

"Don't worry, anyway lovely to see you, ladies. Enjoy lunch and I might see you around again. Cute baby bump by the way. I'm sure Pete would be surprised to see you're sprogged up with someone. Congratulations, and good luck if I don't bump into you again," he says with a laugh. "Sorry, I do have a sad sense of humour."

I can see that, Dan. I smile, "Thank you," I say. "Take care, Dan." I turn to walk away and I feel distraught – not only because if Pete is alive, will he probably not remember me, but the reality is my baby's father is most likely not with us anymore.

"Oh look! Wahacca, we'll go here," Sarah says, probably because it's the nearest place to us now. I love Mexican food, but I do believe she can see I need to sit down badly and if there was ever a time I needed a drink, it would be now.

"So, how are you feeling and why were you acting so strange with Dan? You know about Pete already!" Sarah asks.

"I honestly don't know. The initial reaction was if he found out that Pete and I were together he'd automatically assume that the baby is Pete's. I don't know, I just want Pete to hear the news from me, if he's still alive. It's stupid I know. I guess the hormones made me do something stupid and weird just now. I don't know what I'm feeling …I'm numb."

"I can imagine. This is the first time you've had to really talk about Pete, to someone you don't really know, isn't it?" Sarah asks.

"Yes, it is, and it felt really strange Sarah. I didn't like it. I felt like I was talking about him like he is dead... but I don't believe he is," I say, feeling very low.

"Well, you know what we have to do now don't you? We have to find Pete and let him know," she says.

"I don't know Sarah, the likelihood is that he's dead, gone. How could this happen? Even if he is still with us something has happened to make him cut ties with everyone. I can't really turn up on his doorstep and say "Hi remember me? This is your baby? You left me nine months ago, pregnant, but you didn't know at the time, and then you had an accident, and now you can't remember anything about me. Well, you didn't know about the baby anyway, but I just thought I'd drop it all on you today," and I'll hand him the baby? That would go down well I'd say."

"Don't be so dramatic. Look, come on, be positive. He hasn't been found so he could still be alive. You've been in torture for the past three months or so not knowing what the hell happened to him. If he's alive, who knows what happened to him? He may have suffered trauma and lost his memory. We don't know anything. But if that did happen, and he gains his memory back, you know he's going to come looking for you. How upset do you think he'd be to learn he was a dad and you never told him?" she asks.

"I know, but where the hell do we start especially if the Search and Rescue team can't even find him? I am trying to not think about him right now. That's the best thing to do," I say.

"Hmmm, I don't know, I think you're making a mistake. Think about it properly ok? You have time anyway, six months or so," she says with a wink. "Actually, you know what, surely he must have told his brother how besotted he was with you? Maybe we should find him. I'm sure he'd be delighted to know he's going to be an uncle!" Sarah roars with enthusiasm.

"I'm not so sure. You know we never really discussed family a whole lot as he wasn't very close to his, not even his brother. I'm surprised they even had contact before he left, but obviously he did. Maybe he didn't get a chance to tell him about me yet as this all happened on his first day after all."

"Hmmm, maybe, maybe a lot of things, chicken, maybe a lot. I still think it's a day of good news as opposed to bad, though. Baby is very healthy by the sounds of it. Daddy may just be out there wandering around looking for you, but not knowing exactly who or what he's searching for. You're in a far better position today than you were yesterday, so embrace it and enjoy the fact that you've had good news. Now, let's order, because we have a waddling duck here who's eating for two," she says with a giggle.

"Wagon!" I say with a laugh, "I hope I'll get to mock you one day when you're fat. I'm ok, Sarah, I am good. I think the baby is too," I say, smiling.

20

"*I* can't believe I've managed to persuade you both to do this," I say with a smile.

"It's a great idea Katie, and if anything, it might help you put your mind at ease as you'll feel you've done something to go in search of him. Laura, you're in agreement, right?" Sarah asks.

"Of course darling, my goodness we are on a mission, and while we are going for serious reasons, we will also have a laugh I'm sure. It would be difficult for us not to laugh I think, we are always cracking jokes whatever the situation. It's good to keep the spirits high. I think this is a great idea Katie. It'll be good for you," Laura says.

"Oh, I don't know girls, maybe this is a mistake?" I ask.

"Mistake, smishmake! This is the right thing to do, and who knows what will come of it, but at least you'll have tried. I have a good feeling about all of this though, a very good feeling, so stop with the negativity lady, this is meant to happen," Sarah says.

"I think so too, I just feel bad as I feel like maybe I've pushed so hard that you feel obliged to come with me," I say hesitantly.

"Flight 2430 to Rome is now boarding, can passengers please have their boarding cards and passports ready for inspection," shouts the voice over the tannoy.

"Right, that's us. Let's do this," I say with a smile.

"Hurrah, whoop whoop! Girlie mission underway," Sarah roars.

I wonder would you be so enthusiastic if you knew what Pete said about you to Jarvis earlier in the year. I know he was joking, and to be fair he didn't know you were my friend either then, but I do wonder what you'd say if you knew. Oh, I need to forget that, it's in the past. I have to stop with all of this stupid worrying over nothing. Who knows, I may not even find a trace of him anyway, so no need to get excited just yet.

I smile at Sarah and look at Laura, who seems even more excited at the idea. *Ok, I need to loosen up. I'm on a mission to find the man I love and hopefully I will find him, and he'll remember me as clearly as the day he left me. It's a very long shot, but my gut feeling is that he's still alive, but I'm just not sure if I'll find him.*

We board the plane and thankfully Laura knows one of the aircrew and arranges for us to get seats in the first row. I need the space to stretch my legs as they are a bit swollen of late, and I want to do my leg exercises during the flight.

"Katie, I feel mean doing this, but would you mind if I have a drink? I know you can't, but I love the auld buzz you get from a bit of alcohol while flying. You know I'm no pisshead, but I do enjoy that sensation," Sarah says.

"Oh would you stop. You don't need to ask me, Sarah. Listen to me now you two, we might be on a particular mission here, but don't feel that you can't enjoy yourselves some bit. Now, I don't want to hear a word about this, if I say the mission is aborted at any time, then the mission is aborted, ok?" I say.

"Ha ha ha ha, you sound like a commander there Katie. Ok boss!" Sarah says as she pulls a diary from her bag. "Now, I've made a plan. Since you came up with this idea Katie, I decided I'd see if we could narrow down the searching process. Seeing as we have a week, I've outlined the areas I think he'd be most likely to be, judging from the information you've given me already. I reckon his course was based around this area on the map which I've marked in black. The flight was around this vicinity which I've marked in red, and they jumped from this point. I don't know, but I think he's alive still. I really do and I reckon he can't have landed too far off this area," she says with a grin as she circles another area on the map. "Now, if he landed in the sea, well, people can survive that, can't they? So, I think he could be in one of these towns here. Someone could have found him and helped him. You know how you read about these things happening," she says with great hope. I'm hopeful too.

"Please fasten your seatbelts ladies, the cabin door will be closing shortly," the air stewardess says with a strong Italian accent and a smile.

I smile back and do as she asks then turn my attention back to Sarah. "Ah, you've kind of thought about this a lot haven't you?" I say.

"Too much?" she asks.

"No, it's not too much, I suppose. I love your enthusiasm, but I'm just trying to keep it real also. I'm just worried that we might not find him, as we haven't heard anything in months after all. Let's wait and see as the detective who's worked on it all has been told to close the case as they believe he's gone and will never be found at this stage. I don't want us to get our hopes up if they have searched all of these areas already, Sarah. Even if we do find Pete, he might not remember or he might just not want anything to do with me or the baby," I mutter.

"Yes, but remember, no one seems to know you were with him, except for us. His friend Dan even thought you were just acquaintances, and you let him believe that too. That, my friend, might actually be a good thing!" Sarah says with glee.

"Listen to me, for starters, a negative attitude is not going to help you," Laura butts in. "Secondly, this man was in love with you. That love will be there in his eyes still, and you will jog his memory somehow when he sees you. I can't guarantee that, but I believe when two people are meant to be together, it all works out, and if this is meant to be, he will see something in you the minute he meets you again. Now, we are going to find him, we have a whole week, and I don't want to hear another negative word out of you, ok?"

"Ok, but..."

"No Buts!!! Zip it, pregnant or not, hormones or not, I will not listen to negativity. You are not allowed to encourage negative thoughts on this journey. It's going to be fun with a wonderful outcome. End of story. Now, how long do we have to wait for that drink?" Laura says.

Oops! I've pissed her off now. I'd better be quiet or she'll dump the drink over my head. Keep your head down Katie girl and say nothing.

I sit back and relax. The journey is quicker than I thought it would be, and my ankles, although swollen, are nowhere near as bad I thought they'd be. As we touch down, I can feel the heat before the doors are even opened.

"I'm sweating like I'm in a sauna. I hope it's not going to be this hot for the time we're here," I say. "Sorry, sorry no negativity, I know... sorry!" I say before Laura berates me.

"I wasn't going to have a go at you for that. I can imagine it must be highly uncomfortable for you, I'm feeling a bit sweaty myself. Don't go all scared to speak to me now. I know I had a go at you earlier, but that was because you need to think of this as a fun challenge rather than something that you might come out of disappointed," Laura says.

"Sweating? I'm the fairest of you all and I'm drenched! I'm not built for this heat at all," Sarah says. She's not wrong, she has sweat patches all over, poor thing.

"Ok, let's get this show on the road. I need icy cold water to cool me down and a bit of air soon," I say as the door opens. "We're lucky we're sitting at the front, first off at least."

"I know, none of us are sorry about that fact," Sarah says.

We walk towards the baggage collection area and I run to the ladies quickly while the others watch and wait patiently for the bags. When I return, I'm surprised the luggage has arrived so quickly and they've managed to collect mine also.

"That was fast!" I proclaim.

"I know, good that things are on our side. Right, I've booked us into the Boscolo Exedra Hotel," Sarah says.

"Excellent! A nice five star! I'm happy! So, when we start our travels do we know where to start?" I ask.

"Not really, but that's all part of the fun, fun, fun," Laura says.

"Right, let's hop in a taxi and get our asses into some air conditioning," Sarah says.

I'm not sorry to hear you say that, I'm bloody exhausted already, but I know not to complain as I'll get my arse kicked.

"Woohoooo! Look at that for a snazzy hotel," Sarah says as we pull up to the Exedra.

"Wow! Well done Sarah, nice work. It looks like there's a spa attached to it too. Great, treats girls, treats! I badly need some sort of facial or a back massage would be divine!" I say.

"Yes well, I had you in mind when booking it. You need a break and one where you can relax with others to look after you, besides us of course. Thought this would be ideal," Sarah says.

"Well done, very well done lady. I'm very impressed. I could do with a few treats myself, especially my nails, they are in such a dreadful condition lately. I lost my letter opener weeks back and I've been using my nails to open everything. I keep forgetting to buy a new one but look at them, just disgraceful, chipped and discoloured. This will go down a treat now," Laura says.

"Good afternoon ladies, how can I help you?" the man at reception asks in a thick Italian accent.

Mmmmm, look at you with those smouldering eyes. I'd fancy you if I were single.

"Check out yer man," Sarah says. "I'd fancy him a bit."

I snigger as Sarah and I normally don't go for the same type of guy. Jarvis may have been the exception to the rule, but this is the second time we have an interest in the same guy. "I was just thinking the same thing myself, if I were single and less pregnant," I say with a laugh. "Go for it girl, nothing to lose and we are here for seven nights. It gives you time to work that charm of yours on him," I say with a smile.

"What are you two sniggering about?" Laura asks with a grin. "Oh yes, I think all three rooms are booked under Sarah's name, O'Sullivan is the surname," she says with confidence to the man behind the desk.

"Nothing, Laura, we'll fill you in later," I say with a grin.

"Ladies, would you like help with your bags?" the concierge asks.

"That would be fantastic," I say with a smile. "That saves this poor pregnant lady a job."

"Oh, who's taking the piss?" Sarah says laughing. "She's getting into the spirit of it all now I see. I can imagine what else you'll chance your arm with while you're here."

"Ha ha ha, well you were whinging earlier that I was negative, I'm just showing a more positive side now and enjoying the fact that I will have people out there who will be willing to help a pregnant lady out," I say with a grin.

"Of course, madam. I will, of course, take your bags too, ladies, it's all part of the service," the very attractive concierge says.

Sarah and Laura grin at me. I can't help but laugh, "I'll get special privileges elsewhere I'm sure, bitches," I say with a laugh.

We all squeeze into the lift, which seems quite small. "Maybe the pregnant lady should take a lift by herself?" I ask.

"Ha ha ha would you stop, get your arse in here now, there's plenty of room," Laura says.

I never hear her use the word arse really. I think it's something she's picking up from being around us a lot more of late. I can sense the concierge feels a little uncomfortable.

"Are you ok there, we aren't making you uncomfortable I hope?" I ask.

"No madam, not at all," he says with a smile.

"He's a bit young for you," Sarah says. I blush and give her the death stare. She sniggers and snorts while trying to keep it under control.

"I wasn't you know, trying to seduce you or anything there," I say to him, making matters worse. *I feel so awkward now.*

He grins, "it's ok madam, I get ladies of your age coming onto me all of the time. I am a good catch so I understand," he says in a very sexy accent.

Cheeky little sod, you're only about five years younger than me! Age is just a number after all! I can't help but notice his naturally curly black hair and blue eyes. His very muscular physique is definitely to be admired and he's the first very tall guy I've seen since I arrived. He must be at least six foot two. *I wouldn't mind running my fingers through those curly locks of yours.*

I'm glad when we reach the eleventh floor because I'm starting to feel uncomfortable in the lift after what was said. Sweat beads are forming on my forehead and I'm not sure they would be there had Sarah not opened her big mouth.

"Now madam, you are in the last room on this corridor, so I'll save the best for last," the concierge says with a cheeky grin.

"Ohhhhhh, ha ha ha ha, best for last Katie," Sarah and Laura say with a grin.

"Ah, she is only next door to you ladies, 1109, 1110 and 1111 for Ms. Katie," he says.

"I'm in 1111?" I say. "Ooohhhh nice number, eleven is a very lucky number you know?" I say to them.

"Yes, we can see it's working already before you even get to the room," Laura says giggling.

The concierge laughs, "Oh you ladies are a fun, I like when we get customers like you here. You know how to have the laugh with staff,' he says.

Oh you're a little sweetie, I like you.

"Please, ladies, settle in, make yourselves at home and please call me should you need anything. And finally, here we are Ms. Katie. We have special treatment for you as we cannot allow you to lift anything heavy. I hope you enjoy your stay and please call to me if you need anything. My name is Enrico."

"Thanks, Enrico, you're very kind, I really appreciate your help," I say.

"Do you mind me asking Ms. Katie, when do you have your baby?"

"Oh, not for another four months approximately, Enrico. I'm here searching for the father," I say.

Oh feck, that came out wrong. I need to explain myself now. "That sounded all wrong. It's a bit of a story Enrico, and please call me Katie, not Ms. Katie," I say.

"Ah sorry. Ok, Katie. If you like to tell, I like to hear it," he says.

This is weird, but sod it, I'll tell you.

I sit down and tell Enrico the brief version of the story.

"Wow, Katie, that is one sad story," he says.

"Yes, I know. That's why I'm finding this whole situation a bit strange but yet comforting," I say.

"Well, Katie, I like to help you any way I can. If you need help on my day off, please call me. I like to help you. Please forgive my English is not so good."

"Your English is fine Enrico, and you know what, I might just ask you if we do need help. Thank you," I say with a smile.

"You're welcome, now I must get back to downstairs or they might call to police for missing person," he says.

Cute! You're so cute.

I give him a tip of twenty euros as he was so good to listen to me. A sweet guy, who has just made me realise that I've not really spoken to anyone about my situation except for the girls. It feels good to speak to someone and let it all out. Once he leaves, I lie on my bed for a few minutes and drift off to sleep.

"Katie, Katie, are you ok in there?" I hear, accompanied by loud banging noises on the door.

Oh no, what time is it? Oh no! Dinner time and I'm not even changed!

"Hi, hi," I say as I open the door. "Sorry girls, I fell asleep which oddly enough is something I do a lot of lately. Come in," I say as I hold my back. I'm aching and the angle I slept at hasn't helped.

"Are you ok? You don't look too good, no offence," Sarah says.

"No I'll be grand, I just need to freshen up. I fell asleep after Enrico left and only woke now, forgive me please?"

"Of course! You're pregnant hon, we aren't going to berate you for sleeping. Do you want to come out or maybe we can get room service if you prefer?" Laura says, looking at Sarah and nodding.

"No, no, this is a holiday too, girls, not just a mission. Let's go out," I say.

I can see they both look pleased at my response. Part of me wishes I could join them in a drinking session tonight to make it feel more like a holiday. I know my whole reasoning behind this is to find Pete, but I do need a bit of a sun holiday too. And I certainly know they are up for a bit of holiday partying. Once I get ready, we make our way downstairs and out onto the piazza. The sun is just setting and such a beautiful sight it is.

"The guy on the desk told me this bar next door do great cocktails, and virgin ones for you," Sarah says.

"Virgin ones? I'd doubt that would be appropriate for me!" I say as I rub my bump which feels like it's expanded over the past few days.

"Ha ha, that's the spirit girl, oh you're on fire tonight. Come on let's head in here so and have a bit of a giggle. You must both be starving, are you?" Sarah asks.

"Yeah, I think baby needs a bit of grub now alright," I say as I rub my belly furiously.

We take a seat at a table in the corner and the girls let me sit on the inside where there is plenty of space between me and the table.

"So come here to me miss, what did you mean earlier when you mentioned about when Enrico left, you sounded very close to him or something. You didn't shift him did you?" Sarah asks.

"Ha ha ha, I did not!! Jesus, Mary and Joseph, what do you think I am? He's a young fella!" I say.

"Although, he's not that young, maybe five or six years younger maximum? Age is just a number love. So, what did happen as I think he's got a bit of a crush on you? Don't they say that men find pregnant women very attractive?" Sarah says.

"Yes, they do say that. I have a colleague at work and she found it very amusing that most of the men in the office kept looking at her as she passed by. And a few times she looked up from her desk to see some of them staring at her. They'd just smile nervously when they got caught out by her," Laura says.

"Is that not a bit weird though?" I ask.

"Well I suppose in some instances it could be, but most just think it's a naturally beautiful sight, which they can't help but admire," Laura says.

"True, I suppose. Ah well now, I couldn't be telling you what happened between myself and Enrico then, that would just be too much information for you to handle," I say with a peal of laughter.

"Hang on a second, you can't say something like that and then not tell us!" Sarah says.

"Indeed, spill it, lady," Laura spurts out.

"Ah I'm kidding girls, seriously like, he's probably what thirty-three max? He was really sweet, actually. He asked me if we were here for a fun and sun kind of holiday and I explained why we were here. He was really adorable and offered to help us out with searching for Pete if we needed help. How sweet is that?" I ask.

"No way! That was lovely of him. Did he mean it, though? He wasn't just sweet talking you to get a few quid out of you as a tip?" Laura says.

"Hmm no, I don't think so. I didn't look at it like that. I gave him twenty euros as he was so sweet. Still, surely he wouldn't if he knew he'd be seeing me around over the next few days?" I say.

"Possibly. He did seem like a nice guy I have to say. My first impression was a good one and you know me, I always go with my first impressions of everyone," Laura says.

"That you do! I remember when I brought my first London boyfriend to your house and you turned to me and said 'get rid of him, look at the shoes'. He had arrived before me and I felt disappointed you'd say that, but when I looked down and saw he was wearing socks with sandals I nearly collapsed on the spot. Remember, he kept asking all night what was wrong and I just couldn't speak without nearly laughing into his face. Socks and sandals... such a no go for a man in his twenties," I say with a laugh.

"Ah, feck off! Are you serious? Such a no go for a man full stop!" Sarah exclaims.

"Hah! Yes, sadly, he arrived twenty minutes before me, and it was a summers evening. I told Laura he was on his way and to keep an eye out for him as he wouldn't be the type to join them of his own accord when he didn't know anyone. So Laura, being Laura, invited him in and when I arrived, there he was in a pair of board shorts, and his socks and sandals. I didn't see them first as it was dark, but Laura kindly pointed them out to me. I was stunned as he seemed a pretty cool guy, very eccentric, but that really took me by surprise," I say laughing. "Oh happy days, girls, happy days."

"Indeed, you've had a few dodgy ones from what I recall," Laura says. "Although I have too so I can't talk. Remember the guy who refused to drink anything unless he had a yellow straw. Oh goodness me, I thought it quirky at the start, but it started getting very embarrassing after a while especially if he was given a different coloured straw and I had to ask for a yellow one specifically. It was quite mortifying I have to say."

"I've had a few close calls too," Sarah says. "One we all know!"

"Oh, Jarvis? Well, I do apologise to you for that. I was highly disappointed with his behaviour, he's let me down badly I have to say," Laura says. "Highly disappointed I was," she repeats with an air of disgust. "Still, he's David's friend and I can't just ignore him, can I?" she says sounding annoyed.

Can we change the subject, please? Because if you ask Sarah what happened exactly, I'm going to be very red-faced, even though it's not my fault.

"Oh girls, let's move on from Jarvis to someone who's not in common with any of us," I say hoping they will.

"Ha ha ha, oh look, look at him! The guy with the navy shorts, and the Hawaiian shirt! Does he remind you of anyone? The one near the flag, can you see him? Oh, that damn plant is blocking your view," Laura says.

"Where, I can't see. Oh my God, it's not is it?" I say.

"No it's not, but it looks very like him," Laura says.

"Who, who are you talking about? Tell me, girls, don't keep me in the dark!" Sarah says.

"Member maaaaaaaan," I say with a roar of laughter.

"Who the hell is Member Man?" Sarah asks.

"Member Man is this guy who I saw for around a year. He was hot, really hot, but he had this thing for sending pictures of his member to my phone," Laura says with a giggle.

"Oh no, really? One of those guys?" Sarah asks.

"Yep, he was a lovely guy, but for some reason had it in his head that I really enjoyed getting these photos. He'd send one first thing in the morning, again at lunchtime, dinner time, and when off to bed. Honestly, I just couldn't believe it sometimes. I opened one of them one day in the office as didn't know what it was, I thought it was just a regular picture of him saying hi, and you know to just say he was thinking of me or something as that was the first time he sent me a photo. Well, he was thinking about me alright, and not in the way I wanted him to," Laura says.

"Ha ha, that's just awful, but so funny!" Sarah says.

"Wait, Sarah, this gets better, Laura, tell her the rest of the story," I say trying to hold the laughter back.

"Well, I got all excited before I opened the message, and my colleague, ah she's a good friend, but I said to her, 'Oh look he's thinking of me, he's sent me a picture, how sweet.' She got excited and ran across to me. 'Show it to me, I'm dying to see this guy you've been talking about,' she says. So I open the picture and there it was in all its glory, I nearly died on the spot. I never ever went so red in my life. Jackie nearly fell over with fright, she didn't know where to look and burst out laughing. 'Well isn't he just as handsome as I thought he'd be,' she said, typical smart Irish woman, love her to bits. I couldn't help but laugh, but I swear I couldn't help but look at it either. Neither could Jackie, she came back to me saying, 'Don't put it away yet, let me have a proper look.' It was quite funny, but he continued to send me pictures out of the blue. So, I had to open them in private any time he sent a picture as I was afraid what it could be."

"Oh stop, that story is just brilliant, but what happened in the end? I take it that Member Man is not David then, or that guy standing there?" Sarah asks.

"Goodness no! It's definitely not David, nor is it that guy, but he really does look so like him. In the end, we just realised we weren't compatible at all and we went our separate ways. Although he pops into my mind every now and then," Laura says.

"I'll bet that's not all that pops into your mind," I say with a giggle.

"No and I shouldn't say this, but I kept one of them. I've no idea why, but I did. Am I a dirty bird for doing that?" she asks.

"Whatever takes your fancy Laura, nice to know what you like hoarding, though. I'll know what you want for your next Christmas present now," I say with a laugh.

"Cheeky girl, I do no such thing. He was just an interesting character and I couldn't resist keeping a little memory of him. I know that's bad, maybe I should delete it?" she asks.

"Do not ya big eejit! Keep it, and the next annoying fella who comes your way, show him the picture and tell them that's what you're going back to if he doesn't behave himself," Sarah says with a laugh.

"I'd like to do that, but the only annoying fella I can do that to is my husband, and I don't think he'd appreciate knowing that I have a photo of Member Man on my phone as a fond memory. Maybe I should delete it. I love David, he's my one and only for definite."

"Well, I see the memory side of it all for you, but it could cause problems if he saw it. Maybe we can have a farewell Member Man party tonight and you delete that photo?" I suggest.

"Hmmm, true." Sarah says. "I guess that might not work out too well, unless you fancy getting a divorce maybe? Oh, that's a funny story. Aren't men strange though in comparison to us? For instance, I wouldn't dream of sending pictures of any part of me to a man, even if I was going out with him. I know there are women out there who probably would, but it just doesn't seem right at all."

"Yeah, I guess everyone is different. I thought when I met Pete first he'd be like Member Man actually. Thankfully he wasn't at all, but he has that kind of personality. A cheeky chappy guy, who might do something like that, or at least that's what I thought! Thankfully he was an absolute gent, caring, giving and very loving," I say. "Sorry, I don't want to bring the conversation to a stop, I didn't mean to come out with that," I say.

"No it's fine, you haven't spoken about him much, it's good to talk and if you want to, then do. We're both here to hear you out, chicken," Laura says.

"Thanks, girls. I'm sure I will talk about him over the next few days, but that's enough for now. Not a very good first impression I'm giving you of him is it, telling you he came across as a member man."

"Hah oh don't worry, we know he's not, you're a fussy bitch. You'd have that knocked out of him in no time anyway if he had been like that," Sarah says with a laugh.

"Ok girls, kiss Member Man goodbye, I'm deleting him," Laura roars.

"I hope you actually don't mean that literally, I'm not kissing a photo of that," I say.

"Ha ha ha, of course I don't mean literally, oh darling you're on top form. Ok, here goes, a toast to Member Man. Thank you for the memories, especially the ones which I think will be forever embedded in my brain. Alas, it is time for me to say goodbye and leave you well in the past. Cheers, ladies," Laura says as we clink our glasses and she presses the delete button on her phone.

I smile. "Right girls, don't know about ye, but I need food, and now. This little baby has just given me a good kick for the first time," I say with a big grin on my face.

21

*I*t's late, later than late actually, 3:30 am and I can't believe I actually went clubbing with the girls. "Don't you love that song 'Groove Is In The Heart?' When I heard it tonight I knew I wouldn't be able to sit still," Laura says. "I do love a good daawwwnce darlings, you just cawwwnt beat it," she says in her overly posh English accent.

"You do know you sound very posh as it is Laura, but have you ever noticed it comes out far more exaggerated when you're after drink?" Sarah says.

"Really daaaawwwrling I've no idea what you mean," she says with a grin.

"Yeah, it does get exaggerated after a sipeen of alcohol. It's like that song, when she sings it's like 'Murder on the Daawwwnce Floor', that's how you sound," I say with a giggle.

"Oh here now, are we going to mock me for the night? What about you with your accent? Don't even staaaart me," she says with a roar of laughter.

"We won't because you'll do that really rubbishy Irish accent you do, and that's just embarrassing," I say with a giggle. "Oh come on girls, we're nearly there and I'm absolutely knackered, I can't wait to get my shoes off as my feet feel really swollen," I say.

"Good job you're not wearing these then is it dawwwrling?" Laura says as she lifts her five inch heel off the ground and topples over as she does it.

"Oh fuck, that wasn't supposed to happen," she says with a laugh.

Sarah bends down and offers her a hand up, but instead of pulling her up, Laura ends up pulling Sarah on top of her and the two of them are rolling around on the street giggling like two school girls.

Ok girls, this is very amusing admittedly, but please get up as I need to get to bed. "Come on ye gobshites," I say as I walk away.

"Help us up Katie!!" they roar after me.

"I will not. I've no plans on ending up on the floor. I've got another human being rolling around inside of me thank you very much," I say.

"Ok, that's true. Laura, come on. Get up or try and hoist yourself up somehow," Sarah says as she rolls over onto her side and then onto her knees.

You're both in some condition. Is this how I am after a few drinks? If it is I'm never drinking again, that's for sure.

We slowly make it back to the hotel, it's only what should be a five minute walk, but it takes us twenty as I have to try to keep the girls in from the road. *I suppose I should get used to babysitting.*

"Buona Sera sexy lady," roars a man from a car.

"You want to make fun time with me tonight?" he asks Sarah.

"Yerah go on and feck off with yourself ya dirty clown," she says. I snigger. She can be quite funny after a few drinks.

"Sarah, be careful, we don't know him so don't draw him on us," I say quietly.

"Oh, but I don't talk to you, you are not attractive, I like sexy lady with baby bump," he says.

Lovely! Is this what I'm going to be subjected to for the rest of my pregnancy?

"Well bugger off because sexy lady with baby bump thinks you're not attractive so feck off into the sunset, it's that-a-way!" I say. *Creep.*

The girls erupt into hysterics. "Oh Katie, that's the funniest we've seen you in ages. Well said and how dare he say I'm not attractive. I am, aren't I?" Sarah asks, sounding hurt.

"You're a big ride," I say sarcastically. "Now, come on please because I'm tired and very narky, as you've just seen. I need my bed. I don't have your stamina for drinking and dancing right now, please remember that," I say trying to sound as calm as I can.

"I know. Sorry Katie. Have a lie in tomorrow and we can head off on our journey in search of Pete a little later. Although, my coordination may not be so great tomorrow so just bear that in mind," Sarah says with a smile.

"What are you talking about there?" the voice says from the bushes we had just passed.

I turn around to see Laura squatting in the middle of the bushes.

"Laura, what are you up to?" I ask.

"Sorry dawwwrling, I couldn't hold it any longer. It's fine, no one can see me," she says nonchalantly.

"Doesn't she normally wear glasses?" Sarah whispers to me.

"Yes, she does, and yes I know she's not wearing them tonight. Laura, no one can see you apart from us and maybe, just maybe the entire police station that's well lit across the street," I say in an angry tone. "Get up now!" I shout.

"Shhhhhhh, you'll wake them from their sleep," she says. "I'm not wearing my glasses so it looks like there's no one around."

I stand there patiently waiting for her to finish emptying the contents of her bladder which seems like the entire night's drink intake. *I can't take anymore. I want to go home now!!*

"Girls, I'm getting very pissed off now and I might just abort this mission and fly home tomorrow if you don't cop on. I need some sleep and you two are pissed as coots. If you don't hurry up, I'm going and you can take another fifty minutes if you want to walk the twenty second journey to the hotel! ' I scream.

I storm off. *The hormones are really taking over tonight. I feel like crying now too. Where is Pete when I need him?*

I finally get to the hotel and the two girls in tow behind me. It's only a two minute walk, but I have no idea what they are doing now, they are taking so long to catch up.

"Ah Ms. Brown, I have a note for you. It's from Enrico," the night duty concierge says when I approach the desk.

"Oh, thank you," I say with a smile, the first smile in the past hour probably as I'm so frustrated with the girls.

I open it.

> Dear Katie, It was a pleasure to meet you and your friends today. I mean what I say that I would like help you look for your man. I am not working tomorrow. I work nights, and am free most days while you are here. If you want to start search I am happy to help? I have boat too, and we can go to islands if this is necessary, but have car for driving mainland. Please leave note at desk for me and they can call me to let me know. Thank you. Enrico.

What a sweetheart. I walk back to the concierge and ask for a pen and paper. *I'm such an eejit! Why didn't I give him my number and we could WhatsApp instead.*

> Dear Enrico, thank you for your kind words and it was a pleasure for us also to meet you. That's so kind of you to offer your car and boat to help us in our search. If it's not too much trouble, it would be a massive help to us. We will be ready to leave the hotel probably around 10:00 am tomorrow. Please let me know if that time doesn't suit as we are very happy to work around you. Thank you Enrico, you're an absolute gentleman. Katie.

"Hi, would you mind leaving this here for Enrico please? He's kindly offered to help us tomorrow, and I want to take him up on his kind gesture," I say to the night concierge.

"Of course, madam. Enrico is a good guy, he is well liked around here. I will call him now to tell him so he has notice. He has made me aware that he may be coming to collect you all tomorrow," he says.

"Thank you and sorry, what's your name please?"

"I am Paulo, madam," he says with a smile.

"Thanks, Paulo, your help is greatly appreciated," I say as I turn to walk away from the desk.

I manage to get the morning more or less arranged before the girls reach me in the foyer. "Ok bitches, get to bed as it's nearly 4:30 and Enrico is collecting us at 10:00," I say.

"What? 10:00 am? For God's sake Katie, we'll be dying," Sarah says.

"Hmmmm, true, but self inflicted and we would have been home a lot earlier if you hadn't kept downing those damn shots. I, on the other hand, will probably feel like I'm hungover in the morning, but won't be. Girls, come on, get to bed," I say as I usher them to the lift. "Laura, are you ok, you're gone very quiet?" I ask.

"Yes, I'm tired and feel sick at the thought of that early start," she says.

"I know, but look Enrico has been kind enough to offer and we can't let him hanging around waiting. It's not fair! It's his time off, and I'm sure he'd like to spend it doing something else, but he's offering to help us. You can sleep in the car if necessary. I'll be of sound mind to tell him where we want to go. Ok! Can you put your key in the door?" I ask as she keeps missing the slot. "For feck sake! Give it to me!" I grab the key and place it into the slot and remove it, *click*, "Go on, go to bed and sleep well," I say.

Sarah goes into her room and closes the door without uttering a word to anyone. *They are going to be in some state in the morning.*

22

The alarm rings. I turn it off and leave a massive yawn from my mouth. *Oh, stretch stretch stretch! I wonder how the girls are. They better be getting up shortly now. I'm full of life, what has made me feel this good after such a late night out?*

I get myself ready and head out, grabbing a sneaky pastry from the breakfast room to help keep me sustained until I get back again. *I shouldn't be too long I'd imagine. This detective won't have much to tell I'm sure.*

I reach the coffee shop and sitting there is a very official and distinguished looking gent. I walk towards him. "Detective Cannavaro?" I ask.

"Si, si. Katie, welcome to bella Roma. How are you? It's very nice to meet you after our conversations on the phone," he says.

Oh, you're a bit of a handsome man!

"And you, thank you," I say with a smile.

"Ok, let me get a coffee and what would you like my dear, perhaps some pastries or fruit as I see you are having a baby," he says.

"Oh, I'm fine, thank you. I had a pastry to keep me going until I meet the girls later. Maybe some fresh orange juice would be nice, though, please?" I say.

"Of course, I'll be back," he says with a grin.

"Ok Arnie," I reply. Thankfully he got my joke and laughed out loud.

"Ah, funny Irish. I love Irish," he says as he walks away.

When he returns, he brings me a large glass of orange juice, and a pastry. I don't complain and eat it. I'm still hungry after the one I had as it was like a mini one.

"So, cara Katie, I'm afraid I don't have anything further to tell you about Pete. We still have not found a trace of him and as I explained, they have ordered me to close the case now. I don't want to until I find at least a body, but I don't have a choice. I am in this job a long time and I've seen many go missing, but they all turn up, either alive or there's a body, which I hate. However, it is the nature of my job. In this case, though, I don't feel it's right to close the case, I believe Pete is still alive and is hanging on in there." he says with a smile.

"Really? It's weird, because I have this feeling he is too, but to be honest, the chances are so slim. If he landed in that sea, he would have drowned surely, and I really don't know if I can cope with thinking about this every day for the rest of my life. Maybe it's best that the case is closed and that I close it from my side too," I say feeling sad.

"I see your point, but as long as I am alive, I will never give up hope of him turning up, and you should do the same. For now, though, as you have a little baby on the way, it might be better, so as not to cause stress. Pete's baby, yes?" he asks.

"Yes, Pete's baby," I say with a smile. "Thank you for meeting me. I feel bad dragging you out at such an early time and especially as you could have told me this on the phone," I say.

"No, it's my pleasure. I feel better telling you this to your face and I am very happy to finally meet you," he says.

"I'm happy to meet you too. Maybe we should stay in touch?" I ask.

"That would be good, and if anything crops up I can let you know," he says with a broad smile.

"I don't mean to be rude, but I've got two hungover girl friends back in the hotel who I need to wake. I managed to persuade them to come and search for Pete with me. They probably don't think it's the best idea, but came nonetheless. I suppose there's not much point now is there?" I ask.

"Of course there is. You may not find him, but at least you'll know you tried. Go and search for him. You might learn something new, you will see new places and meet new people. Katie, this could be a journey for you. Go and enjoy it. But make me a promise please?" he says.

"What's that?" I ask.

"I urge you to do this and you'll at least feel you've given it your best efforts, but please try not to get your hopes up too high as I would hate to see you disappointed. Remember you're carrying a child also, so please don't push yourself too hard," he says.

"Thanks for your concern. I know I may not find him, but I feel I'm actually doing something now and not just sitting back in London, waiting. Thank you Detective Cannavaro," I say as I stand up and shake his hand.

He shakes mine and looks at me with a smile and for some odd reason, we hug each other. It's lovely, he feels like an uncle giving me support.

I leave quickly and head back to the hotel, it's still early thankfully.

I pick up the telephone and dial Laura's number first.

"Hello," says the mouse like voice at the other side.

"Oh God, what way are you?" I ask.

"Sick, I'm at deaths door and the sunlight is breaking my head."

I stifle a laugh. "Well my sweet, it's nine o'clock now, and Enrico is collecting us at ten. Maybe go for a shower, and I'm sure you'll feel much better after. Rinse yourself off with cold water, and that will wake you up well," I say.

"Ok, bye," she hangs up.

Great, this should be a fun day. I'll be navigator and commander today.

Sarah's turn. I pick up the phone. *Hmmm, I wonder should I knock on the door instead? Maybe not, she probably won't get up, at least the phone is next to the bed.* I dial the room number. No answer. *Oh for God's sake. Where the hell is she now?*

I try again.

"Hello, ah Katie, how are ya girl?" she asks.

"You sound chirpy!" I say.

"Yes, I can't believe it, I woke at eight o'clock and decided to head for a swim, and I feel so much better for getting up. I'm sure I'll have a delayed hangover later, but feel great right now," she says.

"Fab! That's not what I was expecting, but delighted to hear it! At least two out of three being coherent isn't a bad start!" I say.

"Oh God, is Laura in a dire condition?"

"Sounds like it, I just called and she could barely talk. We might have some moving her later I'd say," I reply.

"Ok, leave it to me, I have something here which might give her a boost. I come prepared always," Sarah says.

"I'll leave it to you then, I'll get ready and meet you for a quick brekkie in ten minutes?" I ask.

"Sure, we can take a few croissants for Laura as I've a feeling she's not going to be wanting brekkie now," Sarah says. "I'm starving myself so I'll see you in ten downstairs." She hangs up.

I feel relieved, although I can't help but think maybe she's still under the influence so I don't get too excited.

I get ready and make my way downstairs. Sarah is sitting in the breakfast room waiting for me when I get there.

"How's herself?" I ask.

"Slow and painful death. She looks like crap. I gave her what I had to help cure her, and she was going for a cold shower to wake up. I've wrapped a few croissants up in a napkin for her, we could take a few sausages too maybe, or will we look like gobshites if we do that?"

"No aren't we paying for them?" I say. "Let's take one of everything," I giggle.

"We'll leave the eggs, that could get messy like," Sarah says.

I laugh. "Yeah, I think so."

"You look fab today honey, you obviously got a great sleep?" she says.

"I did, I don't even remember if I brushed my teeth last night. I think I must have just shoved the pyjamas on, and conked out on the bed straight away. Fantastic sleep," I say with a grin. "And I'm actually excited about starting this search today Sarah. I'm just so worried I'm getting my hopes up, though. I want nothing more than to see, hear and feel Pete again, and have him put his hands on my belly and feel our child inside me, kicking, but I'll be devastated if it doesn't happen."

"I know love, but look, if it doesn't we'll cross that bridge when we come to it, but for now, think more positively. You know how a positive mind brings a positive outcome," Sarah says.

"You're right. Ok, positive thoughts. We will find him, he will want me and the baby, and I will go back happy. One week isn't a lot of time for that to happen, though, hon."

"It's plenty I reckon if we look in the areas I've outlined on the map. Maybe some people might recognise him from the few photos you have and can point us in the right direction. We'll definitely get some information, I just feel it," she says.

"Ok, the photos aren't the best, as he's distant in them or else they are blurry. Even you have to admit it's not easy to make out exactly what he looks like in these. I wish we had taken some close up selfies, as much as I hate them," I say. "Look it's nearly ten o'clock, will we just grab this, run up to the room and drag Laura out and feed her? I don't want us to be late, this guy is doing us a massive favour," I say.

"Sure, well we can treat him and pay for petrol, we won't just let him do it out of the goodness of his heart," Sarah says with a smile.

We get up and leave the breakfast room. I ate a little too quickly and can feel slight indigestion taking place which is making me very uncomfortable, but it will pass.

"Do you want to wait there and spare your legs and I'll run up for Laura?" she asks.

"Sure, why not," I say.

I sit in the foyer patiently and Enrico comes in with boundless energy.

"Katie, how are you today, you look beautiful. Where are your friends? Are you excited about your mission?" he asks.

"You're lively for this hour!" I say with a smile.

"Yes, I am always lively, I am a morning person and it is beautiful, beautiful day outside. I cannot think more nice way to spend it than to show you sites of this wonderful country in the sunshine," he says.

"I'm excited Enrico. Oh look, here are the girls. They are a little ill today I'm afraid, too much alcohol last night," I say.

"Ah ha! I have good cure for that, it is something my mother made for me when I first got very sick from alcohol. It is nice, and we can collect some on the journey. They will feel good after taking it," he says.

Hmmm, I don't know now if we should be taking something from you Enrico, nice and all as you are. I wonder what it is.

"Hmmm, I don't know Enrico, we'll see as they may not feel up to taking something if they don't know what it is," I say.

"No Katie, it is safe all natural, it's just ginger tea, but mama makes it fresh and not from tea bags. They will like," he says

I'm going to get sick at the thought of it. I'll never manage to keep anything down if I smell that as my sense of smell is one hundred and fifty percent amplified these days and certain foods or drinks are having bad reactions. Oh God.

"Hmmmm, let's see about that one. With my sense of smell at the moment I could be likely to join them in the sick stakes as ginger isn't agreeing with me at the moment," I say with a smile. "Girls, are we ready, how are you feeling Laura?" I ask.

"I'm just getting too old for this. I need to stop partying and act my age. It's just gone way beyond a joke now, too old altogether," she says.

I look at Enrico and he whispers, "I think you might be right, maybe we forget about the hangover cure," he says with a smile.

We make our way to the car.

23

"And this, ladies in front of us is the famous Colosseo," Enrico says.

I gaze up to see the most beautiful ancient building I've ever seen in my life. It's structure so strong, gigantic and overpowering. I get a shiver down my spine as I suddenly feel transported back in time, back to Roman times. It's the first time I've heard Laura speak since we left the hotel.

"Oh, goodness me, look at that wonderful sight. I've never seen anything more beautiful in all my days. Enrico, how in God's name did they make that? Look at the size of it and the size of the...," Laura says. "What are those, blocks or bricks? No man could carry them surely?" she says in awe.

"Oh, Laura it amazes most today about how they created building. It must have taken ten men to carry each stone they are so big and heavy. Molto Grande! It's incredible it's still standing. We are very proud of building, very proud," Enrico says as we stop at the traffic lights.

It's such a mix of old and new, it's strange. A huge ancient ruin with traffic lights situated next to it, with cars and vespas zooming in and out, darting and weaving like little bullets. It's just odd, but beautiful. Enrico jams on the breaks.

"Where the hell did he come from?" Sarah yells.

"Ah Katie, are you ok?" Enrico says with worry in his voice.

"I'm fine Enrico thanks, although that idiot did come pretty close to causing a major accident there," I say nervously.

"Ah I'm a used to these idiots, it's a normal driving here in Roma," he says and then continues muttering in Italian.

"What's he muttering?" I hear Sarah whisper to Laura.

"Damned if I know, something Italian, maybe he's swearing?" she replies.

"Ok, we're all fine, no damage caused," I say.

"Let's get out and take some photos," Sarah suggests.

"Have we time? Remember we are on a deadline to find Pete and we don't have endless hours," I say.

"True, but just a few minutes, I mean who knows when we'll get back here again and we might not get time to take some pictures at the end of the break. Just a few minutes?" Sarah pleas.

"We have a time, we have a plenty of time. Where I take you today, is not very far away from here. It's a thirty or maybe forty kilometres, no more than that. Please I park, we go take pictures? I take them of you and the girls. Here we go, I can't a stay long here, but it's a Roma, and Polizia don't take a notice most of the time," he says with a laugh.

"Thanks, Enrico, you're the best. Do you need to stay in the car just in case?" Sarah asks.

"No, no, it's fine, I come to take the photo."

The three of us stand with stupid grins on our faces and the girls point with one finger to my baby and the other to the Colosseum.

"Your best smile ladies please?" shouts Enrico from a distance.

"Formaggio!" we all shout and erupt into laughter.

"Beautiful, you all look very, very happy in this. Please, look. Are you happy?" he asks.

"Awwwww, look at baby bump and big smiley head on momma. You look so cute with a bump," Sarah says.

"Oh sweetie, you are glowing, absolutely glowing. Oh dear, look at me, I'm paler than pale. What did I do to my poor liver last night? I'm going to get more serious now for the rest of the trip. I want to enjoy it without big hangovers each day," Laura says with a grin.

"Oh, enjoy yourselves, you're only young once girls. I love this picture. I feel the happiest I've felt in months, girls. I feel really positive and I think baby is agreeing as he or she has just given me a good old kick," I say.

"Is good, is good! Baby is happy, we are all happy!" Enrico shouts.

Oh bless you, Enrico, you are such a good guy. I owe you a lot for doing this for me.

We all pile back into the car. "Next attraction, to your left and right, you see the Fori Imperiali, the ancient ruins, more beauty. Ladies, soak this up, it's a rare city and it will stay in your heart for long, long time, maybe forever," he says, looking quite reflective.

I can see why. I look with awe at the beauty that surrounds us. The clear blue sky and blazing sun just adds to the entire atmosphere. If we weren't in a car, I'd think I was back in ancient times.

"Do you have vandals trying to knock all those ancient poles to the ground and putting graffiti all over them?" Laura asks. "It's just shocking in London. They actually employ people to get rid of the graffiti. I mean something as wonderful at this wouldn't last a day in London, they'd have attempted to just destroy it by looking at it," she says with an air of disgust.

"Ah, you know, we are a proud people and we know all the people travels the world to see our beautiful city and country. This is told to us from young age, and we respect that this is heritage. You don't touch or destroy something which has a, hmmmm, how do you say...a natural beauty for the eye? But there is always one person who don't agree and make graffiti. It's disgusting. Graffiti have its place, but not on national monuments and history," he says very matter of fact like.

"Yes, I understand completely and that is exactly how it should be. This is what should be drilled into every child from birth. Are you listening to this, Katie," Laura says with a smile.

"Oh, don't you worry, this baba is going to be brought up with fantastic manners. He or she will be well behaved and most certainly will not be doing anything like vandalising national treasures or they ll hear about it," I reply.

Sarah giggles. "You go, girl. Poor baby... all sounds lovely and regimental to me," she says.

I laugh.

"Ladies, the building on left is the grave of the unknown soldier. It is called Vittorio Emmanuele and its nickname is "The Wedding Cake.""

"Mother of God, look at the size of that! That's some grave!' Sarah says.

Mother of God? Has Sarah turned seventy all of a sudden?

"You wait because we now enter Piazza Venezia and when you turn to look back, you see why it's called the wedding cake," Enrico says.

We all turn with excitement and what a sight it is. Such a modern day monument in the heart of an ancient and very rustic square and city, yet the mix works.

"It looks good enough to eat," Laura says. "Actually maybe not, my stomach is still slightly delicate. It's beautiful, though, a modern type of beautiful and not something I'd personally put in the middle of such a rustic square, but yet I can see how it all oddly fits. What a truly spiffing city."

Spiffing? What is wrong with these girls today? Must be the alcohol affecting them still.

"Really, Laura, spiffing?" I quiz.

"Yes sweetie, sorry I've no idea where that came from," she says with a giggle.

"Like, that just looks massive really. Enrico, why are there two guards at the back of it, standing by the wall?" Sarah asks.

"Ah ha! I was wondering if you could see them. Yes, this monument is guarded twenty-four-seven as it is grave of unknown soldier. And something else of interest maybe? You see horse, big horse at left side. Hold on, I go around so you can see from front again. Is worth it. Ok so you see horse now?" he asks.

"Yes," we all say in unison.

"Inside stomach of horse is a dining room," he blurts out.

"What?" I ask.

"Yes, it is true. Many years ago they used have dinners in the stomach of the horse. This give you idea of how large this whole monument is."

I look at the others and we are all just speechless. *I want to live here. In fact, looking at that horse, I'm ravenous now, I could eat one.* And with that thought, I get a very unpleasant kick from my gut. *Ok baby, are you reading my thoughts now?*

"Enrico, can we stop at a shop, I know it's not long since I've eaten, but I think the smell of the bakeries around here is making me hungry. I can smell fresh croissants and baby can too it seems. I just got a good old kick when I thought about the pastries."

"You're hungry again? Well, you are eating for two, and you didn't have a massive breakfast to be fair," Sarah says.

"Of course, we can stop wherever you want to stop. I can recommend this café on the corner. I will have to stay in car, but when you ask for pastry, it's not croissant here, it's cornetti. You want to learn some Italian while here girls?"

"Yeah why not, might help us pull a few nice men," Sarah says laughing.

"Si signore, per favore," Laura says.

"Si, si," I say as that's the only Italian I know.

"Hahaha, eccellente! Ok, so remember croissant is cornetti. Se si desidera un cornetto?" he pauses and looks at me.

"I've no idea what you just said," I say.

"I know. I am testing to see if you understand. I say, if you want cornetto, cornetto for one, cornetti for more than one. So what do you fancy now?"

"Oh I don't know, could you not come with me?" I plea.

"I can't, I have to stay in case Polizia come. This is centre, I cannot park here. If I sit in car they know I wait short time for someone. Sorry, I would, if I could."

"Ok, what do you recommend? I like ones with cream or custard in them," I say.

"Ok, you say, voglio un cornetto, or cornetti con crema per favore, if you want a plain one, you say voglio or posso avere – this means can I have, voglio is more a demand like - I want. Be polite as sometimes they get annoyed. Say for a plain one posso avere un cornetto semplice, per favore?"

"Right, I'll try it. Girls, you stay here as you'll only mock me. And don't' even think about following me!" I say.

"No way! We're there, let's buy a big bag. Coffee, Enrico?" Sarah asks.

"Si per favore, un espresso. Grazie," he says.

We rush into the café and I order ten in total. The girls are giggling as they tell the girl on the register that they are all for me. I don't find it very amusing as she nods and says, "Ah baby," as if she knew and understood – which she might have done.

I can feel my face blushing. "Can a poor pregnant woman not get a break around these parts?" I ask.

"Sorry, we couldn't resist. You're a good sport anyway. You're not overly emotional to be fair, and you can take a joke, thankfully," Laura says.

"Did someone get the coffee?" I ask, trying to change the subject. I'm a little put out actually by their piss taking session. I know I shouldn't be, but I am a bit on the hormonal side today I have to admit.

I take the pastries and head towards the car. Enrico looks at me and laughs. "Katie, are you feeling extra hungry?" he smiles.

I just can't get angry with you. What is it about you? "Not just for me, Enrico. I hope you like 'con crema'?" I ask.

"Ah, you don't need buy this for me, I can look for myself," he says.

"The girls are bringing your coffee now," I say with a smile.

"Enrico, here you go, we got you a double just to keep you extra alert," Sarah says.

"Oh ladies, you are very very kind to me. Thank you," he says.

What a lovely guy you are. Wouldn't you be perfect for Sarah.

24

We hop into the car and Enrico slams back his espresso as if drinking a shot of tequila. I'm not sure how he can drink it so easily. It would take a lot for me to even sip coffee that strong.

"And this, ladies, is via Nazionale. I love this street, one of my favourites. I can't say why, it always make a me smile when I walk or drive here. Nice feeling, yes?"

"It is nice. I think I'm getting that nice feeling on every street though, I have to say," I reply.

"Just a very relaxed kind of feeling here isn't there, it's rather splendid. The traffic is a bit crazy, but people seem so chilled out in comparison to at home. I could live here," Laura says.

"So, girls, if you're looking for the romance, you need to pay a trip to this location," he says as he stops the car. "We'll be two minutes. I just need to show you this."

We step from the car and there's such an amazing view over the city.

"And here, if you look down, you will see we are standing at the top of the Spanish Steps and over to your left, you will find Trevi Fountain."

"Ohhhh," we all say in unison.

"Ha ha, I thought you girls have this reaction when I tell you where it is. It's very beautiful, but we don't have time to go today as you have to walk there from here, and I think you are too tired maybe?" he says looking at me.

"Too big more like!" I reply. "Definitely I'd be far too tired to walk anywhere that would be a bit of a distance today. I need to get used to the heat also. Maybe we can come back before we leave girls, what do you think?" I ask.

"Well, I can drive as close as possible next time and will be five minutes maximum for you," Enrico says.

I nod in agreement and right now I don't want to leave this place as the view is captivating. I feel in such a happy place. Straight ahead of us is the beautiful dome of St. Peter's Cathedral. Its enormity is like nothing I expected. On the left we see a similar dome which is smaller in size, but I'd imagine many must mistake if for St. Peter's.

"Ah, that one is St. Paul's outside the walls, it's a very beautiful also. If you have time I recommend St. Peter's. Maybe not the dome for you as it's a bit narrow and, well," he says as he points to my ever growing belly and smiles. "Ok, ladies, we need to go if we get to Castel Palocco per pranzo. I take you to a wonderful restaurant there, but first we go to beach in Ostia."

"Hold up, hold up, beach sounds wonderful, and while we're here for a holiday too, I think we need to not lose sight of why we're here in general...to find Pete?" Sarah says.

"Yes, I understand, but Castel Palocco is less than forty kilometres away, and we will make it in a plenty of time," Enrico says.

Pranzo, pranzo...what's that again. I remember learning that word before. I flick through the dictionary and see lunch. *Ah yes, lunch. Well, I'll be delighted to have a bit of that later!*

"That's fine with me," I squeal with delight as the realisation hits me that I might actually see Pete again for the first time in months, and pray that he will see something in me that sparks recognition. This baby deserves its father to be around. *Positive thoughts, think positive thoughts.*

As we head out of Rome the countryside looks a bit burnt and crusty, but it is a different country and I know not to expect the greenery of

Ireland or England in such a sun drenched area. I'm soaking up the beautiful sunshine with the windows lowered to the maximum as the girls sleep in the back of the car, clearly hungover and lacking of sleep. *At least you aren't missing out on the sights of Rome right now.*

"Ladies, wakey wakey, wakey wakey," Enrico exclaims. "Is that what you say, yes? I heard someone use these words once when they want some-one to stay awake, yes?"

"Ha ha, yes that's right," I say with a giggle as I hear the girls ma-noeuvring in the back of the car and mumbling.

"We are taking long route as we are in good time. I take you for a glimpse now of beach at Ostia. You can swim to wake up if you like," he says.

"Oh lovely, beach," Laura snorts and falls asleep again.

"I think we'll just leave them sleep for now and wake them when we get there," I say to Enrico.

As we approach Ostia, I can hear slight movement from the girls.

"I smell sea air," Laura says as she lifts here head from her makeshift pillow.

"Oh goodness, look at that. Oh just smell that air," she says as she elbows Sarah to wake up.

Sarah lifts her head and squints to see. I can't stop smiling. *This feels like the most exciting trip I've ever been on and I'm totally sober for it. Amazing what you see without any alcohol involved.*

"Ok, ok, all out, breathe it in ladies, fresh sea air on coast of Italia. Enjoy and go swim, go soak up the sun. I'm stripping off and going to water now. Come with me if you like?" he asks, directing the question at me.

"Are you asking me?" I ask.

"Well yes, of course, will be good for baby, and for you," he says.

"Oh I don't know, I've not really shown anyone my baby bump yet, not even the girls have seen it this large," I say.

"What? You cannot be serious Katie. You need to show the world the beauty of your pregnancy. You have swimsuit or bikini yes?" he asks.

I look at the girls who are giggling as they have been emphasising of late how men find pregnant women attractive. They usher me to go with him with their hands.

"Well yes, I have a bikini," I say.

"I have changing hut on the beach. Take your bikini and towel and change there. You need to enjoy this. Then in one hour, maybe if you are having fun one hour and half, we go to eat in that restaurant. You will be starving by then!" he says.

"Ok, Enrico, let's do this," I say as I walk towards the beach with him.

I can overhear the girls chat as we walk towards the water.

"Come here, he's gorgeous like. I wonder if she doesn't find Pete will she find love with Enrico?" Sarah asks.

"Funny, Sarah, I was just thinking the same thing myself. He might be a couple of years younger, but he's rather dashing isn't he?" Laura comments.

"He's gorgeous! Wish he fancied me," Sarah says.

I feel bad now. I'd prefer her to get a man, and for me to find Pete. Not sure about Enrico and I, as a couple. He'd be a rebound case anyway probably. No, forget that notion Katie, forget that notion.

25

"We need to make a plan, a proper plan," I say as I tuck into the heartiest plate of pasta I've ever seen. "Thanks for bringing us here Enrico, this is possibly the best pasta I've ever tasted," I say with great enthusiasm.

"Ah yes it's a very good here, but I think a maybe you're a little hungry now too," he says with a smile. The girls laugh.

"Ok, so what do you think we should do? We only have five towns where we think he could be, so now we need to, I don't know, start asking locals?" I ask.

"Well, it depends, because if that photo you have is anything to go by, he could be dramatically different by now," Laura says. "Maybe we should get one of those photo fit things done," she says.

"He's not a freaking criminal Laura!" I say in hysterical laughter. "I just wish we had taken more selfies as I don't even have an up to date one of him. I know the only close up one I have is a bit blurry, but we have to do what we can with it.

"I know he's not a criminal, but I'm just trying to make the point here that he could look very different now, it's a possibility. He might have a massive beer gut, have long hair, and speak like an Italian. If he's lost his memory he might not even remember how to speak like an Englishman," she says.

Wow! Hit me with a stick there why don't you Laura? You're right, though, what if he has forgotten everything and he's just living his life, trying to put the pieces together. I'm not sure I could cope with knowing that.

"She's got a point," Sarah says. "I know," I say with a sigh as my positive thinking starts to wane.

"No, no, no. We have to find this man. No sad faces ladies, no sad faces. We will find! Come on be positive please?" Enrico says. "Come on, we are a team, we are on a mission to find someone who means a lot to Katie. It's a beautiful weather, eating a beautiful food, you must be happy. When you are happy he will come to you. I am positive person, no negativity please?"

I laugh. "You're right, Enrico. We need to be more positive and believe we will find him," I say.

He is right! Good things come to those who wait, and I'm sure if I think more positively, he will come to me. I have to put the girls' negative comments far from my mind. I wouldn't mind, but they were the ones having a go at me for being negative at the start of the trip. Talk about contradicting themselves!

It's three o'clock, and at this stage the girls are absolutely blotto. *They haven't even drunk a lot. It must be a mix of last night's alcohol, and the heat that's getting to them. I can't handle sitting around any longer.* The searing heat from the sun is really affecting me. Even though we haven't even started exploring yet, I need a nap. I'm half- heartedly wanting to continue with this search for Pete. The girls look like they're heading for sunstroke as they haven't even bothered to bring hats. Maybe having a baby isn't so bad in terms of being more sensible.

"Ok girls and boys, I have had enough of this heat. I say we move somewhere shaded or go for a quick snooze somewhere as I'm boiling up here and really can't take much more of this," I say.

"Agreed!" they say in unison.

Why the hell didn't I say this an hour ago?

"I'm sweating. I need to get out of this heat. I feel like I've been in a sauna," Laura says. "Who's got deodorant?"

"Here," I say as I hand her a can of sweet smelling spray. "Think we might all need a bit of that. I've everything but the sink in my bag these days as I never know what to expect," I say.

"I've just brought a bag the size of my wallet today," she says. "I didn't really think the whole day trip/beach thing through, did I?" she says.

"I'll have a spritz off of it too if you don't mind, please Katie?" Sarah adds.

"Go for it girls, just hurry, please. I can't take this heat any longer," I say.

"Ah Katie, we must make our way to the town centre and see if we can find your man. I think this is not right town, though. Gut instinct tells me this is not the right place," Enrico says.

Your gut instinct? Since when do men go with their gut instinct? Not much of a gut there Enrico, I've been gawping at your six pack for the past two hours, and shouldn't be.

"Oh, Enrico, to be quite honest now with you, I don't feel like going in search of anyone at the moment, I just want to sleep."

"Don't worry we don't have to search for long. In fact, we don't even have to walk as you don't look like you're able. We can take the car through this town, it make things more simple for us, for you," he says with a very charming smile.

Such a cutie.

"Ok, refreshed and ready to go walking around this beautiful spot. Don't you love small picturesque towns like this where there are no tourists, only ourselves?" Sarah says.

"I think we might take the car, Sarah," I say. "Sorry!"

"No that's fine, it's exhausting in this heat, nice air con in the car to cool us and you get a rest as you look a bit uncomfortable at the moment," she says to me.

"I don't just look it, I feel it too," I say. I try to launch myself from the seat — as that's what it feels like I'm doing, I'm getting so big. "Toilet call, and then I'll be ready. Here, Sarah would you mind getting a few litres of water in for us while I jog off to the toilet?" I say with a smile.

"Course love, jog off," she says laughing.

When I return they are all cooling themselves in the car, and it looks so inviting. Enrico has his ever smiley face on and the girls are in the back using those paper type fans you'd make as a child. We all thought we were very artistic. They were so simple to make.

We drive through the winding streets and it seems very quiet. As we turn a corner there are some locals standing drinking espresso. Enrico stops the car.

"Ciao, siamo alla ricerca di una persona, il suo nome è Pete come Pietro. Lui è inglese e il fratello crediamo vite in questa zona," he says.

"What's he saying?" Sarah says.

"Don't look at me! As if I bloody know darling. He said something in Italian, I know that much," Laura says with a laugh.

"All I caught was Pete and Pietro and Inglese which I think means English," I say.

I look and they are all shaking their heads. *I wasn't expecting too much from this journey anyway. Still, this is just a few people, and the first town. No time for negativity as Enrico will be disappointed. Snap out of it, why do you even care if he's disappointed? Oh no, is this my hormones kicking in?*

Enrico turns to me and laughs. "I can hear you all wondering what I ask the mans! I say we are looking for person, his name is Pete like Pietro in Italian, he's English and his brother lives here. They don't know who I talk about, sorry! But, this is only three peoples, there is more streets to go to yet and we have more towns, so don't look sad, please."

"Ohhh Katie, isn't Enrico such a lovely guy?" Laura says. "Enrico, can you please come back to London with us? You're such fun and so loveable, just like a big squishy bun," she says.

"Squish bun? What is?" he asks.

"It's something you eat, and a very odd way of expressing that you're cute," Sarah replies. "You are very cool, though, and cute," she says with a giggle.

She's right. He is both cool and cute. Not to mention a very sweet guy for caring so much about me, and my reasons for coming to Italy.

"Enrico, that's very sweet of you and thank you so much for thinking of me like this. I have to say I'm of positive mind, but I really don't have any expectations from all of this and just saying, if nothing comes of it, we'll have made a new friend for life in you. You will have to visit us in London by the way, that goes without saying!" I say.

"Oh now we have time yet Katie, we have time yet. I will like to visit London one day. I save my money to visit at the moment. It look magnifico, like nothing I see before. I look forward to the day I visit, and I hope it will be soon. Now, I see more people to ask questions to," he says with a smile.

You're starting to make me feel squishy inside now with that smile of yours. I have to stop thinking like this, but you're hotter than a bag of chips to me right now and that trickle of sweat rolling down your forehead, I want to wipe it with my already sweat covered tissue!

"Katie, are you ok, you look a bit lost there?" Sarah asks.

"Ha? What? Sorry, what are you saying?" I ask.

"Nothing, you just kind of zoned out there for a second. I just asked if you're ok?"

"I'm grand, grand girl, grand, couldn't be better. The heat must be affecting me," I say.

I can't tell the girls what's running through my mind right now, they'd laugh at me and mock me forever more!

"Ok, just make sure you tell us if you need anything as we have to be careful of you in this heat. We can't let you get heatstroke," Laura says.

Oh I'm not thinking heatstroke girls.

I smile and try to stifle a laugh as my brain is working overtime. "I'm fine girls, no bothers at all on me," I say.

We carry on with our travels and as seven o'clock approaches, people are leaving work. We see far more action around, and more bodies to ask if they might know Pete. Even though we don't speak Italian, the girls and I just use the photo to try to explain to people that we are looking for Pete. It's just getting a little too late for me now, and I'm starving again.

"Let's call it a day and go eat again," I say.

I'm drained and it feels like it's past my bedtime already. Oddly enough I don't feel saddened in any way that we haven't found Pete. I

know we still have more time and while I don't have any major expectations anyway, I thought I'd feel differently.

— ~

It's four days later and we've tried most of our target towns at this stage
and to be honest, I'm ready to go home. It was a silly idea to come all of
this way for no reason. It's the final day before I give up and I have a two
day relaxation time in the Spa of the hotel to look forward to, with the
girls. I'll miss Enrico. The one thing I know I've got from this entire
time is that he's become someone I look forward to seeing each morning.
Although, I only know him five days, there's just some sort of bond after
forming between us, which I can't really explain.

"Buongiorno Principessa," he says.

I melt at the sound of it. "Oh, hi Enrico, how are you? Lovely day
isn't it?" I say in a very odd high pitched tone. *What the hell was that?*

"You look stunning, ah how you say in the English...em...blooming?
Is this good thing to say?"

I laugh as I wish I was still the skinny bird I once was as I feel like
a whale at the moment, even though I'm still relatively small. Yet, I'm
growing at a fast pace. "That's correct Enrico and thank you, that's very
sweet of you to say. However, I don't feel too pretty right now," I say.

"No! Stai bellissima!! Bellissima!!"

"Oh, she does look bellissima doesn't she? Honestly, you are probably
the best looking pregnant woman I've ever seen. I remember when my sister had Jonathan, she was just dreadful looking. She had a chin on her that
looked more quadruple than double and she just looked fat!" Laura says.

"That makes me feel fantastic, thanks, Laura," I say.

"Oh darling, I don't mean you look like that at all! What I mean is,
you're the complete opposite! Look how slim your arms are, and those
legs of yours are still long and slender. You are literally all baby, and
no fat. No wonder you're getting so much attention while we are here.
You're a babe who's pregnant and looks like a babe still!" she says.

I don't really feel like such a babe Laura, I feel fat, and that quadruple chin is starting to creep up on me.

"Quadruple chin? She had a quadruple chin? How is that even possible?" Sarah asks.

"It was! It was nearly down to her knees! Absolutely huge," Laura says.

"Ok girls, can we have less chat about the chins now please as I'm not exactly feeling very slim at the moment and we don't want what was my good mood to change at the flick of a switch, now do we?" I ask.

"Ladies, ladies, please, we are all friends, you are all beautiful, but Katie is the most beautiful. No offence, a woman with a child is a natural and beautiful thing to see. Beautiful," Enrico says as he stands there with that lush smile across his face.

We all stand there looking at him. *You are beautiful!!!!*

The girls look at me and smile.

"Eh, we have to go to the bathroom, we'll be back in five minutes," Laura grabs Sarah and rushes her off, not even in the direction of the ladies.

I blush. He's still smiling at me. *I wasn't expecting you to say something like that! Do you have feelings for me, Enrico? This isn't even your baby. You find me attractive and I'm having someone else's baby? You're not right in the head surely.*

He blushes. "I sometimes cannot help myself when I want to tell my feelings for someone. It's your last few days here, and I grow very, how you say, fond of you. I wish you don't have to go," he says.

"Wow! Enrico, I wasn't expecting this at all. I'm not sure what to say as I'm very shocked to be honest with you," I say. However, I feel so incredibly flattered and while I'm trying to convince myself that I don't feel the same way, I know inside that I do. *What should I do in a situation like this?*

"It's ok, I don't expect you have feeling for me like I have for you. You are looking for your man, and I am here to help you find the man. I wish it was different though. You are beautiful, charming woman, and I would like to see you again after this, but I know, Katie, that you live in other country, and is difficult for this to happen. It's ok, I understand."

How do you know I don't want to jump your bones, Enrico? Don't assume anything, but for now, I feel I need to keep whatever these feelings which are bubbling inside, just there, inside.

"Enrico, if circumstances were different this could be a very different situation. I feel incredibly flattered by what you've said, but you're right. I've come here for a reason and I cannot forget that reason now or lose sight of the fact I came to find the father of my unborn child. It's not the easiest of situations, but until I find him and see him again, I'm not sure I could really think or focus on anyone else," I say with a niggling feeling of regret, already.

As the girls return, looking a bit sheepish, I put a smile on my face and greet them, but inside I feel sad. I feel like I've just let my possible future go and all for the love of a man who may not even remember anything about me. However, I know it's a risk I have to take.

Our final journey as we head to Castel Romano. There's silence in the car for most of the journey. Enrico looks sad even though he passes a brief comment every now and then and flashes a little smile which would melt the hardest of hearts He's a handsome man. As we step from the car, Laura pulls me to one side.

"What's going on here? You could cut the atmosphere with a knife. I've been trying my best to talk, and get a response from you both, but I'm getting a simple yes or no answer. Tell me...now!" Laura says impatiently.

"I can't here, I'll tell you later. It's a bit awkward. He likes me and well you know why we're here, so I can't look at him like that right now, maybe not ever. He's lovely, but look, I'll fill you in properly later. You have the gist of it now. Come on, we need to catch up or he'll know I'm telling you everything," I say.

"Oh damn it anyway and you know what, I know it's a dreadful thing to say, but damn that Pete too. This guy is lovely and perfect for you and he likes you. Pete, who I know we came here to find, but as you'd say for feck sake, he might not even recognise or want to know you when or if you find him. Sorry for being so blunt, but it's true. Aghhhhhh," Laura stomps off.

I know she's feeling frustrated as I could see she wanted Enrico and I to get together if possible over the past few days. I know she's regretting saying yes to my suggestion of us coming here. This entire trip has played with my emotions big time, and I know all she wants is to see me happy and finding Pete would make my family complete. That is all I want, too.

"Ok ladies, this is it. We have our final chance to find Pete today. I'm a sure I can a search for him if I visit other towns on other days and will ask to people when I see them, if we don't have happy outcome today," Enrico says.

I smile. "Come on, let's get to work. No pressure. If I'm meant to find him, I will. If not, I'll go home and live my life as it's meant to turn out," I say. *Oh Dear God, please let this be a good outcome, I'm not sure how I'll react once I get home to an empty flat knowing I've nothing to look forward to.*

We manage to walk a fair distance as it's not as warm first thing in the morning. However, as it approaches midday, the sun becomes far more intense and it's not a great idea to be walking around in it, especially for me.

"Time for a cake I think," I say with a giggle.

"I was wondering when you'd scream for cake!" Sarah says.

"Ah yes, cake or pasta, which one you prefer?" Enrico asks.

"Oh cake for sure, let's do it backwards because I just saw the most spectacular pasticeria a few doors back, you know my beady eyes when it comes to cakes," Laura says. "Cake first and then lunch in an hour anyone?" she asks.

"Hmmmm, I'll wait for the pasta and eat the cake later," Enrico says with a smile.

"Hmmm, we all know he won't eat any cake with the body he has," Laura whispers to me. "You're a fool to let him go if you do girl, an absolute fool!"

We lag back and let Enrico and Sarah continue in front of us.

"Laura, look at me! I'm five months pregnant, craving cake, and if I haven't put the pounds on now, I will, and quickly towards the end of the pregnancy! I've read about all of this already. Trust me, he's not going to even glance at me in a very short space of time. AND you know the reason we came here. Please don't upset me now. I'm already feeling apprehensive today knowing that this is the last chance I have to find Pete. I just want my baby to know its father, that's all. Right now, he might as well be dead."

"I'm sorry, I'm so sorry, I didn't mean to upset you in any way. I'm sorry, I just want to see you happy Katie. It's just, while I know you came up with the idea of coming here, I thought we'd be more successful than we have been. And well, Enrico's not a bad person, and he's hot to top it all off! He's crazy about you. I can see the way he speaks to you, it's with love, infatuation maybe, call it what you want, but he is serious. I think these Italian men are very into love and expressing their feelings. They seem far more mature than the gits we put up with at home, game playing ferrets. I realise what I'll say now is not going to impress you. You'll probably want to beat me up or something, but, just on the off chance we don't find Pete today, please don't discard Enrico. He's one not to be discarded. Now, I'll say no more, I'm walking into this lovely cake shop and I'm going to stuff my face with cake to shut me up. But think about it, long and hard before you make any drastic decisions. Remember, we still have two days left after today, and it's to relax. Some of that time could be relaxing on your own with Enrico," she says as she walks ahead of me.

Maybe you're bloody right! Oh, frustration!! I really can't make any decisions right now, at least not until I know the situation with Pete. I walk into the shop. The cakes that surround me just make me want to hound each and every one of them down and fast! Baby is kicking and I can't be sure, but I have a feeling this baby is going to be a bunter by the time it's ready to come out of me.

26

nother unsuccessful day and as we pull into the petrol station to fill the tank, I feel deflated.

"Are you ok, Katie?" Laura asks.

"Yeah, I'll be fine. I shouldn't have come here thinking I'd find him. I must have been mad," I reply.

"No! Stop thinking like that, we still have two days here, and he might just happen to be where we will be over the next few days, who knows?" Sarah adds. "I'm not giving up the fight for finding Pete," she says in a matter of fact way.

"Sarah, relax, you sound like you're going on a protest march or something there. Look I'm trying to be real about this. You know me. I'm a realist, not a dreamer. I knew I could go home disappointed from all of this, and it looks like it might be the case. But, we've tried and there's no more we can do. So, I suggest we just try to enjoy the last couple of days and not think about it anymore. To be honest, I'm getting tired of all of this travelling," I say.

"I know darling, you're right. I think you should still spend time with Enrico though, just give him that chance now that you know as much as I hate to say it, that Pete is most likely gone from your life," Laura says.

"Maybe you're right Laura, maybe you're right," I say as I rest my head on the car seat head rest. *Hmmm maybe she is right, but I don't know. Pete, if you're out there, can you please, please come to me?*

I spot Enrico returning and he smiles at me as he sits in the car.

"I got this for you, I think your energy is low now so some nice Italian chocolate will pick you up, until I get you back to bella Roma," he says.

He divides the chocolate out to all of us and we heartily eat it. I feel like such an animal today. I ate so much cake and even ended up buying a box of them to take back to the hotel with us, in case 'we' got hungry. I just can't stop eating.

We arrive back to Rome within the hour and darkness is starting to fall. This city is so incredibly beautiful and each time we pass by the Colosseum, I get a warm fuzzy feeling. The streets are alive with locals going to pizzerias and trattoria restaurants. The tables and chairs arranged beautifully outside for those who wish to soak up the summer heat at night time. The red and white table cloths on the tables set the scene for what I always imagine to be typically Italian in my mind.

This is just so beautiful. Do I really have to return to London? Could I not stay here and continue my search for Pete, and have my baby here? Bring him or her up in the Italian way of life. It's definitely a much better way and lifestyle, the food, the drink, the moderation. Few if any binge drinkers to be seen. The young people seem so well behaved, and just go out at night to sit in a café to enjoy a chat or to a pizzeria to enjoy their typical dishes. Am I dreaming? Am I no longer a realist? I don't know, but I do know I'm highly confused. And then there's Enrico! What do I do about Enrico? I glance in his direction and I admire the contour of his face as the street lights shine on him as we drive slowly through the city.

"Are you ok, Katie?" he asks.

"Yes, Enrico, I'm ok, thanks," I say and we return to silence again.

I can sense the awkwardness for the girls in the back of the car and then Sarah says, "You know what, I'm destroyed, you look destroyed too, Laura. We should probably retire. Why don't you go for dinner with Enrico, Katie as you need to feed little bambino or bambina there. We can't have you going to bed without something to eat. I could quite happily go, though," she says with a smile and a wink.

"Eh, um." *I don't know what to say to that!*

"Well, Katie, if you would like to have a dinner with me, it would a be my pleasure," Enrico says.

I think my mind has been made up already then! I want to go for dinner with you Enrico, most definitely. "Ok," I say with a smile. *Ok? Is that all you can say? Fool!*

"Right, that's settled then. Please, drop us here and let you both go have a nice evening together," Laura says.

"Yes, we can walk from here as it's only ten minutes and it's a lovely evening. Thanks very much Enrico, we'll see you before we go I'm sure?" Sarah asks.

"Are you sure ladies, I want to be sure you are safe at hotel?" he replies.

"Oh, don't you worry about us, we are big girls, we know where we are going," Laura replies and taps me on the shoulder as she leaves the car.

Enrico starts the engine again, and revs it like a lion roaring. I laugh. *Such a man thing to do, God! You're damn cute, though. I really can't figure out if I fancy you or just like you as in friendship, though. I'm seriously confused here. What if Pete pops up now out of nowhere, what do I do then? Aghhhhhhhhhh, I'm going crazy!!*

"I'm now going to take you to see a most wonderful view. Are you hungry now or you can a wait for a little while?" he asks.

"Enrico, I've a whole box of cakes there since today which may go off if I don't eat them soon. So, you've nothing to worry about in relation to food," I say with a smile. "I'm not actually hungry yet, but I will let you know when I am!" I exclaim.

"Hah! Very good Katie. I'm a glad we have this time together. I know, I know it's a friendship and you love someone else and that's fine with me. Just know that one day, if you ever feel differently, I'll still be happy to be with you, and your baby. I'm not a very good with a expressing in the English, but I've never met a woman as beautiful, and with a such passion. It's very beautiful, you are very beautiful."

I've a never had a guy say something so lovely and with such passion to me before! Am I still in love, though, am I? Am I really in love with Pete still, or am I in love with the idea of having loved him and that everything will be hunky dory between us when we meet again? I honestly don't know!

"Enrico, thanks for being such a gentle and kind man. I have to be honest, I don't know how I feel about Pete. I think I might still love him, but I won't ever know until I see him again and I don't know when that will be, if ever! All I do know is I want what's best for me and my baby and before I came here, I thought finding Pete was the answer to that. I would feel the happiness that I once felt with him again, and we would be as we were before he left. But hindsight is a wonderful thing Enrico, and now that I've spent a week searching for him and finding not even a trace, it seems like the most idiotic idea we've ever had, as in the girls and I," I say.

"Idiotic? What's a mean?"

"Stupid, we were stupid," I say with a giggle.

"I understand what you mean, but you are not stupid for having idea. It was love that make you come here, not stupid," he says.

Oh, you're so cute with your broken English. "No really, we were. I mean, how big a country is Italy? Had we been more realistic, like I normally am, I wouldn't even have entertained the idea of coming here, but I was a bit stupid to think we could find him. The upside though is that I also think maybe we all needed a holiday, and it seemed like a good excuse to come as we could kill two birds with one stone," I say.

"Why you kill birds with a stone? They are harmless," he asks.

I'm not sure I have patience for this conversation right now. "Sorry, it's an expression, Enrico. It means to get two things done at once, if you understand? So we managed to have a holiday and come to look for Pete also?" I say.

"Ah, I understand. Now this stupid expression for sure. Poor birds, why not say a larger animal because birds cannot defend themself? ' he asks.

"Fair point! Fair point! I've no idea, it's just an expression. Forget I even mentioned it," I say with a giggle. "You are lovely Enrico. I wish circumstances could be different, but right now I can't say what I feel because I'm very confused and I don't know where my life is going, to be honest with you," I say.

"I know and I understand. But, you must also think of it positive way. If you did not come to bella Roma, we would not meet. And I know you think of Pete now, but one day, you might come to Enrico. I always how you say optimisto?"

"You're always the optimist? I like that. It's a good way to be and stay that way please?" I ask.

"Certo, I will," he says as he stops the car. "I'm now going to show you the entire cita of Roma from this point. It's my favourite view, and I come here to be alone and think or sometimes to just enjoy the view," he says as he takes my hand to help me from the car. I nearly need a JCB to move me these days, I'm getting so big.

I look around and we are far outside the city and near the Sheraton Hotel. We are on a height, and I've never seen anything so spectacular. I can see St. Peter's Basilica in the distance along with St. Paul's, and the lights which lead down to the Fori Imperialli. I never thought I would get to see such a beautiful view of Rome and so close to the city itself. I can see why this might be Enrico's thinking ground. I breathe in the fresh air and the searing heat of the sun is still lingering from earlier in the day. It's such a balmy night and as Enrico stands there holding my hand, I can't think of anywhere else I'd rather be.

"Well?" he asks.

I look upwards to his face and smile. "I have no words," I say.

He glances at me. "I know I should not do this, but it feels right and if you don't want me to, you will stop me right now," he says as he bends down to kiss me.

I don't stop him.

27

9 wake to someone banging on the door. "Katie? Katie? Are you ok in there? It's half past twelve."

I must have slept at least twelve hours. I'm still in my clothes, what the hell? I must have collapsed into the bed once I got back. Where's Enrico gone?

I spy a note on the bedside table. I reach out to grab it and read it.

> Dearest Katie, I hope you feel better when you wake. I will return shortly. It's 11.30 now, I've just gone home to shower and change and will return again to take care of you. Please stay in bed and get the rest you need. See you soon. Enrico x

"Oh fab! I'll bet she's up and gone out with Enrico already," I hear Laura say.

"Girls, is that you? I'm here! Sorry, give me two minutes please?"

"Oh, she's there. Sure, take your time," Laura says.

I walk to the door and open it. Both girls are standing there looking at me in awe. "Were you sleeping until now, love?" Sarah asks.

"Yeah, it seems so," I say. "And I still have my clothes on, which is a good thing in one way, but a bad thing in another."

"Are you ok, you seem a bit lost?" Sarah asks.

"Yeah I had a little episode last night."

"Hmmmm, ok. What do you mean by episode? I assume Enrico dropped you off?" Laura says.

"Oh, he did. We had a lovely night. We kissed and then we went for dinner. I didn't drink anything, though, with the exception of water of course, but I became really faint while we were out walking and ended up in hospital," I say.

"Hospital? What do you mean hospital?" Sarah is looking agitated as she grabs my arms and checks me up and down. "Ok, let's call Enrico and see if he can shed some light on this. You look a bit disorientated, love. Go back into the bed there now, change into something more comfy for starters especially if you've been in those clothes since yesterday!" Sarah says.

"I'm ok, but so tired. Look, Enrico can explain it all," I say as I wave the note in her face. "He'll be back soon."

What the hell happened last night? I feel like crap after that little episode. I remember Enrico bringing me home safely after a trip to the hospital.

I look across the room to see Laura dialling a number. "I'm not waiting. I'm calling Enrico right now and then a doctor as I'm a bit concerned now," Laura says.

I'd normally put up a fight, but I feel drained and so I just agree.

"Enrico, darling, it's Laura, how are you? Yes, yes we are in the room with Katie now. Do you know what happened to her last night as she seems a bit unsure? Maybe you can call around?" She pauses. Enrico seems to be talking a lot. "Ok darling, ok, thanks for that. Should we call a doctor to have her checked again?" Laura asks. "Yep, of course, yes. Right, fantastic! You are wonderful Enrico. We'll see you shortly." She hangs up.

"Ok, Enrico is on his way and he can explain more when he gets here, and just for the record, I did note that you said you kissed when you were retracing your steps earlier. I want to hear all about that later," Laura says with a wink. "It sounds like you were lucky he was there as you were heading front down onto the pavement and baby could have been severely injured or worse, but luckily he was able to hold you up and call an ambulance," she says.

"God almighty Katie! Ok, you're staying there for the day and we are watching you like hawks," Sarah says. "I feel so bad that we left you alone, can you imagine if something happened to the baby?" she says with a gasp.

"Sarah, relax, I'm fine. And the hospital released me, so baby is fine too," I say.

Within twenty minutes, there's a knock on the door. "That'll be Enrico, I'll get it," Laura says as she rushes to the door.

"Hi Laura, how are you today? You look like you have a fresh colour, have you been to the sunbathing this morning?" Enrico asks.

"Ah yes, I was up at seven o'clock today Enrico, fine and fresh so off I went to the pool. It's rather warm out there now, though. I'm glad it got hot, otherwise poor Katie might have been here on her own, had we not checked," she says with an air of concern.

"Oh please everyone, stop fussing. I'm fine, look I'm fine. I'm in one piece and that's all that matters," I say.

"Hello Katie, how are you feeling?" Enrico asks as he holds my hand and runs his hand over my cheek.

"I'm ok, just tired Enrico, thank you. I can't believe that happened last night. You've been so great to look after me," I say.

"Ok, I tell the girls the full story now, you sit down and rest," he says with a smile. "We were a walking down the Fori Imperiali, it was beautiful, probably a bit extra hot for that time of night and you were saying you felt really warm. It was all very romantic and lovely. You told me you were really enjoying your evening and suddenly you just became really faint and started to fall onto your front, but I manage to catch you, just in time. I worry straight away and call ambulance because I worry for baby in case something wrong, but worry for you because I care about you, a lot."

"Oh that's so sweet, thank you," I say as I hold his hand. "So the ambulance arrived then and took me to hospital? Sorry, I do recall it, but it's a bit blurry as I feel so exhausted today even though I've slept so much."

"Yes ambulance arrive ten minutes later, which is a miracle for this part of Roma! Trust me! They take you to hospital and I go with you in ambulance. They do tests on baby and on you and everything is fine. But they say you have heat stroke and you need to have more water as dehydrated. You also had drop in a how you say the pressure of the blood?"

"Oh dear, her blood pressure dropped suddenly?" Laura asks.

"Ah yes, the blood pressure, sorry I say the pressure of the blood as it translate from Italian to English this way," he says with a laugh. "So the blood pressure drop and they keep Katie in for observation for couple of hours. This is probably why you are tired today. You slept lots, but they say you may sleep even more and right through the night. I stay here on the couch until ten this morning and then go to home to change. I look for Laura and Sarah to tell them, but could not find anywhere. I do not want to leave you alone, so I leave you a note, and tell maid who clean room to check on you every ten minutes, to make sure you are ok. I'm sorry to leave you here alone, I need to have shower to wake up and change the clothes. I come back straight away, and here I am," he says with a grin. "You are ok yes?" he asks.

"Oh bless you, Enrico, you're like a little angel sent to watch over us since we got here," Laura says. "You know, you're just going to have to visit London once we get back, I won't hear of you not visiting," she says.

I can only look at him in amazement. This wonderful man sitting in front of me, who I know little under a week, and he has fallen so hard for me — and my baby it seems — and I'm starting to realise that I do have feelings for him. I have never met anyone who cared about me in such a short space of time, like this before, except for Pete maybe. "Thank you, Enrico," I say and I squeeze his hand.

"So do you prefer I leave you here with the girls?" he asks.

"NO!!!" I shout. "Sorry, ahem, no, I'd like you to stay," I say in a softer voice. *Don't get too carried away, act some bit disinterested.* "You must be tired, I think you should sleep a bit," I say to him.

"Laura, Sarah, girls you're fab, but I've ruined enough of your day and we only have today and tomorrow left. Go have fun. I'll be fine here," I say.

Laura winks. "Of course you will, but are you sure?"

"I'm sure. Enrico and I can catch up on some lost sleep," I say with a smile and a wink.

"That's fine, we'll carry on and go shopping like we planned then. Would you like us to bring anything back? Cakes maybe? We need to keep you fed and watered now!" she says.

"Bring me back a surprise," I say with a giggle.

"Are you sure that's what you want? You do know a surprise might not always be a pleasant one!" Sarah says.

"I think, since I arrived here, I've had nothing but pleasant surprises," I say with a smile. "Thanks, girls, enjoy and don't worry about me or bringing anything back to me. I'm good."

"See you both later then," Laura says and Sarah waves and smiles as they leave the room.

"So, my beautiful girl, what are we going to do with you? Collapsing and falling over, ambulances, what else can happen? This is most eventful holiday I think anyone I know have!" Enrico says.

"Oh, trust me Enrico, this is eventful, but nowhere near some of the eventful holidays I've had," I say with a giggle.

I lay down on the bed again and I can feel a slight pain in my arm. I look and see it's badly bruised, I turn on my side and try to snuggle up as close to Enrico as possible. It's not easy with my very rotund belly. He puts his arm around me and rests his other hand on my bump.

"You know I will look after you no matter what?" he whispers to me.

"I know you will," I say as I close my eyes to go to sleep.

28

My last day in Rome and I don't know how to feel. I'm sad about not finding Pete, overwhelmed by the way I've become so close to Enrico, and just generally don't feel like I want to leave at all. It's such a spectacularly beautiful city and the way old meets new in terms of its architecture is just amazing. The cakes!!! The cakes!!! I have to leave the cakes behind. *How will I survive without a bomba or two for breakfast every day? No wonder baby is growing at a lively rate!*

We depart this evening at eight o'clock. *I wonder if there's some miracle that could happen to enable us to stay a little longer, or maybe just for me to stay a little longer. I don't want to leave Enrico. Oh God, what's wrong with me? Was this a holiday romance? How could it be? I'm over five months pregnant, and there is no way it could just be a holiday romance. Nothing happened between us apart from a few kisses, but it feels like it's so much more.* I feel a nudge to my arm.

"Hey dreamer, I got you an ice-cream. It's hot today isn't it?" Sarah asks.

I smile. "Thanks, pet, you're very good. Could do with something to cool me down now," I say as I enjoy what will probably be the last few rays of sunshine that I'll see for a while. It's raining back in London.

"How are you feeling about leaving?" she asks.

I smile, a smile which gives away my sadness. "I'm ok. I'm not sure how I feel really. It's all been a bit crazy, Sarah. The whole touring around, looking for Pete, and not finding him. Enrico telling me how he feels, us kissing and acting like a loved up couple for the past two days, like what's it all about?" I ask.

"I know, I know, it has all been a bit crazy. And here I am, heading back, man-less again. Laura, of course, has her own lovely man at home, but you know, we barely had anyone hit on us. Then look at you Ms. Sassypants, five months pregnant and attracting every man who walks past. Nearly makes me want to get pregnant just for the attention from them," she says with a laugh.

"Oh stop! You've had plenty of attention here. It's just all a bit weird, though. I mean I know the whole trip was so we'd try to find Pete, and it would all work out fantastic. We'd even tie a holiday into it too, but I got far more than I bargained for. I feel the whole holiday revolved around me and I wasn't really expecting that," I say.

"Ladies, what's happening?" Laura shouts as she approaches with some drinks. "Last of the holiday drinks girls, a few cocktails to send us on our merry way and of course a virgin one for yourself," she says as she hands me the fruit juice mix. "So, what's going on with Enrico and how are you feeling? Should I purchase ten boxes of tissues due to the tears for the journey home?" she asks.

"Ha ha, no I'm not that bad. I do feel a bit sad, though. I don't know Laura, I was just saying to Sarah I feel this whole holiday has revolved around me, and I didn't want that to be the case. It's like so much has happened, so many crazy things and the whole reason for me coming was to find Pete. Instead, I end up with Enrico, who's lovely and just wants to give me the world, but I can't help but feel that I'm letting Pete down now. That he hasn't shown up and I'm just moving on, dismissing him for the next best thing to come my way. That doesn't feel right. How can it be right for my baby? If something happens here, do I let my baby believe that Enrico is his or her father? Do I tell them the truth? Are they going to hate me? God, so many things going on in my head, I feel I'm going crazy!"

"Blimey woman, relax. Get a grip. Right, first things first. Pete, we haven't found Pete. We knew from the start it was a long shot, and I admit it was a bit of a crazy idea and I feel bad as I probably got your hopes up way too high telling you to be positive all of the time. I didn't realise how big Rome is and the outskirts with all the beautiful towns we've visited. I wasn't expecting it to turn out like this and I'm sorry. I'm sorry because you're disappointed..."

"I'm not... I,"

"Wait, I'm not finished," Laura says.

I smile. "Sorry... go on," I say sheepishly.

"Ok, so we meet this amazingly charming, intelligent Italian man instead, who has happened to fall head over heels in love with you AND your baby. This man is special, rare and bloody handsome. If something hadn't happened between you two, I'd have been bloody disappointed going back. Now, as you always say, everything happens for a reason. You need to go with this Katie. This guy is real, and rare, as I said. He's besotted with you. It was plain to see even from day one when he took the lift with us in the hotel. So, you can sit back, enjoy it, and make a fool of him — which I sincerely hope you don't as I'll be disgusted with you. Or, you can enjoy it with him. Enjoy that feeling you get when you're around him, and how he makes you smile. Girl, we haven't seen you smile like this in almost six months and it's something we miss. So, I suggest you spend some time with Enrico later, and you spill your guts on how you really feel. Now, I think we should give you a little time and space to think about it all and let you soak up what I've just said, particularly the part where I said he makes you smile so much!" she says, and winks.

"She's right, she tells it as it is," Sarah says. "I'm heading for a quick siesta before it's time for dinner and we have to go. Go call Enrico now so you get to spend time with him, and tell him how you really feel," she says as she taps my leg and smiles. "He's good for you Katie," she says as she walks away.

At this point, Laura has wandered back to the poolside bar and is sitting on a stool reading the paper.

Maybe they're right. I haven't thought a great deal about Pete for the past couple of days. I wake in the morning thinking of Enrico, and he's the last one I think of before I go to sleep at night. He does make me smile and makes me feel happy. I haven't had that feeling in so long. Do

I have genuine feelings for him, or am I feeling like this because he's the first man who's shown me love or any kind of affection since Pete went missing on me? I think maybe I do have feelings for him, and I need him to know before I leave.

I head towards my room and call him from the hotel phone.

"Hi Enrico, it's Katie."

"Hi beautiful, how are you feeling?"

"I'm good, thanks. Enrico, I really need to see you before I go. Is there somewhere we can meet?" I ask.

"Of course! I was hoping you would want to see me or I would feel a breaking heart."

Damn you anyway and that broken English, I love it, it's so cute! "Do you want to meet here or we can meet outside somewhere?" I ask.

"No, I come to you, I will be there in twenty minutes? This is good?"

"Sure, see you then," I say and hang up.

True to his word, there's knock on the door, twenty-five minutes later. When I open the door his beautiful Mediterranean face just makes me smile so much and it's very apparent to me then, that this is one man I don't know how to or want to say goodbye to.

29

"What the hell is wrong with me?" I ask.

"Nothing, you've just got the looooove bug, love," Sarah says.

I look around the airport feeling a bit sad, and stupid at the same time. *I shouldn't have got myself into this situation. Why didn't I just let it go and go home having not listened to my heart. Stupid, stupid, stupid!!! I feel my eyes fill up with tears. Fecking hormones! I can't handle this now.*

"Ohhhh darling, don't cry. Come on we need cake and we have three hours to hang around yet," Laura says.

We head to the nearest pasticeria in the airport. I sit there listening to the girls and their good, in fact probably excellent advice, suggesting I let things happen naturally. If it's meant to happen, it will. I keep thinking back to the way Enrico grabbed my face in his hands before I left him, and kissed me so softly on the lips. I felt lost again, like it was the last time I saw Pete, the night before he left and then I never saw him again. That is one thing I never want to go through again.

"So, I reckon he's going to come over. I know we said let it happen naturally a few minutes ago, but I think he's not going to be able to stay away from you," Sarah says.

"Well, darlings, if I'm to be honest, I think the exact same and no, before you go off on one Katie, we aren't just saying this to make you feel better. It is what it is and I think that he's not going to be able to resist staying away for too long. Let's see," Laura replies.

"Thanks, and I know you wouldn't say this unless you honestly thought this, but I really feel that I should just let it all go now. I have to try to get on with life, and what the future brings with this munchkin," I say as I rub my belly. "Kicking baby means liking cake girls. Maybe I need to have just a little bit more," I say with a giggle.

It's Friday night and I'm back home with three days. I thought Enrico might have text me at least, but nothing. I got it all wrong, and the flash in the pan romance or kiss I shared with him, was just that. *Where do I go from here, though?* "It's just you and me kiddo," I say to my ever growing stomach. Not to mention my boobs. I've never had a pair like this before. It's one part of pregnancy that I'm totally enjoying, I just hope they stay when baby comes!

There's a knock on the door. My heart skips a beat. *Enrico?* I get up as quickly as I can, which isn't quickly at all, and I make my way to the front door. I open it with a smile spread across my face which quickly fades, but shouldn't.

"Oh, Sarah," I say sounding disappointed.

"Sorry, bad time? I came as thought you might need cheering up as haven't heard from you since we got back and that's not like you so figured you need a bit of love and friendship?" she says.

"Oh sorry, no, no, not at all. You know what, it's a good time. I could do with a bit of company. You're right, I've been sitting here wallowing in my own self-pity. I probably shouldn't have taken the rest of the week off. It would have done me good to get back to the office, even though I'm allergic to it," I say.

"Ahh, I know. Sometimes the worst thing to do after a holiday is to take even more time off and especially after this trip. You need something to keep that brain of yours occupied girl. I brought your favourite DVD and very appropriate I think. It's yours to keep as I know you get a giggle out of it, especially at the moment," she says.

"Ahhhh ha ha ha ha! I love this, you know my favourite line and Seth Rogan is just so cute in this. It's very appropriate indeed. Thanks, Sarah, you're a good pal," I say.

I can't help but think to a few months back when she was with that idiot Jarvis and for what reason. He messed her around so badly and she was so down in the dumps after him. It's lovely to see her back on form. I think the holiday did her the world of good, but I know she's super excited about the baby coming as she'll be an 'aunty' for the first time. This little bunter is going to be spoilt rotten and deservedly so. If dad isn't going to be on the scene then I want to make it up to him or her, in the best way. My friends certainly won't let me down on that front.

"Popcorn at the ready, crisps, malteasers, twirl, all your favourite things. Sorry, I got nuts too but know you can't eat them...do you mind if I have a few?"

"Go for it girl. I'm used to not eating them now. I'm missing fish more than nuts to be honest though and my new obsession for cake is making up for all of them...as you can see!" I say.

"You have kind of acquired a bit of a heavy craving for cake, haven't you? Maybe it's a good thing that I brought this with me also then?" she asks as she produces a massive chocolate fudge cake. I have to say I'm almost more taken with the box as it's pink and pretty, and I love pretty things. Not at all what Sarah would normally go for, but then again, she's thinking of me here, and it's very me.

"You beauty. It's my favourite too, I can't live without chocolate fudge cake these days. Sarah, I've been thinking, should I text him and let him know I'm thinking about him?"

Oh God, your face says it all. It's blank looking!

"Should I take that as a no? You're looking at me very blankly," I say.

"Hmmmm, I'm not sure. Have you heard anything in the time you've come back?"

"Not a whistle. I text him to let him know I got back safely the other night, but he didn't reply to me. I suppose that's a 'forget about me' reply by saying nothing, is it? I was trying to convince myself otherwise, and that he just needed time, but now I realise that's it. Especially after your reaction," I say with an air of sadness.

"Hey listen, get more of that cake down your throat now, it'll make you feel much better. Don't go on what I say and I haven't actually said anything yet so now I'm going to say what I do think," she says.

"Ok, I'm all ears, but I know it's not good obviously! Go! I'm listening," I say.

"Right, I reckon he's giving you space actually. He probably should have replied with a 'thanks for letting me know', but look I don't know how he's thinking. I would imagine though that he is thinking of you, as he was quite a caring and sensitive creature from what I knew of him. He knows you're hormonal, he knows you're getting closer to the big day, and he knows that you still have a chance of Pete turning up in your life again or making a grand appearance at your front door. He too could be trying to figure out what would be right or wrong in this case, and on top of that, you know us girls, we over analyse everything!"

"True, fair point Sarah. That's quite a lot for him to think about isn't it, in comparison to what I have to think about," I say. "I hadn't thought of it like that before. My life is a bit of a mess for someone to take on board really, isn't it? How the hell did I get myself into this mess when I think about it all now?" I say as I stuff more cake into my mouth. "This is very good cake and hitting the spot nicely."

"Look, all I know is you are in this situation, it's not a mess. You have a beautiful bundle of joy on the way, who will change your life dramatically admittedly, but don't forget that we are all going to be here for you no matter what. We don't know what's going to happen, but you know my method of thinking, everything happens for a reason and you are meant to be this baby's mother. You're going to be an amazing mother. This is probably a lot for someone to take on board, but there are guys out there who will and Enrico might just be one of those guys. However, for now,

183

hold tight and let's see what happens. He will come to you if he's meant to."

"Ever the optimist! Thank you, Sarah. You're right, I think I just needed someone to clarify what I was actually thinking in the back of my mind," I say with a smile. *You're right! I need to get a grip I think. I can't be selfishly thinking of myself right now, I have a baby to bring into this world and be the best mother I can be to it. Cop yourself on woman, cop yourself on!*

I sit back on the couch and press the play button, I love this film. Probably more now because of the situation the main character finds herself in, is not too dissimilar to mine.

Another three days pass and I feel much better after the weekend. I'm heading back to work today. Something I'm not particularly looking forward to, but it will keep me occupied and will take my mind off other things. As I walk into the office I'm greeted with an encore of "Ciao Bellisima". *What is that all about, do they love me all of a sudden?* Greg, one of the guys sitting opposite me gets up and pulls the chair out for me to sit down.

"We've missed you, lady. What would you like, tea, water, the beverage of your choice?" he asks.

"Are you feeling ok?" I ask. "Maybe I should disappear for a couple of weeks more often if this is the treatment I'll get on my return?" I say with a smile. "I'll have a nice cup of tea please Greg, no sugar, little drop of milk, literally a drop and I'd mangle a biscuit with it," I say with a grin.

"Biscuits, at this hour?" he asks.

"I eat them at any hour these days, it's all part of acquiring that JCB to lift me from point to point," I say with a giggle.

"I normally wouldn't say this, but you've grown over the past couple of weeks definitely. Tea and a packet of biscuits it is then," he says with a laugh.

I punch him playfully. "My punch is getting stronger too so be careful, and I won't say no to a packet of biscuits, I just won't eat all of them now," I say with gratitude.

"I was joking, but I'll get you a packet. I have to be nice to you now that you're back. I had to do a lot of work myself while you were away. I need to get you back on side now," he says.

I smile. *Nice to know they missed me.*

I walk towards my boss' office and knock on the door. "Hello, hello. I'm back, eventful time I hear? How are you?"

"Ah Katie, wow you've grown, you look positively glowing though I have to say."

"Erm, thanks and thanks. Had you said that under normal circumstances, I'd want to punch you, boss," I say with a smile.

"Ah, you know how I meant it. We've missed you. Yes, eventful is right. I think Greg had a lot on his plate. He's definitely pleased to see you're back!"

"Sorry to hear that, so you didn't bother with a temp then?" I say.

"No, last one we had, she was a bad experience, thought we'd be better off just working away on things ourselves. We managed, but we are all very glad to have you back now. Besides everyone misses a genius in the office," he says.

Who's kissing arse today? Although you're a good guy, I know you mean what you say. I can't wait to see what some of the others spout out at me, though. This is going to be fun. My last few months at work might just be plain sailing.

30

Three months later...

I open my eyes to what seems to be a miracle. Sunshine! Sunshine!! Something I hadn't seen in London in about six going on seven months at this stage. With a massive stretch and a struggle I manage to hoist myself out of the bed, with severe backache in tow, and make my way to the shower. I'd give anything for a bath, but I just physically can't get in or out of it at the moment so a shower is welcoming. *Baby scan, baby scan, we are going to see you for the final time before I see you in the flesh, today! I'm so excited baby, I'm so excited!*

I start getting myself ready when I hear a loud banging sound coming from my front door. I know it's one or both of the girls. When I open the door, the girls are there with flowers and balloons. I'm a little confused.

"Ha ha! What are you two up to?" I ask.

"Well, seeing as it's your last scan before we come back from the hospital with a little baby in our company, we thought it might be a nice little surprise for you. And we brought cake too!! Can't forget the item most worshiped at the moment," Sarah says with a grin.

"Oh, how I love you, girls. This is a great surprise, thank you. Will we have it now or after? How are we doing on time?" I ask.

"Well, I think we should go now. Parking will be chaotic in the hospital grounds. And you know how long it takes in the waiting room sometimes? The earlier we go the better and you can dream of having the cake on return, or we can just take it with us. Although I warn you, this is one we will all make disappear very quickly!" Laura says.

"Ok, I'm curious now. Let's wait until we get home though as I've a feeling I'll want it beforehand otherwise, and I know if I start I won't stop. Aw, thanks, girls, you're such little stars," I say.

"I don't want to keep bringing the subject up, but any news from Italy?" Laura asks.

"Nothing. I've sort of forgotten about him now. I think it's for the best and you know it's good being back at work now. Everyone is falling all over me as they missed me so much. I'm enjoying it all, and it's taking my mind off what's happened. Besides, Italy was three months ago now. He would have contacted me by now if he was really as interested as he said he was," I say. "Hang on, you are talking Enrico and not Pete, I take it?" I ask.

"Well, both really. Any news of either would be good and welcome news," Laura says.

"Oh well, no is the answer," I say with a smile. "That lovely Detective Cannavaro called me yesterday to see how I was doing. He said he guessed I'd be with baby in arms soon. He didn't have any news of Pete, though. I have to be honest, I'm very excited this is the final scan, but absolutely terrified also. It's scary knowing that I'll have a little one to look after in four weeks," I say.

"Oh you're hardy, you'll be fine. You've got us nutters to help you with everything anyway. Or are you more scared about the giving birth side of it?" Sarah asks.

"Both, I'm really not thinking about the whole birth scenario as that would really freak me out so early on. The unknown is scaring the life out of me, though. Pippa at work told me that her experience was horrific. The epidural froze her from the waist up and not down. She couldn't feel anything in the upper half, and felt every part of the birth. That's something I definitely don't want happening to me. Then Diana said that she had hers in the damn hospital car park. Imagine it, some random strangers passing by looking at my bits while I'm screaming, trying to push a baby out. Jesus, Mary and Joseph, I'd die of mortification. I just couldn't cope with that," I say.

"I'm sure that won't happen to you. Besides, darling, you'd scream enough profanity to scare anyone off who might even remotely glance at your bits. You do know that Sarah and I will be there with you, don't you? However, I guarantee I've no interest in looking there. I just want to see the baby after it comes out. I'd feel a bit strange otherwise. Just to put you at ease," Laura says.

"I hope so, I'd be wondering about why you've been giving me flowers otherwise," I say with a grin. "Did I mention Mary is coming over to help with the birth?"

"Mary? Mary McCarthy?" Sarah asks.

"Yep. She'll be fully qualified then, and she's requested permission to attend. From what she's said the midwives here are quite happy to let her join in the party. It'll be good as I do think she'll help me feel more at ease during the whole process, at least I hope so!" I say.

"That's excellent. She's absolutely hilarious, but she makes an amazing nurse don't you think? I think she'd probably be even better as a midwife! She loves babies too, but she's such a joker, do you think she'd be serious in the midst of you giving birth?"

"I'm not sure, I'm hoping not as that's what would put me at ease! One of my friends in New York is hoping to have her at hers, too. She's a popular chick in fairness," I say.

"I have no idea who you're talking about darlings, but she sounds like fun and you know how I feel about fun. However, I'm sure we don't want party land either on the day right?" Laura says.

"It won't be like that, don't worry, Laura. No, she'll have her serious head on that day, and I know she'll want to make an impression as I'm sure they'll invite her back again. She's got a knack with people in general, she's a real people person so it'll be good to have her on board," I say.

"Sounds like a good plan to me. For now, though ladies, it's time to get out of the car and enjoy the short walk to the hospital in this sunshine. Do you need help getting out Katie?" Laura asks with a smile.

"You're hilarious! You know I do," I say with a laugh. "I swear, I'm finding it a major struggle at the moment that I'm not even sure a JCB would move me, I'd need something far larger. Maybe a crane would be useful, to help me get out of this seat. Laura, did you put bucket seats in the car since I last sat in it?" I ask with a laugh.

"I did not. Although now I'm thinking I should tell you I did as I don't want you getting upset as it's kind of suggesting that you are very large, which you are, but not that large."

"A waddling whale would be a good description of me right now I think. Ouch!!"

"What? What? Are you having the baby now? Sarah, she's ready, what do we do? We were joking about having it in the car park, maybe we've tempted fate?" Laura says in a panicked state I've never seen her in before.

"Would you stop panicking? I'm not ready to go yet! Baby just gave me a bloody good kick. It's getting stronger and heavier by the day. Must have been insulted by the whale comment," I say with a giggle. "Laura, I've never seen you panic like this before. That was funny. Sarah, are you ok? You've gone very quiet?" I ask.

"I... I'm grand thanks. I just got a bit of a fright there as I only realised now, I have no idea what to do if you do go into labour! I won't be able to do anything because if I freeze like I just did now, I won't be of any help to you," she says.

"Oh stop! Girls, come on I'll get there before you both at this rate. Keep up for God's sake," I say with a laugh.

We are sitting patiently in the waiting room and my belly is rumbling like a loud peal of thunder. Laura is looking very impatient. I don't think she believed me when I told her I'm not going into labour. She has nothing to worry about now that I'm in the waiting room of the hospital anyway. If it happens here, I'm in good hands. It's very busy and I feel considerably smaller in size when I look at some of the women walking the corridor. *I wonder if I'll expand to that size at some point or is this it? I do have four weeks left. I hope I don't get any bigger or I won't be able to walk soon.* I watch a lady pace the floor as she holds her back. I look at her legs. They are so swollen, and I really feel for her. I've had very little swelling, and little or no fluid retention. I now realise how lucky I have been. The worst part was the morning sickness at the start when I thought I was just dying.

"Now, Ms. Katie Brown?" says the nurse who thankfully looks very friendly.

"Yes, that would be me!" I say.

"Come this way Katie. Do you have people with you or are you going in alone?"

"Well, I've got the girls with me and would love them to see as they are going to be there for the birth with me," I say.

"Great! Come this way then. Have you ladies seen the scans before?" the nurse asks.

"I have!" Sarah says with glee.

"No!" Laura utters.

"Well, you are in for such a treat then. Follow me ladies. The sonographer will be with you shortly.

The girls take a seat in the room and I get myself up on the bed as best I can, trying not to shuffle about too much for fear of falling off. One lob sided move and I'd be on the floor.

"Hellooo ladies. How are you all? And Katie, well haven't you grown since your last scan! You look fantastic and just about ready to go I'd say," she says.

"Ha! Thanks! I'll take that as a compliment shall I?" I ask.

"Of course, you know how much I love when new mums follow the rule and eat like they should. You've got all the signs for a healthy baby on the outside. Are you ready for me to check on the inside?" she asks.

"I certainly am. I think the girls are scared, but excited about this. This is Sarah and Laura by the way. Sorry I can't see you girls at the moment, but I think I introduced in the right order. Baby is preventing me from seeing your beautiful faces," I say sarcastically.

"Yes, you got that right," Laura says.

"I'm Kay, yes I recall meeting Sarah once before. This is will be the last time you'll most likely meet me, but you'll be in for a treat from this point onwards I'm sure," she says.

"They might be! I'm not so sure I'll be in for a treat, though," I say apprehensively.

"Don't think about it too much Katie. Ok, just a bit of gel going on, this could be cold, you know that already, though, I don't need to remind you," she says.

She presses the probe to my stomach, and baby starts kicking. There he or she is on the screen. My little pride and joy, and I cannot wait to meet him or her.

"I can't remember if I told you the sex the last time, remind me please as I don't want to spoil the surprise if I haven't?" Kay asks.

"No you didn't. Please don't tell me!" I shout.

"I won't, don't worry. Ok girls, come a little closer if you want to see what's going on. So, it's quite obvious I think. Here we have the head. Oh, this little baby is no longer little, he or she is ready to come out soon I think. I don't need to explain this area, arms, legs, all very visible. Heartbeat is good. We're looking very good here, Katie," she says.

I look at Laura who has tears streaming down her face. "I've never seen anything so beautiful before. I mean think about it, what we're looking at now is going to be physically in Katie's arms in a few weeks, it's just amazing when you really think about it all. Gosh, I'm so emotional right now. It's making me want to have a baby and that's probably the first and last time you'll hear that out of me!" she says.

Laura has never been a fan of kids. Her career and lifestyle always came first. Always one to enjoy a party, mainly hosting dinner parties as she loves fussing over people, but this is the first time I've ever heard her even mention an interest in children.

"Laura, is it possible you're getting broody?" I ask.

Sarah is just sitting there in silence, watching, looking, like as if she's waiting for baby to arrive right now. "Sarah, relax, don't look so panicked, it's not coming yet," I say.

"I am not getting broody, I just passed a quick comment, but that moment has passed now again," Laura says.

"Sure, you say that now!" Sarah comments.

I get dressed and wait for Kay to give me the scan pictures.

"Are you going to put them on Facebook?" Sarah asks.

"I am not! This is private to me and it's going to stay that way. Why would someone want to see my baby scan pictures, I mean really like, why would they?" I ask.

"Hmmm, well, people who are close to you might, your relatives, close friends?" Sarah says.

"I'm not convinced. I can text or WhatsApp them to those I think might want to see them. It's a shame that Pete and myself never became friends with each other on Facebook. We didn't think it was appropriate to share with the world we were a couple yet, so just left it go. I wonder would it register something with him now if I did send him the scan and would he remember me?" I say.

"Well, if he's alive he's most likely lost his memory darling, so I don't think he'd know his password anyway to get into Facebook. Besides that, he most likely doesn't remember any of his friends either, unfortunately," Laura replies.

"It's just not right really, is it? Sorry, I shouldn't be getting upset, he's gone from my life for eight months now, but I still can't help but wonder what could have been," I say.

"It's only natural and we were expecting this might happen today. The time is getting closer so it's a normal reaction for you. It's stress related too, I'm sure, as you don't know what to expect," Laura says.

"True, I don't. I am shitting myself I have to admit," I say.

"You don't need to do that, my dear girl, you have a friend coming in to help out the midwives don't you?" Kay says as she walks back waving an envelope in the air.

"Yep, I do indeed. I'll either batter her or hug her like a maniac when she's here. I'm hoping the latter as she is funny, and I've a feeling if I'm crying it won't be with pain. She's great, I know she'll take my mind off of it all, well she'll try to at least," I say.

"Great, you'll be fine, it's never as bad as what other people say, depends on your pain threshold. How is that?" Kay asks.

"Not too bad, could be better, could be worse. I think I'll be fine, I'm sure I will be. I'll keep a positive mind, which will get me through it. Are those my baby scan pictures?"

"They are indeed. Here you go. Advice would be to have your overnight bag packed from here on. I don't want to scare you, but you are looking pretty ready for baby to arrive, and baby looks more than ready to make an appearance. Just to be on the safe side, get yourself organised now," she says.

"That's just mad, we'll be aunts soon Laura, imagine that," Sarah says as she walks down the corridor towards the exit.

I take my time behind them chatting to Kay, and as I pass all of the other women who are also looking forward to their big day, I realise I'll be ok. Some of them look like they've been through it before. Others look just as scared as I do. *Ok, I can do this. I can be strong and it will all be fine.*

31

Two weeks later...

I cannot stand this!! I hate this bloody attention. Why does this always have to happen when someone leaves an office? Everyone is just standing there, expecting me to give some form of speech. It's not a freaking Oscar I'm receiving!!

"Thanks, thanks very much everyone for the lovely gifts and flowers and the cake. It's important you remembered cake. However, you should have bought another one just for yourselves as I'm going to eat this one," I say jokingly. *I bloody would! It's my favourite too.*

"We are going to miss you Katie, but we'll look forward to hearing your good news. Make sure you text, ok? We'll all be anxious to know the outcome and that you're well," Joe says with an air of sadness, like he'll miss my no nonsense smart arse attitude.

I hope they all do. To be honest, they've been amazing to me for the past three months, really looking after me and were quite like family to me. I feel slightly sad myself, however I manage to hold the tears back and a large slice of cake is making me feel better.

I make my way home early in the afternoon and try to get on with last fiddly bits and pieces which need to be sorted before the big day arrives. I'm finding it hard to concentrate, though.

Look at the size of them! I'm holding the teeniest of baby clothes you can possibly imagine. *I hope this baby is tiny, although I've all the signs that it's not, this will never fit him or her. Maybe I should go shopping for slightly bigger clothes and it might take my mind off the fact time is ticking a lot faster than I thought it would.*

I make my way out to the nearest shops which are a ten minute walk from where I live. I'm inside in one of the main baby clothes shops when a wave of sadness suddenly hits me.

I'm staring into space and as I hold out the tiny baby-grow in front of me I realise that in a couple of weeks, I'm going to be a single mum. *Oh, Jesus!* I take a deep breath and feel my eyes well up. *How am I going to cope? Am I really secure enough financially to bring this little one up on my own?* I hold myself up by leaning against one of the clothes railings. I spot the shop assistant coming towards me as my breathing becomes heavier.

"Madam, are you ok? Do you need me to call an ambulance for you?" she asks.

"No, no, I'll be fine, but thank you," I say.

"Please at least take this seat for a few minutes," she says.

"Thank you," I say with a smile, as I feel a tear escape from my eye.

"Would you like some water?" she asks.

"No, really I'm fine, sorry I'm just having a moment," I say and manage to giggle as I now feel slightly stupid. "I'll just rest here for a minute," I reply.

"Take your time," she says and touches my shoulder gently.

I have to stop these thoughts. I can't be thinking negatively. I know something good will happen, it always does. I'll be fine, I always am. I'll be fine.

I remove myself from the chair and thank the shop assistant. *I need to go home again. I'm not able for shopping today.*

━ ﹏

I make my way home and when I get there, there's a man hovering around outside. He looks familiar, but I'm not sure who is standing there, as I'm not in full view yet. I make my towards the entrance and as I get closer, the now bearded man looks very familiar.

"Enrico! My God, what are you doing here? I didn't think I'd ever hear from you again, especially at this stage," I say.

"I know. I took some time to figure out what I have to do, and I keep coming back to same answer. Go to her, go to her, go to her! So I come to you. I hope it's a good decision," he says with a smile.

Oh My God! You couldn't have made a better one. Now that you're in front of me, I realise I still have feelings for you, and I couldn't want for anything more than to have you here right now.

"I'm pretty sure it is," I say with a smile and I greet him with a big hug, as big as I can give him without my rather rotund belly getting in the way.

"Wow! Are you having the twins? That baby has grown a lot since I last see you!" he says with surprise.

"Ha! No, no twins just one big, bouncy baby. Yeah, I think I've expanded a great deal more since the time you last saw me. Come on, come in," I say as I grab his hand. I can't believe this has happened. Such perfect timing as even though I'd never admit it normally, I really could do with a man's help right now. Someone to keep an eye on me, and be there for me is what I need, as I'm not sure how I'll react once those waters break.

"You look good with a beard, Enrico," I say with a smile.

"Ah, you like? It a something different and it's a how you say, a hipster look?" he says with a laugh.

"Oh, so you're a bit of a hipster are you?" I say, smiling.

"No, not really, you know me now Katie, I like nice things, and I sometimes follow the fashion, but I'm not typical Italian man, which you know."

"Oh I don't know about that, you're quite romantic from what I recall. And just turning up like this, out of the blue is very romantic. This has been the most beautiful surprise I've had in a long time, Enrico. Thank you for coming to London. So, how long will you stay for?" I ask.

"Oh! You want me to leave again?" he asks.

"No, no!! Nothing like that, I'm just wondering will I have you here for a while or is it just a holiday to see how I'm doing?" I ask nervously. *I can't believe I just asked that. Am I sounding needy and desperate now? The woman with the unborn child who's just dying to get a man! Oh no!*

"I stay forever if you like, Katie. It take me three months to make this decision, I think long and hard about it and I make the right one, for me at least, and I hope for you and baby too. I never fall for someone I just meet like I do with you. There was a, hmmm how do you say it, when two people have the same feeling, the look in the eye?"

"Connection, we made a connection, a strong one," I say.

"Yes, connection! I never have connection with anyone before like I have with you when I meet you. You are different. When I see your eyes, it's a like I see your soul. I know you are caring, loving person the minute I meet you. I am here for you, and I don't leave until you tell me to, but I hope you won't," he says. "I understand, that if something happens between us, it will happen slow because you are nearly having baby. I am happy as friends, and later you see how you feel. None of the pressure from me," he says smiling.

I can't believe this, I've waited three months to hear these words and finally after I have given up, you arrive on my doorstep. The fact I'm having someone else's baby has never seemed to bother you in the slightest. This is too good to be true surely. I didn't think men like you existed.

"What? You are looking in deep thought, but you say nothing to me," he says.

"I'm sorry. I'm just a little overwhelmed. I've thought about you every day since I left you in Rome. I wanted to contact you every day, but when you never replied to my text, I thought that was it and I was wasting my time. I understood if you didn't want me, especially when I'm carrying another man's child, but you've come to me now and it's like a dream coming true for me. I thought I'd never meet anyone, and put thoughts of it happening out of my mind a long time ago. I'm just really surprised and happy that you're here. Sorry for the vacant look, it's not actually vacant, it's just disbelief. I suppose, I'm afraid you'll be taken away from me again," I say.

"I'm not going anywhere. It's been tough three months for me too. Do I come to you? Maybe I cause trouble for you because you are unsure and with baby, maybe not thinking right. I don't say properly, I think you know what I mean?" he asks.

"Ha ha ha, you mean my hormones are all over the place? True! They are, but right now seeing you here in front of me, they have never been so intact and I feel so overwhelmed, yet happy and I really believe this feeling will not change for me Enrico. Thank you for being here," I say. "For now, yes I think we might be better to stay friends, until we are sure and I'm of more stable mind," I say with a smile.

He kisses me slowly and it sends shivers through me. This man, who I have merely kissed a few times while on holiday, has left his country to come find me. That says a lot and I'm going to do all I can to make this work. He's something special for sure.

"You know the baby is due within the next two weeks?" I ask.

"Yes, I thought it would be soon, I was not a sure when. I take a chance to come here now, and please, don't be upset with the girls, but they know I come here to be with you. It's how I know where to go today. I would be lost otherwise," he says with a smile. "I have contact them two weeks ago, and they tell me you have baby very soon. I think it's very difficult for them to keep this secret from you. I am happy they do, and it's a good surprise for you," he says as he sweeps my hair from my face.

"They knew? My God, how did they manage to keep that from me? They can't keep secrets ever! Wow! Actually, maybe they can. That's just crazy. I must congratulate them when I see them," I say with a laugh.

"Yes, they tell me also you have baby scan a couple weeks ago and that baby is doing very good. Well, I can see baby is doing good. You look incredible!"

"Do you want to see that scan?" I ask with excitement.

Fool, of course he doesn't, it's not his baby! Not everyone is going to be excited like you are!

He smiles. "I would love to. Katie, I know it's a very soon for me to say these things to you. But I am here for you and for baby, ok? I come for that reason, not just for you. I have the strong feelings for you, but with you comes baby, and I am more than happy to treat baby like my own, if you will have me do that?" he asks. "But, I know it's just friends and kissing maybe now and then, for now?" he asks with a smile. "I understand this is difficult situation for you."

"Thank you, Enrico. I won't object to kisses," I say as I hug him. I can't say anymore as my eyes are filling up. With that, I feel a good strong kick.

"What is?" Enrico asks.

"What do you think? I think baby's just given his or her seal of approval," I say with a teary eyed smile.

32

A week has passed, and I love having Enrico around me. He literally won't let me lift a finger. It's been lovely, so relaxing for me, yet I think he's stressing out a little as he doesn't know what he's let himself in for. I'm standing in the kitchen when all of a sudden out of nowhere, splash - all over the kitchen floor.

Oh! I look down to see the floor flooded and so am I, my waters have broken and while it was the strangest sensation I can't help but giggle and giggle hysterically. "Enrico, I think you should come in here," I say with a laugh.

"What, what? What's going on?" he says rushing into the kitchen. He looks at me wide eyed. "Oh fuck! Baby is ready?" he asks.

"I didn't think I'd be this calm, but it looks like my waters just broke," I say.

"Oh My God, I need to get you to a hospital now, hurry or you'll have the baby in the car," he says panicked.

"It's ok, it's odd, but I know the baby isn't arriving just yet. We can take our time a while," I say in a very calm voice, which really isn't me.

"Right, ok, how you know? Baby might just come now this second! Oh where did I put the keys to my car. Shit!!" he says as he runs into the spare bedroom and starts rummaging through his things. I follow him.

"Calm down! Honestly, there might be nothing happen for a couple of days yet. And my baby just isn't ready to move yet, I can feel it. I was going to say in my waters, but I can't use that expression now seen as they've broken," I say with a giggle.

"Katie, please don't laugh, you're a making me very nervous, please?" he says.

"Oh come on, it's fine. Look the keys are here. Seriously, we might go to the hospital now, and they could tell me to go home again and come back another day. That's normal sometimes," I say.

"Ok, I just prefer to get you there, I'll be happy then, knowing you are definitely in safe hands as I don't know what to do if baby comes. I wish I came here earlier now, I could have gone to natal classes with you." he says.

"You mean anti-natal classes? Yes, that would have been nice, and you'd probably be more clued up for what's ahead, but look I'm just glad to have you here, because it was a huge decision for you to come here, and thank you. It really means a lot to me," I say.

"That's ok, you know I'm happy when you are happy. Now, I love this chat we are having, but it's the wrong time to have it. If I see a baby head coming shortly I don't know what to do. I'm a not a doctor so please, let's go and we chat another time Katie, yeah?"

Oh bless you, you're so panicked. I'm so calm! Why am I so calm? This isn't me, I normally panic like crazy about situations where I don't know what I'm doing. Oh Katie girl, just go with it. It's better to be like this.

I go to grab my hospital bag.

"Stop! No lifting. Just go, open the door and go out, I have the bag."

I start laughing again. This is so funny. I haven't had a laugh like this in a long time. "You know, we could clean up my burst pipe from the kitchen floor before we go, ' I say.

"Katie, get in the car please, and try to keep baby happy and inside you until we get to the hospital."

Ok, I'm just going to have to go the extra mile on this as it is giving me a good laugh.

"Ok, I'm in, baby is in. Actually, it's funny. I was just chatting with the girls on the way to the final scan a few weeks back," I say.

"What's funny?" Enrico asks.

"Well, we were coming into the hospital car park and we were giggling over what would happen if I had to have the baby in the car park, if I wouldn't make it inside the hospital. When we stopped the car, the girls thought I was going into labour and nearly died of fright. It was so funny, though," I say with a smile as I look at his face to see the reaction.

We stop at traffic lights and he looks at me. "Katie, please listen. I am not joking, these beads of sweat rolling down my forehead are real. Please don't actually make me to shit myself!"

"Ha ha ha ha, sorry! Ok, I won't make you do that as we'd be a right pair heading into the hospital then, me after destroying the kitchen floor, and we have no spare trousers for you. I'll stop now," I say as I purse my lips together trying not to laugh. "It would be funny, though," I say.

He's silent.

Ok, enough is enough Katie, stop now or you'll really piss him off. Poor fella, he's so good to me and so handsome. Like what the hell has happened for me to deserve this beautiful creature?

"I am hungry with you now," he says.

Don't fecking laugh, do NOT laugh.

He laughs. "Sorry, I mean I'm angry with you, these stupid English words are too the same, why not change them to something that sounds different?"

I say nothing, but close my eyes as a dart of pain goes through my stomach and out my back. "Oh, Jesus Almighty!"

"See, this is what happens when you a joke about these a things! We'll be there in a five minutes. Just keep the head inside, please?"

I breathe and breathe and breathe. The first contraction. *This is not pleasant, not pleasant at all. And this is just the start. I'll need one of those stress balls that we have at work, to bite on.*

"Ok, it's easing, it's easing. As I said, I've a bit of a way to go yet I'd say before the head comes down. I don't even know how far dilated I am." *That was a sharp pain and I really want to shout at you now, because all you're worried about is if the head comes out! It's supposed to!!!! Stay calm Katie, stay calm.* "Don't forget to ring the girls! I'd ring them now, but I don't want to be contracting on the phone to them, it'll probably freak them out. Your reaction is bad enough," I say.

"I'll ring the girls, don't worry about the girls. I know you want them there, we will make sure they are. I'm sorry beautiful, I've never gone through this before, and it's a bit scary. But I try my best to be a good support in whatever way I can."

How can I possibly be angry with you? My hormones are all over the shop today and I really don't know what way I'll react to you, handsome. I hope I don't shout at you, kick you or scream at you. You don't deserve that. Maybe I should apologise in advance, just in case?

"Enrico, can I apologise in advance to you?"

"What? For a what? Wetting the kitchen floor?"

"No, in advance... sorry about that too," I say with a giggle. "That couldn't be helped, though. No, I mean, well I have a feeling that things might get a lot more difficult and painful for me as this goes on. I'm concerned I might say things or do things that I don't mean to. Can I just apologise now in case I do? Just so you know, I'll be pushing this baby out of me and it is going to affect me in some way," I say.

"Ha ha, oh my beautiful, you don't need to worry. I don't know what will come my way, but I'm sure you won't mean anything bad you might say. Please, Katie, just do what you have to do and I'll be there no matter what. I am here for you, I mean that."

"Thank youuuuu. Oh for feck sake, it's starting again already, I don't know if they should be this close together and so soon!!" I shriek.

"Breathe, breathe, breathe. We are almost there. Here we go through the gates. Breathe Katie, breathe," he says.

"Shut up! I am breathing!" I say in a narky tone.

"And a here we are. Ok, stay here, I get wheelchair, and we get you inside," he says as he runs into the main area of the hospital.

Oh please hurry, please hurry! Right now it feels like the head is out already. Oh just please let the pain stop, just bloody stop!!

I see Enrico return with two emergency room people.

"Ok, now Katie, I know you're in a lot of pain right now, but I'm going to need you to give me some information, ok?" one of them says.

I look at them grimly. *Information, do I look like I'm capable of giving information right now?*

"What kind of information?" I ask trying to keep calm.

"Right, well, how long ago did your waters break? Are you having proper contractions yet?"

"Proper contractions? Well if these aren't proper contractions, I don't want to have them because these are bloody painful feckers," I say. "Waters broke around forty minutes ago, had my first contraction about eight minutes ago, and another started just as we entered the hospital around three minutes ago," I say.

"Ok, so roughly only five minutes apart? Very good. Ok, ease yourself into the chair now, darling. Very good. Right, we are going to get your papers sorted and we'll have to ask a few more questions when we get you settled," she says.

"Settled? You make it sound like I could be in labour for forty-eight hours?" I ask.

"Well, we can never tell sometimes. It's different for everyone. You're doing good, though, and it's good for you as you'll have that beautiful little baby in your arms before you know it," she says.

I look for Enrico's hand as I want him next to me. "Will you call the girls, please? I think that you might be right and baby might pop out a lot faster than I originally thought," I say in a regretful manner as I feel I took the piss out of him a little too much.

"Sure, I call them now beautiful. Let's get you into a bed or room at least first," he says.

They wheel me down a long corridor to another reception area. There are pregnant women pacing the hallway and I can hear moans in the distance. *Oh good God almighty, will I be able for what's ahead of me?* My next contraction starts.

"Take no notice of the noise love, some women have a very low pain threshold, you seem quite calm, though. You might not mind it as much as others do," the nurse says as I pass her.

Right now I'm not taking any notice of the others. I've got contractions and I'm just thinking about my own pain!!

As I reach the room and want to climb onto the bed, the sharp pain in my lower back is driving through me again. I hold my back and take deep breaths. I'm noticing the contractions are becoming sharper and longer the more often they come. Enrico starts to rub my back. It's just what I need right now. Once the pain subsides again, I manage to climb onto the bed.

"Are you ok if I go outside to call the girls?" Enrico asks.

"Go for it, this probably won't happen again for another five minutes or so," I say.

I watch him leave the room, and I feel I can smile now. Not because he's gone, but for some odd reason, I just feel happy in this moment. I hear him talking to someone at the door.

"Excuse me, but do you know how long before baby comes?" he asks.

"Well, contractions are less than three minutes apart so could be very soon, or it might take a little time yet," the voice says.

"Ah that's a fantastic, I tell the girls. Friends of Katie, they are meant to be here for the birth," he says.

"Oh lovely, I hope they don't need to catch a flight?" she says.

"Ha ha no, no, they come by car, thirty minutes maximum, depend on the traffic," he says.

Then it registers with me. *Oh no! Mary is meant to be here for the birth!!*

The door opens. "Hello, hello, well aren't you the impatient mother now, coming in a week early?" Jessica, the midwife asks.

"Jessica, how are you? I ask. "I overheard you talking to Enrico. I'm relieved to see you," I say with a smile.

"Where did this Enrico man come from? My goodness Katie, he is certainly easy on the eye. Well done!" she says.

"Ha ha, yeah well I did tell you the story, didn't I? Well, he arrived on my doorstep around two weeks ago. He wants to give this a go with me. We've started as friends, but it's with a view to something more once the baby comes and we are sure it's what we want. I'm as surprised as you seem to be. I can't understand how it all happened, but I'm happy to go with it. He's been amazing while he's been here so far and I really believe he means what he says," I say.

"He seems a lovely chap, but do be careful my lovely. Remember you're in a very vulnerable position at the moment and someone telling you they'll be there for you is one thing, but they need to mean it. I don't want to burst your bubble, but when the baby arrives which I'd imagine will be very shortly, it's a life changing time," she says.

"Ok, so I didn't mishear then, baby is on the ball and arriving way ahead of schedule?" I ask.

"Yep, well you knew that when your waters broke, but just let me check, hmmmm, yep, you're fully dilated already. You'll be pushing in no time at all," she says.

"Oh bugger! My friend Mary is meant to be here for it all, she was due to fly over tomorrow and spend a couple of weeks with me to keep an eye on things, and be here for the birth. She'll be so disappointed. She really wanted to be here for it all," I say.

"I'm afraid you can't put a definite time on these things. Babies come out when they are ready, some can be a week over, some a week before, some a month before. You just never know. But, the upside is, at least you'll have a midwife staying with you for a bit after the baby is born. I know it'll be disappointing I'm sure for both of you that she's not here, but the main thing is that you and baby are both healthy and happy. That's the only outcome we all want in the hospital," she says.

"I know and you're right. Oh for fuck sake, it's off again," I say. "Sorry for swearing," I say between breaths.

"Ok, we're at two minutes apart now, it's speeding up considerably. You'll be ready to go very shortly my sweet. Keep breathing, don't worry about swearing. You're considerably calm actually. How's the pain? I can't offer you an epidural at this stage of labour but you're doing well with just gas and air," she says.

"Gas and air, that's fine," I manage to expel between breaths. "They're just a little more than painful, aren't they?" I say in a sarcastic tone. "It's bad, but is it likely to get worse?" I ask.

"Hmmmm, I think you're probably at the worst part now, to be honest. If you can do that with gas and air, you're doing seriously well. I think you are anyway. Trust me, some of the women here fire abuse at us. They just can't take the pain at all. We know they don't mean it, so take no notice. It's all in a day's work, but you're doing quite well, Katie. Well done and stay calm as best you can. This also keeps baby calm for its journey to the outside world. Be proud of yourself, you're doing extremely well," she says. "Right, I'm going to head out for a minute, I can see Enrico is on his way back now, but I'll be back in to check on you again in a minute or two. Just press the bell if you get another contraction before I come back, ok?" she says.

"Sure, thanks, Jessica," I say.

I see Enrico's smiling face as he walks towards me. "Girls are on their way," he says.

"Thank you my sweet. You're very good. Bad news is that Mary is going to miss it all as it looks like baby will be here very soon by the way Jessica is talking," I say.

"Yes, she tell me as I was going to call the girls. This is good. I cannot wait to meet baby. I wonder if it's girl or boy?" he says.

I love how excited he is, especially when it's not even his kid. I wonder how the real father would feel if he knew. I wonder does he know. I wonder if he is still with us. I think he is Oh snap out of it Katie, he's gone and probably best forgotten. This baby is going to have an Italian father who is going to care for him or her like he or she is his own. I smile at Enrico, but it doesn't last for long.

"Aghhhhhhhhhhhhhhhhhh, Enrico, I think this is where I'll crush your hand," I say trying to keep calm, I press the bell as it's been less than two minutes since my last contraction.

"My my, I think this lady is almost ready to push. Down to the labour room for you, my darling," Jessica says as she enters the room.

33

I hold my hands out. *This can't be possible and so quickly!* I'm about to hold my baby in my arms for the first time.

"She's beautiful and absolutely perfect," Jessica says as she passes her to me. "You've got a fine healthy baby Katie, weighing in at eight pound and seven ounces," she says.

"No wonder I thought I needed a JCB to move me over the past few weeks!" I say as I take her in my arms.

Oh My God, you are such a precious little Angel. I love you so much. My eyes well up, with tears of happiness that I have given birth to such a beautiful and perfect little girl. "I feel so proud right now and happy," I say in a quivery voice and the tears roll down my face.

"Can I come in?" I hear the male voice asking from the door. I immediately smile as I nod at the nurse to allow Enrico inside. He looks funny in his scrubs, and it's really sweet to see him looking so happy and amazed by my beautiful little girl. "Is it a girl or a boy?" he asks.

"Oh sorry, I should have said, she's a girl and perfect in every way thankfully," I say with a massive smile as the tears continue to flow.

"Congratulations Katie, she is beautiful. Just like her mother," he says with a smile. It's weird as his eyes are filling up and I'm not sure why. I can only assume because he's as happy as I am. "I'm so glad you are ok.

I could hear others screaming with pain on the corridor. I could not really hear any noise from here so was a worried. You are such a brave lady to do this without showing pain," he says.

"Enrico, it hurt, but it was worth the pain to have this little angel," I chuckle. "I guess it's called 'labour' for a reason! But I'm fine now. Well, I'm exhausted and sore, but the pain is gone and look at this gorgeous baby." We sit there just staring at my little beauty, fast asleep in my arms. "Does she not need to be fed yet?" I ask Jessica.

"No, she'll feed within the next half hour or so," she says.

"I speak with the girls, they should be here soon. I think they are sad not to be here," Enrico says.

"Oh I know, but it couldn't be helped as you know. I was going to ask if you wanted to come in for the birth, Enrico, but thought it might be a bit, I don't know, uncomfortable for you?" I say in a concerned manner.

"Hmmm, I am glad you didn't. I think I would be uncomfortable, and I think maybe you would be too, Katie. I am here for you, but I know this thing between us will take time to grow and particularly now that the baby is here, it might take longer. I want you to know though I want this to work so you take all the time you need," he says.

"Thanks, Enrico," I say with a smile as I turn back to my baby. *Enrico, you're sweet, I can't believe that all of this has even happened. I feel so lucky to have you by my side. And baby, I'm going to be the best mother in the world to you. You deserve the best and you'll get it.* And then it hits me. While my little angel is sleeping in my arms, it hits me, like a punch into the eye socket. She has no dad. As soon as the thought enters my head, my happiness turns to sadness and I sob uncontrollably.

"Katie, Katie, what's wrong?" Enrico asks.

I can't answer him. How can I explain that while he has the best intention in the world, he will never actually be my baby's father. How can I bring her up with me being her mother and her father? Why can't Pete be here with us?

"Shhh, shhh, it's ok. Here, let me take her and let her sleep for a while in the cot," Jessica says as she takes Eva from me. *Eva, that will be your name.* She walks to Enrico, "I'm sorry, we might need you to leave for a few minutes. Don't worry, it's nothing you've done. This happens to most mothers as it's a very overwhelming situation," she whispers.

"Yes, yes, of course, I leave. She will be ok, yes?" he asks.

"She'll be fine. She probably just needs a little sleep and time to herself for a short while. It's a lot to take in being a new mum," she says.

"Please, I stay outside in case she needs me. Her friends come now too, I will tell them to wait," he says as he walks out.

"That's fine. If you want to make your way down to the ward, you can wait outside as we'll move her there now and she can sleep there," Jessica says.

At this stage, I'm sobbing uncontrollably, and I don't even know myself if I can stop these tears. *I'm lonely, alone and sad. I'm a single mother, and I don't know what to do or how to be a good mother to this child. How do I do that?!*

"There, there darling, let it out. I know it's all very overwhelming. You know you're going to be the best mum out there, Katie," Jessica says with a smile. "Mums like you are hard to come by and I just know Eva — a very pretty name by the way — is going to think you are the bees knees as she's growing up. I've been there Katie. It's all very scary at the start, but you'll be amazed how easy and naturally you play the role of mum. Then as they get a bit older and they come to you for everything, it's then you realise what a great job you've done. I won't lie, it's tough, but you're a strong girl. I know you're well capable of bringing little Eva up on your own," she says as she puts her arm around me and rubs my back.

"Do you think?" I'm not so sure, Jessica. I just wish Pete could be here to see all of this and his little girl being brought into the world. I feel he should be a part of her life," I say.

"Katie, you of all people believe that everything happens for a reason. You need to keep believing that. If Pete is meant to come back into your life, he will. But for now, you need to concentrate on being strong for Eva. A happy mummy is something she will recognise and want. If I can do it, you can do it," she says.

Right now, I find it difficult to believe that I'll be a good mum, but I had no idea you were a single mum from day one too, Jessica. It helps to hear stories like that as you seem like such a positive person. I need to buck up and be there for my little girl.

"Ok, you're right, I can do this," I say with a smile. "Are the girls on their way, I wonder?" I ask.

"They're here. I could hear them outside a few minutes ago. You need to rest, however, so lie back, close your eyes and take a nap. I'll let the girls know you need to sleep for a while. They won't mind I'm sure, they just want to know you're ok. We're just going to wheel you back down to the ward now so you can rest," she says with a smile as she covers me with the blanket. "Now sleep," she whispers.

I can hear the girls talking outside and while I want to shout at them to come in, I can't seem to summon the energy. Instead, I close my eyes and follow Jessica's instructions as I drift off into a deep sleep.

34

*I*t's almost Christmas, three months have flown by and my beautiful Eva is growing so quickly. She's a great strong baby and I never thought I could take to motherhood in the way I have. I feel so close to her, closer than I have to anyone ever in my life. The other person I've grown incredibly close to is Enrico. He's been such a wonderful person to have in my life, and while Eva doesn't appreciate or understand who he is yet, I just know she will have the same appreciation one day.

As I stroll down the South Bank pushing Eva in her pram, it looks like it may snow. Enrico is walking with me. I can see he's enjoying the crisp cool air as we walk past London Bridge. "You know there's a garden at the top of that building?" he asks me.

"What building?" I ask. I'm so out of tune these days with what's going on in London that I need someone who's only just arrived in the country three months ago to update me.

"That one!" he says pointing to what's affectionately known as the "Walkie Talkie."

"Is there?" I ask. "I love that building. I always thought it was just very cool offices or something, but never investigated it. Sure I work in the Gherkin which is just behind it. I need to get out more," I say with a laugh.

"Yes, and on the thirty-fifth floor, there's a garden. But, there is also a very nice cocktail bar and restaurant, I've been told," he says. "Would you like to a visit with me one evening?" he asks.

Are you asking me on a date Enrico? "Yeah Enrico, that would be a nice treat for us one evening. It might have to be a while away yet though as I don't want to leave this little one out of sight for a long time yet," I say nervously.

"Oh, I'm sure the girls would take good care of her, if you wanted to go sometime soon? You know, you watch her all day and all night. I think you deserve a break. Think about it and it's your birthday soon, I think it would be nice to take you for dinner....as more than your friend, if you'd like that?"

Oh my! You ARE asking me on a date!

"Enrico, you're asking me out...I," I stop myself from saying anymore before taking a breath, and a moment to think about it.

Think now, he's younger, bloody hot, and younger, but is this a flash in the pan situation? Oh, I'll just go, it's a date. I have nothing to lose.

"Enrico, yes, I'd love to go on a date with you," I say with a smile and a sigh of what feels like relief.

"I feel honoured you say yes to me, Katie. I know it's soon after baby and difficult decision for you to make, but I put no pressure. If you like me, great, but I am happy to go for date and see how we get along. You take your time, if you are unsure about this."

"Thank you for understanding. Yes, look I know how you feel about me, and I love the fact you are feeling like this still. Even though nothing has happened between us yet, but a simple kiss, I was worried that once the baby got here, you might change your mind, which is why I've been slow to let things happen. I wasn't sure 'us' would be an option," I say.

"Katie, I don't fly all the way from Italy just for the fun of it. I want to help you with baby Eva, yes, but I also really do have great feelings for you. I want to spend the time with you and get to know everything about you. You mean a lot to me," he says with a beautiful and gentle looking smile on his face.

I match his smile and say "Enrico, I'd be delighted for us to see how things go. Let's go on this date and see how it all works out."

I feel good, I feel that I have done something positive for a change and not just moped around wondering what my life would be like if Pete entered it again. He's gone and for the past three months of my life, I've forgotten about him... until now. But now, I feel like there's nothing there inside of me which wants to see him or feel anything for him again. I am making a good decision to move on with my life and possibly create a new one with my little girl and Enrico.

We continue walking along the South Bank and as I shiver and notice the air getting colder, the first snowflakes start to fall. Eva seems happy sleeping and Enrico has a grin on his face since I said I'd go on a date with him. I think I probably do too. It's a nice feeling - a feeling of being wanted by someone again.

35

"Helloooo, hellooooo, it's mad aunty at the door, let me in, I've news!" I hear Sarah shouting.

"Shhhhhhhhh! I've just got her off to sleep," I say in an annoyed tone.

"Oh sorry, I was just dying to tell you the news, though," Sarah says as I step aside to let her into the flat.

"What is it?" I ask wondering what could be so important for her to get this excited.

"Well, wait until I tell you. Guess who called me last night?" she asks.

"I have no idea...Hmmmm, the Queen, she's giving you a title and we'll all have to courtesy every time we see you now?" I quiz.

"Ha ha ha, very funny. Although I wouldn't say no if she did. Can you imagine the Queen chatting to me, though? Sure what would we talk about like?" she asks.

"Sarah, for feck sake, who rang you last night?" I ask, getting irritated as I'm feeling decidedly nosey all of a sudden.

"Jarvis! Jarvis! Jarvis! That fecking tool rang me last night. And do you want to know what he said?" she asks.

"Well, now that you've mentioned Jarvis and the words fecking and tool in one sentence, yes I do want to know," I say with a giggle.

"He says, 'Sarah darling, I've made a rather grand error in letting you go. How stupid of me, and I have no idea what I was thinking when I contemplated cheating on you. You were right, I suppose those times we were in bed, I was thinking of Katie and I don't know why, but I was. But that shouldn't change anything between us. I still have feelings for you, and yes, I know I treated you deplorably darling, will you ever forgive me for my behaviour?' That's what he said to me Katie, can you fecking believe what a tool he is?"

That's a lot of fecking! You're angry girl!

"What a dick. I can't believe, Sarah, that I was actually upset for a while when you got together with him. I never told you that before, but I was. I fancied him that night, but could clearly see you were besotted and obviously, you know I'd never stand in your way. He, however, was such an idiot, I feel like I had the lucky escape, a big lucky escape by the sounds of it. I do hope you told him what to do with himself?" I ask.

"That's exactly what I did. Why Katie, it sounds, darling, like you might have been listening to one's conversation!" Sarah says in a pretend Jarvis voice.

"Really, what did you say?" I ask stifling a laugh.

"Yeah, it felt great too. I actually put on a posh English accent and said, 'Jarvis darling, I'm not one hundred percent sure if I'm going to say the right thing to you now, but are you ready, darling, because it might upset you?'" she says.

I squeal with delight. "Oh Sarah, that's so funny. Did you give him time to reply?"

"Of course, I wanted to hear him squirm a bit or at least hear his voice get a bit nervous," Sarah says. "He said, 'Sarah, what do you mean upset me? You know I'm sincere and I mean what I say?' So I said to him, 'My arse you do, you can join the back of the queue! As it's moving slowly, I don't expect to see you again until you're at least ninety. Good luck to ya,' and I hung up," she giggles. "Was I too harsh?" she asks.

I can't even answer I'm laughing so hard. When I manage to catch my breath I hug her. "Congratulations girl, that has to be the best 'good luck, I'll see ya' I've ever heard from anyone. I will giggle over this for years.

Well done! He deserved it. I thought he was a nice guy, Sarah, and he acted like such a noble and nice individual, but what an idiot he turned out to be. I can't stand that kind of behaviour from a guy, and of his age! Like grow up! Well done, you deserve a glass of wine to celebrate that, I think."

"Oh, are you back on the booze? Are you not breastfeeding anymore?"

"I can't. She's just not interested it seems. I've tried and tried. It's just wearing me out at this stage. I said it to the nurse and she said it's up to me when to stop although she did encourage me to keep trying. That was two weeks ago, and I am trying hard, but she just doesn't seem to want it and I can't let her starve. I've tried bottles for the past two weeks and she seems to be able to take them better so I'm going to stick with them now. I need to know she's getting a proper feed as she'll just get too weak if she was to carry on the way she was. As long as she's happy I'm happy. She was great for the first eight or nine weeks. So, in answer to your question, yes I am back on the wine, but just the odd glass or half glass. I'm not used to having it now," I say.

"Fantastic! I have my drinking buddy back again, although I suppose to be fair, neither of us drink a great deal in general anyway. I'll run to the shop and get some," Sarah says with great gusto.

"You don't have to run anywhere my dear. I am well stocked up as Enrico kindly took me for a massive shop on Friday. I think I got enough food and drink to last for a month at this stage. I thought I may as well get a good shop in while I could. He doesn't have time to take me shopping always because of the shifts he works. We must have spent nearly two hours in the supermarket. Was great though, I really stocked up on the chocolate and crisps too, he he," I say as I just can't help a giggle at the thought of the ridiculous amount of things I bought. *I just hope I have enough people calling to help me eat it all now.*

"Oh, you star you. Do you have any Cadbury's Marvellous Creations Jelly Popping Candy by any chance? Sarah asks. "I'm addicted to it at the moment."

"Are you for real? I can't stop eating it of late, it's so addictive, but sooooo good. Did you try the new one with raspberries and hazelnuts? Just beautiful, but I still prefer the Jelly Popping Candy I think," I reply.

"Hmmmm, I'm on the fence, a bit torn between the two, but yeah that would go down well now with a little glass of wine. So, do you think I'll ever meet a man?" Sarah asks.

"Woman! You have men bashing down that door of yours, but you seem to turn a deaf ear to them! Sarah, they are queuing up for you! You're a stunner!"

"I know I sounded all brave there about Jarvis telling him what to do with himself, but I feel really upset about it all still. Why or how can something one other person does cause so much pain to someone else? It's just not fair," she says with a look of sadness.

"Drink this and I'll play some decent music. Bit of eighties ok?" I ask.

"Yeah, go for it," she says.

I turn the radio on to hear, "Do You Really Want To Hurt Me?"

"Oops! That's the wrong song for this occasion!" I say, and can't help but laugh.

Thankfully Sarah burst into laughter. *Phew! That could have gone either way.*

Changing station quickly I hear a great upbeat song, Jermaine Stewart's 'We Don't Have to Take Our Clothes Off.'

I pour the wine as I dance and sing along.

"Oh, great tune! Shame we can't blare it up, we could have a mini disco," Sarah says giggling.

"Sorry, no can do. Herself will wake and it's taken me long enough to get her off to sleep today. So, Jarvis. Why do you think he's had such an impact on you? From what you've told me about the whole situation, it doesn't sound like he treated you too well in general while you were with him," I say with concern.

"I really wish I knew why, Katie. He's just the first guy I've fallen for in, in forever!"

"Wow! That's a pretty big statement, Sarah. Were you full smack bang in love you think? You weren't with him that long really were you?"

"I know, but there was just something about him. I just melted the minute he opened his mouth, with that posh English accent of his, and he was just so charming all of the time. You know the muppety fools I normally meet? Totally different, as you know," she says.

"Ah yes, muppety fools. Yeah, I do recall a few of them. To be fair, I think you can put him in that category now, too. He was a dick I know I'm repeating myself, but he was, and still is. Yes, he was charming, but he took the biscuit altogether! I did fancy him that night you met him Sarah, I won't lie. I thought he'd be perfect for me. Clearly, I was spared what you went through, and wish you didn't have to," I say.

"You know what? I have to move on from him. He's just no good for me and thinking about him isn't going to help matters. The girls at work said that the right man will come my way when the time is right. Maybe it's true. I need a holiday, Katie."

"That's not a bad idea Sarah, a holiday could just help you out and you'd never know what kind of romance might happen for you! Look at myself and Enrico for God's sake! I never in a million years thought something would come of us meeting that time. Things happen in strange ways, Sarah. We just never know how things will really turn out, do we?" I say, hoping she might see the optimistic side again.

"You're right and you two are in such a speedy relationship. It's like meant to be, he's so crazy about you and to be honest, you seem smitten with him too Katie. You've been very fortunate, especially with everything that has happened over the past year or so. You've been so strong too. I don't know if I could have gone through all of that and just look at you now as a first time mum! Katie, you are like the ultimate warrior or something. I really don't know how you do it. But yes, I agree with what you say and I'm sure that one day everything will work out for me too. So, where should I go on holiday and would you like to come with me?" she asks.

"Oh trust me, there's nothing I'd like to do more than go on holiday with you, but I have a very large responsibility now in the form of a very small girl called Eva. I could do with a holiday myself, but no, I can't, Sarah. Why not ask Laura, she's always up for the craic?" I say.

"Hmmmm, I don't know if that would be a good idea as she's so friendly with that J named fool! I don't know her as well as you do, but from what I'd gather, she's very, very close friends with him and I've a feeling when she discovers what I said, she won't take to me very well," Sarah says.

"Ah no, Laura doesn't take sides in general, Sarah. She's pretty non-biased and likes to keep everyone on the same level, no matter how friendly she is with either party. She also makes that quite clear to people so I really don't think you've anything to worry about," I say with a smile. "Ask her, you've nothing to lose. Unless, of course, you don't want to as you do have loads of other friends to choose from. I only suggested her as I thought that you both had such a laugh on holiday in Italy. You've also got a bit of a bond going on since Eva arrived, so I thought it might be a nice idea. But no pressure, obviously!" I say.

"I understand where you're coming from, but I'd feel a little uncomfortable now I think. I'll let it be. I might ask Janet as she's always good old fun. She's single too at least, so we can go out at night on the hunt for some fine men," Sarah says with a giggle.

"Ah, true! Of course, probably better to go with another singleton so you can let your hair down properly. Sure, let me know what you book. I take it you're not thinking Ibiza?" I ask reluctantly.

"Not a chance! I'm too old for that caper. I'd be telling them all to go home and put some clothes on themselves, acting like their mother. No, I was thinking as I've always wanted to visit Sicily, I might just go there. I might bring Enrico's brother home with me," she says with a laugh.

"Well, Enrico does have a very attractive brother as it happens. I've never shown you the photos of him have I?" I quiz.

"Ah, no. Why have you been keeping him so quiet?" she asks.

"It just never occurred to me to show him to you. Hang on, I'll get my phone," I whisper as I open the door to go to my bedroom.

"Here, but look, he's a bit of a cheat by all accounts when it comes to women so he might not be the best option for you, especially as you don't really want an Italian Jarvis in your life," I say.

She sniggers. "I'm just imagining that, and it's not nice. How annoying would he be? But, wow, he's something special isn't he?" she asks.

"I knew you'd fancy him! Please, do not pester me to get him to come over to meet you, he will ruin your life most likely. I will not be responsible for introducing you to one of the biggest womanisers on the planet.

Laura can take responsibility for Jarvis, but I will not for this! I'm not asking him to come over," I say with a slight smile.

"No, I don't want you to, but he would be nice for a holiday fling alright if he did come to London to visit his lovely brother and his brother's lovely girlfriend," she says with a giggle. "I'm kidding. I couldn't be dealing with another Jarvis no matter what nationality he is! It was hard enough to get over what he did, could you imagine what kind of damage an Italian version would do. He is hot, though, but he can stay in Italy. However, if I was ever to bump into him on holidays, I'm sure a little snog wouldn't hurt," she says.

"Stay clear! Please? It's for your own sake!" I say anxiously.

"I will, you know I'm not looking for any hassles. So anyway, Italy would be nice wouldn't it? Maybe I'll look into it, or maybe even down the coastline of Positano and the Amalfi coast, would be lovely. Maybe a bit too romantic for a girlie holiday, but I can investigate it all anyway," Sarah says sounding happy with her decision that Italy should be the place to re-visit.

"Go for it. Want to check it now on Google?" I ask as I take a large gulp of wine as the pangs of knowing I won't be able to afford a holiday for a long time set in.

"Sure, I might as well, if you don't mind me using your computer?" Sarah asks.

"No, go for it, it'll be nice to at least see photos of nice destinations, as that's about as close I'll get to a holiday for a long time I'd imagine," I say.

"I don't want to depress you Katie, but do you still wonder if Pete will come back to you? The thought just crossed my mind the other day and I was thinking about if he turned up one day and you were madly in love with Enrico – which you seem to be now by the way – how would you react?" she asks.

"Oh, I have no idea how I'd react. I'd definitely get a massive fright or maybe even a heart attack from it all, that's for sure. I don't know is my answer, Sarah, I really don't know. But, at this stage, I'm thinking he's not going to show up, it's over a year since I've seen him and even if he is still alive, why hasn't he turned up yet? To me, I think that part of my life is probably best left in the past now. If he were to waltz back into my life, it could turn it completely upside down," I say with worry.

This isn't something I've thought about in a long time. I've moved on now! What if he did come back, how would I react? Would I still have feelings for him? Oh God, maybe I have to sit and think about this and maybe prepare for it as if it does happen, would I still be in love with him like I was? Would it be a matter of me wanting to throw myself into his arms, or would I be a little more than allergic to him?

"Hello? Earth to Katie?" Sarah says.

"Sorry, I was miles away. You've set my mind racing now thinking about that. I hope at this point maybe that he doesn't come back into my life. Sure, for Eva, it would be wonderful for her to know her father, but Enrico and I have become so close. He treats her like she's his. She responds some bit to him, like as if he could be her father, and I'm not sure what I would do if Pete came on the scene then. It could ultimately mess up a happy family," I say.

"Oh God, Katie! I'm sorry for bringing it up. I'm an eejit of the highest order. If you can, please just forget that I said that to you? I'm such a muppet causing confusion like that. I'm sorry. Look I'll go as the last thing you probably want now is me sitting in front of you looking at holidays," Sarah says.

"NO! Stay Sarah, please? This is the first time in a long time that I can actually relax in company as I feel I've been without female company for so long and I can't have conversations like this with Eva. Adorable as she is in every way, shape and form, but she can't talk back to me and give me advice or just have a general chin wag with me. Here, have more wine," I say as I rush to the bottle of wine to fill her glass. I can't even finish my own half glass.

"Ok if you're sure, then I'll stay. I am sorry, though. I didn't think I'd open a can of worms by asking that," she says.

"You haven't, don't worry. You know it's probably no harm some-one has mentioned it to me, as it is food for thought, I'll say that much. However, I really do need to concentrate and keep concentrating on my life with Enrico now. He's amazing and has been such a terrific guy in every way. I can't imagine life without him, to be honest. So, going on that information, I'd say Pete could see his little girl, but he'd be out of my life romantically, at least, that's how it feels right now," I say with a slight smile.

"Well, that wouldn't be so bad then. However, I suppose you'd never really know unless that situation was to occur, would you?"

Hmmmm, you're right. I could have a totally different reaction to a situation like that, but for now I can only hope that it will never happen.

36

"Happy holidays!" I say with a laugh as I hug Sarah goodbye at the airport. It's April, and she's finally decided to go on her 'holiday'.

"I'm excited now. Am I mad doing this on my own?" she asks.

"Not at all girl, you're a grown woman, and you know what you're doing. That's the main thing. You will have a great time. I know sometimes it's nice to travel with someone, but other times it's nice to go it alone, and just do your own thing. You'll meet so many people too, I'm really jealous. Go enjoy yourself," I say with a smile.

"Oh Katie, you're a star, you always manage to say the right thing. Let me hug my little munchkin before I go. I can't believe I won't see you all for three months!" she says with excitement as she takes Eva from me and squeezes her tight. However, I can sense a twinge of sadness in there too. "Enrico, give me a hug," she says.

"Certo bella, you have a most wonderful time. Bring me back a bomba," he says with a roar of laughter.

"A bomba? Isn't that one of those delicious pastries that has custard exploding out of them when you bite into them?" she asks.

"Ha ha, yes, it is, I joke with you of course. Just find yourself a nice Italian man who you can bring back and I can hang out with," he says.

"I'll do my best, Enrico," she says as she looks at me. "You've got yourself a winner there, girl," she says as her eyes fill up and hugs me tight. She wipes her eyes and walks away. As she continues through the security gates, she turns and waves goodbye. I wave until I see her disappear out of sight. Enrico puts his arm around me, and Eva is just Eva, the smiley, happy baby that she is.

I wonder if you understood what was going on here, would you be upset little one? You're so happy all of the time, I'm blessed to have you. I'm going to miss your Aunty Sarah. She's been amazing since you've been born.

We exit the airport, and head towards the car.

"Have you seen Laura lately?" Enrico asks.

"Not a word, nor a sign. It's funny as she's normally so good to contact me. I'm wondering if it has anything to do with the fact that Sarah told Jarvis what to do with himself?" I say.

"Oh no! I don't believe Laura is like that, is she?" She take the side of a liar and cheat? It don't sound like Laura during the time that I know her," he says rubbing his chin, as if in deep thought.

"I know, but people change. I don't know, maybe I should ring her tonight and see if she's ok. You're right, it really doesn't sound like her. I think I've just been so busy here though of late with Eva that I haven't given her much time, not intentionally, though. She knows she can come around whenever she wants to, and I'd welcome her no problem. Yes, that's it, I'll ring her tonight," I say as we approach the car.

The journey home is peaceful as Eva has gone for a sleep and we are listening to some very mellow music on the radio. However, a sudden pang of loneliness has come over me, and I feel very saddened that Sarah is gone. While I have plenty of other friends here, I feel I've grown very close to her recently, and she's been incredible since Eva arrived. Always there at a moment's notice and never complains about it. *I wonder will she return or will she stay if she finds the love of her life?*

The following day, I get a call from Sarah.

"Ciao bella, come stai?" I hear.

"Ha ha, are you drinking?" I ask.

"I had one glass of vino at lunch, and it's just so hot here it's difficult to not get pissed easily. The weather is just amazing. I feel like I've a tan already and you know me, I don't tan at all!" she says.

"You sound happy, hon, and I'm glad. Well you're missing nothing here. Guess what? It's raining... again!" I say with a laugh. "Sounds like you're going to have a great time. Maybe we should come visit wherever you'll be if the weather doesn't improve here. I can't even see the Walkie Talkie building today, and you know how easily I can normally see that from where I live?" I say.

"Oh, that sounds depressing. Sorry, I'm sure I'm not helping by telling you how wonderful it is here. There are some fit guys around too. I think my fair skin is attracting them to me. Hopefully now I'll find a bit of loving on my journey," she says laughing. "Katie, you know I'd love you to come over at some point, so come over if you want to. I'd be thrilled to bits if I saw your smiley face at the airport. Believe it or not, I'm hiring a car for the first time ever. I'm a bit nervous about driving on the opposite side of the road, but it'll be good to drive again, whether it be the right side or the wrong side. I'm excited Katie, very excited," Sarah says.

"It all sounds spectacularly good my dear girl. I rang Laura last night by the way as I haven't heard from her in ages," I say.

"Oh and what did she say?" she asks.

"Well, I asked if everything was ok as I hadn't heard from her in so long. She said that all is fine, but she was a little confused as to how to handle the situation between yourself and Jarvis as she has great time for both of you. I think she's just feeling awkward Sarah."

"Oh, ok, I thought she was taking sides and just decided to side with the tool. I suppose I can see it is awkward for her. Should I call her or something do you think? I thought she might have called me before I left as I assumed she had been in touch with you and knew I was going?" she asks.

"No, she wasn't and as you know I've been a little extra busy of late so haven't really had or made time to call her. It's my fault really, it wasn't intentional, though. Maybe give her a shout. It can't hurt," I say.

"Ok, that's exactly what I'll do. There's a fit man walking towards me now with a cocktail in his hand, for me. I know, cocktails at this hour, but I'm treating the first few days as a relaxing holiday, and I'll start my travels then," she says.

"Erm yes, I think you'll find that you'll be there for a long enough time, so the entire trip is a holiday," I remind her.

"Ah yeah, true I suppose, but I am taking it a bit more seriously in terms of wanting to see things, and finding myself. Yes, I want to find myself," she says.

"Sarah, are you ok? This doesn't sound like you at all, very deep of you," I say.

"I know, but I need to sort my life out and when I do that, then I'll be happy to return to London," she says.

"Ok, I like the sound of that. I better let you go, this will cost you a fortune," I say.

"It's fine. I'm using an app, but I need to run to the loo anyway before I start sipping on this cocktail of mine. I'll be in touch my lovely. Give Eva a massive kiss for me and hugs to both you and Enrico. Love you lots, byeeee," Sarah says.

"Ok Sarah, off you go, I'll send my love to them and you mind yourself. Stay in touch ok?" I say.

"Sure will. Bye hon. Speak soon," she says and hangs up.

I feel happy. I'm happy that I've heard from Sarah, and she's ok. I'm also happy to know she does plan on coming back to London, and not setting up a new life in Italy for herself. I miss her already.

I walk to Eva's room where she's starting to whimper. *Time to feed you I think, little lady. Aren't you growing fast!* I lift her from the cot and the whimpering stops and a smile appears. As I gaze at her, I notice for the first time how much she's starting to look like Pete.

37

I wake with a start. Beads of sweat are pouring down my face along with tears. I'm crying. *What the hell was that dream?*

"Are you ok, Katie?" the whisper comes from next to me.

"Yeah, yeah, I'll be fine, just a bad dream," I reply to Enrico.

I can't tell him what it was about. It would scare him and that's something I don't want to do. I've fallen for him and telling him that I had a dream that Pete returned would freak him out and he'd probably leave. I have no idea where that dream came from, it's been at least six months since I've had it. It's the same dream over and over. I'm out on a night out and get home and he's lingering by my front door waiting to get in. However, it's like he doesn't know why he's there, he just is. He doesn't know my name and there is no baby on the scene. Then he sees me and knows there's a connection, he grabs me and kisses me and then I wake up. It's freaking me out. *Is he coming back to me? Why does this keep happening?*

"Anything you want to tell me about?" he says suspiciously.

"No, it's fine, it's an old recurring dream that has just reared its head again. It's fine, just a bit weird, but no need for concern," I say.

"Ok, you tell me though if it's something I can help you with. You might have the stress at the moment as Eva cries a lot with teeth coming through. She wake you a lot," he says.

Why are you so nice? Another guy would be freaking out because he's being woken, not worrying about the fact I'm being woken every hour. God, please don't let this dream haunt me anymore, put an end to it, please?

"That could be it," I say with a smile. "I think I'm more worried about you. I'm on mat leave and can catch up on sleep some bit, but you're at work every day," I say with empathy.

"Oh I'm fine, I sleep well all of the time. You know it take forever to normally wake me, I don't hear Eva cry a lot which is bad really, but I sleep deep," he says with a smile.

I just smile at him. I roll over onto my side. I am disturbed, very disturbed by this dream. As I'm just about to settle again and hope for a proper sleep, Eva decides to wake with a very loud cry.

"I go," Enrico says.

"No, no, it's fine, you sleep. You need to get up for work in three hours. I'll go," I say.

I take Eva from her cot and walk to the living room. She's hungry so I heat a bottle. I watch her take the bottle like never before. She seems to be starving and looks like she'd take another one if given to her. However, I'd be afraid to fill her little belly too much and once she's finished, I wind her and she's ready to fall asleep again as her eyes close the minute I start singing to her.

Such a little angel you are. I can't believe you're mine, so small and tiny and with no worries, but a slight pain in the belly or being afraid of going hungry. Something I'd make sure would never happen to you. You look like your dad, you have his big eyes and long legs. You've even got that little dark freckle he has on the side of his face.

"Is she ok?" the voice whispers behind me.

"Don't creep up on me like that, I could have dropped her!" I say in an angry tone. I didn't mean to, he just frightened me.

"Sorry, I can't sleep, let me look after her," he says.

I feel like crap. I can't stop thinking about Pete again after that dream, and just as I was admiring how much my baby looks like him, you creep up behind me. I don't know why I'm so angry towards you. You've shown me nothing but love and affection, and are treating Eva as your own. Why? Why have I found myself in this situation? I'm tired. I need sleep, and badly. I'm going to accept your lovely offer of looking after her and go get some shut eye if I can.

I pass Eva to him and he starts humming to her. Her eyes are closed, but she's gurgling a sound of approval. She seems happy in his arms. I squeeze his shoulder, and kiss his cheek. I leave the room and head for bed again.

When I wake it's 12:30. *Why is there no noise?* I get up from the bed and there's no sign of Enrico nor of Eva. There's a note on the table for me.

> Good morning sleeping principessa! I've taken a day off
> work and I've gone with Eva for a walk on the South Bank.
> I will be back by 1:30 to take you to lunch. x

I smile. I am truly blessed. And for the first time in weeks, I don't feel tired. I needed that sleep and I'm not feeling so paranoid about that silly dream anymore either.

I hop into the shower and spruce myself up as I know Enrico will return in less than an hour. It's nice to have some me time and I get to make myself look a bit pretty again. I haven't managed to do this for a long time.

Once showered and ready to go, I realise I have thirty minutes to spare. This has never happened in my life. It normally takes me over two hours to get ready when I'm going somewhere.

The landline phone rings. "Hello?" I say.

There's silence at the other side. "Hello?" I say again.

Nothing. I hang up. *Hmmm, I wonder who that was.*

The front door opens and Enrico walks in. "Hi," he whispers as he kisses me gently on the lips. "You have a good sleep?"

"Yes, thanks, you're so good to do this. I really needed it and I'm sorry if I was in any way snappy towards you. I've been so tired of late and don't know what I'm doing," I say.

"I know you are tired. You need to rest Katie, otherwise you can't look after Eva and you will end up ill. Now, she's sleeping at the moment, but it's probably good idea to go now and keep her moving so she can get good solid sleep. I booked table for us on the South Bank as it's beautiful day out there today," he says. "You are having relax time today, eat, drink and relax. You deserve it, and I deserve a day off to spend with my two beautiful ladies," he says with a smile.

As we leave the flat, the phone rings again. I run to answer it.

"Hello?" I say.

Silence again. I'm starting to feel a bit paranoid again as I hang up. This is just all too weird, the dream, me over analysing, the silence on the phone. I don't know, something weird is going on.

"Who is?" Enrico asks.

"No one. Literally. Nobody there, probably a wrong number I suspect," I say.

We leave the flat and my mind is off working overtime again. *What if it's Pete calling me? Although why now? Why did I have that dream again and then receive two phone calls with nobody at the other end of the phone?*

"There is something wrong with you. I can tell," Enrico says as we walk holding hands, and he steers the stroller with the other.

"No there's not, honestly. Sorry, I'm just a bit confused as that's the second time I had a silent phone call this morning. It's kind of unnerving you know?" I say.

"Oh, I'm sure it's nothing. Wrong number as you said. Come now, you must have nice day today my lovely lady. Just use this time as I do have to go to work again tomorrow. So you have to enjoy today with me and little sleeping beauty there."

"I know, you're right, it's probably nothing," I say with a smile. *It is nothing, stop being so paranoid. It's nothing!* When we reach the restaurant, I check my phone, a missed call. I dare not tell Enrico as that's something that might just tip him over the edge and he might get annoyed with me. As I put the phone in my pocket, I can feel it vibrate again. No caller ID.

I answer.

"Katie? Katie? Is that you?" I hear.

"Sarah? How are you? What have you been up to, I've sent you numerous texts but they don't seem to be delivering properly. Are you in the back arse of nowhere or what?"

"Yes, you could say that. There's little or no coverage where I am. I tried calling your landline twice this morning and I could hear you, but you probably couldn't hear me. You sounded a bit panicked, like a heavy breather the second time," she says with a laugh.

You're probably right there, at least I can relax now. "Yeah, I had to rush back to answer it as was on my way out, little out of breath," I say. *Oh if only you knew! I was in shock as I thought it was Pete!*

"Ah, sorry. In answer to your question, I am indeed in the back arse of nowhere! Very little reception here, I had to get someone to drive me to the top of the town to see if I could get some few bars on the phone," she says.

"Why didn't you drive yourself?" I ask.

"Long story! Very long story which involves me crashing the hire car, but it wasn't exactly my fault. Anyway, I'll explain another time. I have news, loads of news!" she says.

"You crashed. I can hear you're ok, but are you?" I ask.

"Yeah, yeah, don't worry about that, it's all hunky dory chicken. My news, you'll be delighted to know is that I've met someone! He is lovely and funny and charming and you are all going to love him!"

"Oh wow! Fantastic, so what part of Italy is he from?" I ask. I can see Enrico's eyes growing with interest.

"He's from Sicily. Well, not from there, but he lives there. He says Sicily is his home now. I don't mind as I could make it my home, I love it here!" she says.

"Wow! Is it that serious so soon to say you'd live there?" I ask.

"Well yeah, we just clicked you know? I know, honeymoon period and all that, but he's great and we have great fun together. I really like this one," she says.

"Ok just please be careful?" I say.

"I will don....." the line dies and I smile at Enrico. "Someone's happy. Line went dead. She's met some guy who's from Sicily, but isn't from Sicily. I've no idea how long she knows him, but I know how easily she falls for men," I say with an air of worry. "I can't handle the idea of another Jarvis, and her coming home with her tail between her legs, totally depressed and the whole reason behind her going on holiday being forgotten about," I say.

"She sounds a happy. Let's not worry, she's a big girl and can look after herself. I'm sure this is good for her and if she wants to stay, it's a good experience for her at least, no?" he asks.

"True, I suppose I'm just being selfish really as can't handle the idea of having to pick up the pieces again. She's a sensitive little one like," I say.

Yes, yes but she's fine. She have learn the lesson after the Jarvis situation, I'm sure," he says.

"I hope so, I really hope so. Ok, time to order and I'm starving," I say with a smile.

Why does part of me feel disappointed that it was Sarah calling me?

38

$\mathcal{I}$t's time for me to return to work. I've been dreading this day for so long. As much as I have really grown to like my colleagues, especially from all of the support they've given me, I'm still not looking forward to leaving Eva each day. Still, it has to be done, if I want to keep a roof over our heads and provide for her properly.

I approach the office and immediately I see some of my colleagues on the way in. The ones I don't know too well smile and wave and some even shout out "Welcome back!" Tony Winters, is approaching and I feel a bit allergic. I was hoping he'd be retired by the time I got back. It's literally like a scene from a film every time I see him. He says the same thing over and over. "Good day, how are you today?" and tips his hat. He's a bit of a posh toff type, but I'll never know why he doesn't stop and have a proper conversation. I suppose it's a big deal that he even says hello to me.

With that, all I hear is "Good day, how are you today? I haven't seen you in a long time, where have you been?" he asks.

I smile and say, "Mat leave, I'm good thanks, how are you?" He starts walking away before I can even finish my sentence, though.

Ha! Some things never change! You're one strange man. I walk towards the building with a smile on my face. There are still people saluting me from a distance, it makes it look like I'm super popular. *Maybe I am, and I didn't know it?* If I am, it's after that day I looked like the Irish flag for sure. The giggles and smirks from people as I walked the corridor are something I'll never forget, ever! All down to those damn green tights when I thought I had put black ones on.

I enter the building and walk to my old desk. As I do, I spot a beautiful bouquet of flowers sitting there. I read the card. *"Welcome back Katie, we've missed you!"* I'm touched. I never thought they liked me this much. I always got an undercurrent in the office like I was the crazy Irish woman who no one liked. However, this bouquet of flowers suggests otherwise.

"Katie, matey! Welcome back," Ted says as he gives me a huge hug. "Bloody hell, I've really missed you. I've no one to throw Friday afternoon popcorn at, and you know how dry they can be here sometimes? Honestly, it's fantastic to have you back. You like the flowers?" he says with a smile.

"Ted head! I've missed you too, probably not as much as you've missed me, but such is life," I say as I playfully punch his arm. "Did you arrange for these to be delivered?" I ask.

"Yeah, I thought you deserved something on your first day back, as it can't be too easy after being away for so long," he says.

"Aww Ted, that's sweet. Thank you," I say with a huge smile. *Gosh, hold those tears back girl. These people genuinely missed me. Take a deep breath, you're a little overwhelmed right now.*

"So how are things in babyland these days?" he asks.

"Oh, she's a little angel, Ted. She's really amazing. It's exhausting, but I wouldn't change it for the world. I feel really lucky to have her and well, you know the story so it's nice to have some sort of memory of Pete to hold on to," I say with a smile.

"You seem really ok with everything that happened now. Or is that a brave face you're putting on it all?" he asks.

"No, I'm ok. As you know I'm with Enrico now, and he's been so amazing, I feel so lucky and he's such a great guy. Yeah, I'm in a good place now I think. And I'm glad you got to meet him," I say.

"You think?" he asks.

"Yeah, I mean I have feelings for him, but I don't know. I keep getting these recurring dreams that Pete is lurking outside my door and
that he's coming back to me and Eva. It's just weird. They stopped for a
while, but lately I keep getting the same dream again."

"Hmmmm, that's quite interesting. Do you think it's some sort of
premonition or something?" he asks.

"I don't know, that's the thing, I keep getting this feeling that he is
still alive somewhere," I say.

"It's a bit weird though if he is still alive. Why have you not heard
anything?" he asks.

"I know, I thought that too. I don't know what to make of it all Ted, I
really don't. Still, I just need to forget about him now I think as it could
be a case that he does remember, but doesn't want to. He's probably happy
with someone in Italy now and I don't want to come between that obviously, but I do feel that Eva needs to know who her father is one day," I say.

"Yeah, I agree. But Katie, do me a favour, if you don't love Enrico,
don't string him along. You'd break the poor guy's heart as I've seen you
both together, and he really is besotted with you," he says.

"I won't, don't worry. I'd hate to hurt him in any way," I say.

Ted touches my arm as a sign of support and says, "You know I'm
here for you whenever you need to chat."

"Thanks, Ted, I know."

As he walks away my thoughts turn to Enrico and I realise that I need
to sort my head out. I hadn't thought about it until now, but Ted is right.
*Am I being a selfish cow here? I mean what if Pete was to arrive back on the doorstep at some
stage. What would I do or say or even feel for Enrico when I'd see Pete? Would I fall into his
arms sobbing, and slobbering all over his face because I love him still? Or would I just talk to
him and treat him like a friend as he's been gone so long and I've grown close to Enrico? Oh
God! I need to get my act together!!*

"Katie, Katie, welcome back my dear and how are you?" Joe says with
great excitement and enthusiasm.

"Oh... I'm good, thanks. It's nice to see everyone again today," I say,
managing a slight smile. *You scared the daylights out of me there! I was in the middle of
contemplating if I'm an asshole girlfriend or not.* "How are you doing?" I ask.

"I'm great, but more importantly ecstatic to have you back in the office with us. You're a treasure and we've missed you greatly," he says with great aplomb. I've always got on pretty well with him, but I've never seen him so enthusiastic about me and my work before!

"Oh, thank you. That's a lovely thing to say. It's nice to know I've been missed," I say.

He nods and smiles and walks away looking like a very happy man to have me back. I know I won't do much today, it's going to be a great deal of ohhhing and ahhhing over my photos of Eva and catching up on what's been happening. However, I know in the back of my mind what Ted said to me is going to be swirling around.

He's right, Ted is bloody right as always. I'm going to have to sort this out and figure out if I love Enrico or not. He's a good guy and I don't want to mess him about in any way. Why has it taken someone to say it directly to me though, for me to actually think about this fact? I am one confused woman. I really need to sort this out.

I sit at my desk and log onto my computer. *Why on earth, even though people know I'm out of the office, do they continue to send me emails?* I have over ten thousand emails in my inbox, most are trash, but I can see names being repeated as I study the list. One of the names is Tony Winters. *Seriously, this guy has problems if he can't see that he gets an out of office reply every time he sends an email, there's something missing there.* I trawl through them as best I can, deleting most as they are probably obsolete at this stage anyway. It's eleven o'clock and I decide to head to the canteen to grab a coffee and scone. One of the things I missed is a nice freshly made scone from here; they are so delicious I could eat them for breakfast, lunch and dinner. As I walk into the canteen, I see one of the girls approaching. *Oh no! Why do you have to be the first person I see in here?* Judy Wells, the biggest gossip in the company, and possibly the world, bordering on being the biggest shit stirrer. *I really can't handle you right now. Take a deep breath, here she comes.*

"Oh Katie, how are you? Tell me all about your gorgeous little girl. Eva, isn't that what you called her?" she says.

Well, you don't miss out on much information, do you? "Yeah Judy, her name is Eva, and she's wonderful. She's so bright and funny and I just love her to bits. Thanks for asking," I say as I try to walk away.

"Oh wait, and what about your boyfriend, any news of him? Did you find him, or did he return? Or didn't he want to come back?" she asks.

I can feel my eyes growing large as I look at her. It's annoyed me so much that Pete's accident was on the news. I wanted to keep it quiet as people didn't know I was with him. I wanted to avoid all of these nosey loser types, feeding their gossiping habits. I try to bite my tongue, but she is being incredibly insensitive so I decide not to hold back.

"Excuse me? Did you just ask me a very personal question about Pete? Yes, Pete was, or is his name! For starters, do you know what the word personal means? I don't and won't share anything of my personal life with you, or anyone else who likes to gossip here. It's absolutely none of your business!! So, why don't you go home tonight, look in the mirror and tell yourself what an asshole you are for asking me a question like that. It's insensitive, it's personal and you're just trying to feed your gossiping habits and friends. So just piss off and don't annoy me," I say and run out of the canteen, forgetting about my scone. I run to the ladies, and lock myself in one of the cubicles. I breathe deeply and heavily for a few minutes. I've never lashed out at someone like that before and then I start to cry. I hear a knock on the outside door.

"Katie, are you in here?" the male voice says.

Ted? Is that Ted?

"Yeah, Ted is that you?" I ask before I open the cubicle door.

"Yes, get your ass out here and let's find an office," he says.

"Ok," I say sheepishly. *Oh please don't have a go at me, Ted. I didn't mean to lash out at her.*

I open the door and see him standing there smiling and then he bursts into laughter and starts applauding.

"That was fucking brilliant, Katie, the place erupted with laughter. Someone has finally put Judy in her place, nosey cow," he says as he opens his arms to give me a hug.

"Oh Ted," I say with a giggle. "I actually feel really bad. I've never had an outburst like that in my life and I've no idea why I did now."

"We all know why you did. She's a nosey cow as I said, and all she's interested in is hurting people and causing misery. Honestly, if you stayed around, you would have had a standing ovation. Even Joe had the biggest grin on his face, it was epic work Katie!" he says as he cradles me in his arms.

"Really? Wow, so it's not just me that dislikes the woman then? Hmmm, I don't feel so bad now. Still, she's not crying in some corner or something is she?" I ask.

"No, you don't need to tell that woman to grow a pair. Brass monkey she is. She sat down eating her cake, bold as brass and carried on gossiping. No shame, Katie, no shame. I wonder how sad her own life is sometimes to say she is the way she is. I mean, have you ever realised that absolutely nobody knows anything about *her* life, yet she knows every detail about everyone else's?" he says.

"Yeah that's true and on that note, do you think she knows the full story about me and Pete? How I went searching for him in Italy?" I ask.

"I definitely didn't tell her anything. I wouldn't be so stupid as to open my mouth, you know that, right?" he says.

"No, I know you wouldn't. Besides, I'd punch you in the nuts if you did," I say with a giggle.

"Well, after witnessing what I just saw, I wouldn't be surprised one bit," he says.

"But I'm just trying to figure out how she would know so much. It's not like there was a whole massive story on the news about it. It was all very vague. It must have been one of the girls. I know one of them was there when I was telling Evelyn one day before I went on maternity leave. I know she wouldn't say anything either, but I had a feeling this girl was ear wigging. I've seen her talking with Judy a few times in the past. I think she might have overheard. I really need to be more careful," I say.

"Look, it doesn't matter now. It's out in the open, people obviously know if motor mouth knows and you know what, it might not be such a bad thing if people are aware of your circumstances. At least you won't have to avoid awkward questions now," he says.

"Yeah, I understand what you're saying. Ted, since you mentioned it this morning, all I can think about is my whole situation with Enrico, and what if Pete came back. It made me realise that I need to sort my head out a bit. Thanks for saying that to me, I think it's something someone should have pointed out a long time ago. I didn't realise how selfish I was being, to be honest with you."

"I didn't say it to upset you, ok? You need to know that. You are an important friend and colleague and I'm just looking out for you as you're not a bad person, but I know with everything that happened, you could just be swept up in the whole romance side of it. I know you, and you're probably trying to make yourself believe that this is what you want, and that it's all ok. But I can tell by your lack of talking about Enrico that you aren't that into him. Also from the way you look when someone mentions Pete's name, that look of hope that he'll come back to you. You're a good person, if you don't love Enrico, tell him, Katie. He'll thank you later for the honesty and for not letting it go on longer," he says.

You're right. I don't love Enrico. I never have and never will. I have to finish it with him. How did I get to this point?

"Ok, I'll do it. You're right. I'm probably going to be feeling pretty crap for the next few weeks so going to need that male ear to bend." "That's fine. I'm not telling you to break up with him. I'm asking you to think about how you're feeling and figure out what's right here. If you're not feeling it, you need to think about doing something, however, if you do love him then stick with it all. He's a good guy, just don't mess him around, that's all I'm saying," Ted says.

"Ted, if I didn't know better, I'd say you fancy him!" I say with a smile.

"Oh of course I do! He's bloody gorgeous, but not my type and he's not gay so there goes that idea. Besides, I think Roger would be a bit jealous if he thought I fancied another man. You know what, missy, I think you should go home, as not only do I think you're missing Eva, but I also think you've had enough of this place for one day. I don't know, go shopping on your way home and treat yourself to a new handbag or shoes or something. You need a treat from time to time, and I know Joe won't object to you heading home early. Especially after witnessing the incident," he says.

"Hmmmm, I'm not sure I should do that, but I am pretty pissed off already. By the way, you do realise you're still standing here in the ladies loos for over fifteen minutes now?" I ask.

"So I am. Do you think that would stop them entering? I'm harmless for goodness sake," he says with a laugh.

"No, I think they all know they're safe enough with you. I think we should head out, though. Thanks Ted. I'm not sure what I'd do without you today. You're the best," I say.

We walk out of the ladies and up the corridor into the office again. I feel ashamed as I do enter, but when I see the smirks on everyone's face I can't help but laugh. "Oh stop it all of you, I feel bad enough already," I say.

My boss approaches. "Bossman, would you mind if I head home? I'm sorry, I know I'm just in, but my head is a little all over the place at the moment," I say.

"Of course, off you go, take the rest of the day. I'm sure you're missing your little one already. You know you don't have to do full days for now, if you prefer to ease yourself back into it, that's fine with me Katie. I just want to keep you happy and keep you here as I would be sad if you left completely," he says.

"Thank you. I'll think about it and call you later if that's ok? I just need to get my head around a few things and you know if I can sort that out today, I can see about the hours for tomorrow and the rest of the week," I reply.

"That's fine, take your time, if you want to come in later or earlier or whatever suits and do half days this week, just let me know," he says.

I'm so lucky! Where else would you get people who understand what's going on? I can't believe I thought they weren't keen on me and that I was some sort of gobshite, when clearly they have masses of time for me and adore me. I'm just too paranoid at times.

"Thanks, I'll head now and call you later," I say as I touch his arm in a gesture of thanks.

I leave the office as quickly as I can. I decide a nice walk along the South Bank might just be what I need now. It's the first day in months I don't have Eva with me, and as I have a child minder for a few more hours, I may as well avail of the 'me' time as I don't get too much of that of late. As I cross the river, the sun is hot and there's little air to breathe in. It's a little too hot for me, but my skin is tanning nicely, even with a high sun factor on and I'm enjoying feeling a nice summer buzz around London. As I walk across London Bridge the light breeze that's blowing is very welcome. The bridge is becoming more crowded with tourists who all look a little deflated from the unexpected heat wave we are having. I find it a little frustrating as I try to walk past them, as they stand there like statues on the bridge.

Eventually, I manage to get across, and I decide a little walk along the river bank will suit nicely. As it's a Tuesday, it doesn't seem as crowded as it might on a Sunday, and so I manage to get a bench to sit on near the City Hall. It's been a while since I've had this time out and this is my favourite place to sit. It's my spot. I watch the river boats as they pass by, full to the brim with tourists. They wave at me as they pass by. One of the boats has music blaring from it, the onboard party boat.

Ha! I was on one of those with Sarah years ago, we nearly killed ourselves getting on and off and up and down deck as we were wearing heels. Big eejits we were. That was good fun though. I think I need to start ringing around and getting back out there. I haven't seen a lot of my friends in a while, and now that Eva is a bit cuter and alert, I think I might just be able to swing the odd evening out to see some old friends. Yes, I need to sort my life out. I need to tell Enrico that I don't love him. Tears form in my eyes as I think about him. *I'm going to break his heart. How can I do this to him? But then again, I'm worse to not be honest with him. I have to tell him, it's ten times worse to let him believe that I am in love with him. I need to break up now before he gets too attached to Eva, and before she starts to call him 'dada' like he keeps saying to her. I just don't know how I've ended up here, how?*

I take a tissue from my bag and blow my nose. Thankfully I have sunglasses on so people may just think I have hayfever, at least I hope so. The last thing I want is some do-gooder coming towards me, asking me what's wrong. I look at my watch, and it's almost five o'clock. *Feck! I've been sitting here for nearly three hours.* I look at my arms and they are a lovely dark shade of brown, and my legs have also tanned nicely. I'm so lucky that I tan so easily as poor Sarah is like a milk bottle next to me. While

I get excited for a few minutes about how good my tan looks, I realise I have to go and face the music. Enrico will be back shortly. Maybe I need more time to think though rather than jump right in and tell him. So as I wander home, I decide I'll wait until tomorrow or maybe even the weekend before I make my mind up. *What if I do love him, but I've just taken too much notice of what Ted has said to me? I need to spend more time thinking this through I'm sure I'll come to a decision by the weekend and will know how I'm really feeling.*

When I reach the flat, I can hear movement inside so realise that Eva is up and is gargling and making some sort of noise. I love this stage as it's like she's trying to chat. I open the door and Natalie, my child minder is there smiling. "Oh look who's home, Eva! Mummy is home," she says with a massive smile.

"Oh my little baby, how I've missed you today," I say. *I have missed you angel, but I did need that little bit of time to myself.* "Natalie, you're so good, thanks so much. I hope she didn't cause too much trouble?" I ask.

"Trouble? She's an absolute angel, this one. She's been singing, smiling, gargling and dribbling all day," she says. "Think she has more teeth on the way, but she's just dribbling, no crying out of her, though. She's been in top form," she says with a smile. "But, I can see someone is very happy that mummy is home," she says as she hands her to me.

As I take her in my arms, just the smell of her sends a beautiful feeling through me. I feel like I'm whole again when I hold her and that everything will be fine. I kiss her gently on the cheek and forehead and then say goodbye to Natalie. "Oh beautiful little Eva, what's your crazy mother going to do with her life? She needs to sort herself out, yes she does," I say as I laugh when she gargles up at me with a big grin on her face. *I'm so lucky to have you.*

39

"Morning beautiful principessa," Enrico says as he wakes me from my sleep. *Oh, I know what you want and now is not the time at all. Let me figure out what's going on with me before I do anything with you again, please?*

"Oh lovely, I'm so tired. I need to sleep," I say.

He sighs. "Ok, you sleep. I get up as want to make the most of my day," he says as he throws the duvet back.

You're pissed off now. I need to make a decision. I'm really not feeling this at all. I watch him as he walks to the hallway and into the bathroom. He's definitely pissed off. He never uses the shower there unless he's annoyed with me. It's like he wants his space then so goes to another zone or area. I can't blame him. I'd be annoyed too. We haven't been close in well over a month and it's mainly my fault. *Hang on now, he was tired once or twice, and I didn't get angry with him. Why the hell do men have to be so huffy and puffy if they don't get their way? Oh, who am I kidding, I just need to get this conversation out of the way, I might be less tired at least and get a decent sleep again… maybe.*

I hop up from the bed and go to the kitchen as I know that's where his next port of call will be. I sit there drumming my fingers on the countertop nervously as I listen until I hear the water stop running in the shower. *Oh God! Here he comes.*

"Oh, I thought you were tired?" he asks quite sarcastically.

"I am, Enrico, I am. I do need to talk to you, though," I say in a sad tone.

He rubs his face in his hands.

He knows. Oh, God. Are those tears forming already?

"You don't need to say, Katie," he sniffs. "I know you don't love me."

My heart has just sunk right to the bottom of my body. My eyes fill with tears and I don't know how to tell him that it's true. I sniff and take a deep breath.

"Enrico, I'm sorry. I am trying so hard and you've been the most amazing and fantastic man any girl could ask for, but the whole circumstances of us getting together, I just don't know, it was never right. I don't know if I'll ever get over Pete and I don't think it's fair to you that I continue like this with you. As I said you are a fantastic man and if circumstances were different, I'm sure, in fact I'm certain that I would love you as much as you do Eva, and me. However, in the long term, we both know that if one of us isn't happy, the other won't be either," I declare.

"I won't pretend I am not upset or angry Katie. I have make great efforts here for you, and Eva. I love her like she's mine. But, it's my own fault as I know for a long time that you have not feelings for me in same way I have for you, but I hope that one day you will have this feelings," he replies.

I want to hug you so hard right now. I walk towards him and pull him close and hug him so tightly. "The last thing I ever wanted to do was hurt you, Enrico. You are such a special guy in every way and deserve the best. However, I'm not the best. You'll find someone far better than me. I've got baggage and lots of it. You don't need that or me in your life, my sweet," I utter.

He says nothing, just hugs me tight and his wet cheek brushes against mine. I feel like such a horrible person right now. He pushes me away and wipes his face on his t-shirt. "I'll pack my bags and go," he says.

What have I done? Oh dear God, help me here, have I made a mistake? I stand in the kitchen and watch him walk to the bedroom with his head hung low. I've never seen him like this before and my heart aches to see him in such a state. Bad as I feel, I think this is the right decision to make. He would hurt ten times more if I left it go on for longer and then decide to break up. I hear Eva cry. *Perfect timing, I wonder if she knows that the man she's grown so fond of is leaving her life and it's all my fault?* I go to pick her up from her cot. I sit with her for a while in my arms and cry myself until I realise the more I'm crying, the more she's crying and so, I stop. She's still crying, but it's faint and then her cry turns into a gurgle and a smile. All I can do is smile back at her. Such an innocent little creature, so beautiful and her little smile would melt your heart.

"Can I hold her before I go?" Enrico asks as he pops his head around the door.

I look at him and smile. "Of course you can silly," I say as I rub his shoulder. "You know, I don't want you to stop calling to see her. I mean, if you want to that is?" I ask.

"I will see. She is an angel, and I will miss her so much. I will miss you so much, but I understand. Everything happens for a reason Katie, I'm not sure what the reason of us meeting was, but maybe one day I'll know," he says as he kisses Eva on the cheek and hands her back to me. "Goodbye Katie," he says as he kisses me on the forehead. "I'll never forget you," he adds.

There's a tug in my heart and part of me wants to scream out *"Enrico, don't go!"* But something is stopping me from saying that. He opens the door, and looks at me before he closes it behind him. He has a look of sadness, of heart breaking sadness. He's gone.

I head back towards the kitchen with Eva, cradling her close to me as the tears fall. I realise that I am now on my own, and I feel lost. I look at Eva who's smiling up at me. She seems to sense when I need her to smile, and cheer me up.

I smile down at her in my arms, "Just you and me now kiddo. I hope that I've made the right decision, and can give you all the love that you need my little cherub," I say to her as I look at her cute chubby cheeks. It's like she senses what I've said as she smiles up at me. She starts to gurgle and tell me a story.

I do wonder what's going through that little mind of yours, are you trying to tell me what you think? Do you understand what I'm saying and doing? I wander back to the living room and sit with Eva in my arms. She seems content and as she dozes off again, I can't help but feel that sense of loss again. *What the fuck have I done?*

40

*I*t's Monday morning and I'm feeling a bit apprehensive about having a full day at work today, especially after the weekend's events. I wander into the office and immediately Ted approaches.

"He's gone isn't he?" he asks.

"What? How can you tell? Have you seen him?" I question.

"No, but your poor eyes look puffy, like you've been crying, and you look sad. Let's grab a coffee in the canteen," he says.

"Ok, as long as Judy isn't around. I'll be likely to box her today if she comes near me," I say, and manage a smile.

"Oh, you're still in there, good to see you haven't lost that fiery side of you. No, she's on holiday thankfully. Coffee?" he asks as we enter the canteen.

"Yes please, could do with a whole pot to myself today!" I declare.

"Here, a whole pot just for you," he says with a smile. "Ok, my lovely, tell me all. What's gone on, I do hope it was your decision?" he asks.

"Yes, yes it was all my doing, and now I'm wondering if I did the right thing. I haven't slept in a week practically. I was thinking about it all up to now and well, you saw I wasn't feeling it one hundred percent. So, I mentioned it to him on Saturday morning. He was upset. He knew it was coming, but I think he was hoping for the best rather than the worst," I say.

"Aww bless him, he is a sweetheart I have to say, but only you know yourself if it was the right thing to do my love," he says.

"I know, and part of me thinks it was the right thing to do, but when I saw those tears running down his face, and then when he walked out that door, with me left holding Eva, I started to regret it immediately. Now, a couple of days on, I'm still upset and crying a lot and I'm wondering if maybe I did love him, but it took this for me to realise it? Am I mad?"

"Of course not look everyone has regrets when they break up with someone, and it's not always regret, it's just sadness, a sadness you're bound to feel because you've spent so much time with that person, and because they were a big part of your life for a while. Don't worry Katie. I think you've most likely done the right thing. And if you feel sad or different about it all in a few weeks, then maybe you can contact him and ask to meet up. See how he feels then, because you know, if he's out on his own now, he might be making more effort to make more friends and meet new people and may discover he's happy like that," he says.

"Thanks! Make me feel ten times better telling me he's probably going to prefer having a life without a woman with baggage," I say.

"Noooooo silly! You know I don't mean it like that. I mean that in a few weeks, you might or might not decide that this was a good decision. It could turn out that you might think it's great. You could always contact him and see how he feels later. He might feel the same after the dust settles. But, it could also mean that you love him, and realise what you had. You might want him back, and he might gladly come back. Or you both might just end up as good friends yet, wait it out. Give it time. Sorry, I hope I made myself a bit clearer there as that's what I meant?" he says.

"Yeah, I understand now. I get what you're saying and you speak sense as always. Thanks Ted. You're a good pal to have. I'm not sure what I'd do without you as you know what, Sarah is gone with months now and I'm not sure she's coming back. Laura has still been a bit distant since Eva was born and since that run in Sarah had with Jarvis. I only have three, what I would class as very good friends that I would tell anything to and you're one of them. Thank you," I say as I hug him.

"Oh Katie, you know you're my favourite female and if I was straight I'd want to marry you. You are such a perfect woman in my eyes," he says.

I grin. "You make me feel like trying to turn you now," I say with a giggle.

"Oh honey, it'll never happen. I love men. Sorry, I love a man, my boyfriend. I have to be careful what I say, he might get jealous," he says.

"Ok, so what do you suggest I do next? I had that weird dream about Pete again last night," I say.

"Really? Katie, I don't know, I think that means something definitely. Maybe you're meant to go in search of him again?" he suggests.

"No way! Ted, there is no way on this earth I'm going trekking to Italy or anywhere else again in search of him. I feel like an idiot at this stage for doing it initially. I most certainly am not going to take a baby with me this time. I'd be a lunatic to do that. Tempting as it sounds," I say.

"Come on Katie, I'll go with you," he says enthusiastically.

"No! Final, no, no, no! It's too much hassle and then the result will be that I'm upset again at the end of it all," I say.

"Fine, but don't ever say that I didn't offer to help you try and find him. I suppose you're right though and I couldn't handle knowing that I upset you making you go there in search of him," Ted says.

"It's a nice idea, but no, I need to let sleeping dogs lie as they say, for now anyway. You know, it might not be such a bad idea when Eva is a bit older. I don't mean like seven or eight where she'll understand completely. But, one day, I wouldn't mind going to see if we can track him down when she's still not old enough to understand what's going on. At least then if it backfires again, she won't be too upset because she never knew him anyway. I want her to know her father, though, I feel she needs to know him," I say. "I just have this gut feeling he's still alive you know? I can't explain why I feel this, but it seems really positive," I say.

"True, I think she needs to know him too. They say the gut instinct is never wrong Katie. I'll happily go sunning myself in Italy with you two whenever you want me to," he says with a smile.

"Oh Ted, I do love you. You know sometimes I do wish you were straight. We'd make a good husband and wife," I say with a giggle.

"Hmmmm, I fear I might not be man enough for you, even if I were. You like muscley manly guys and even if I were straight, I wouldn't fall into that category I'd say. For now, though, let's leave it as best buds, what say you, sexy lady?" he asks.

I giggle like a child. "I say yes, baby!"

We both start laughing and I feel slight relief come over me as I feel like I'm releasing the negative energy that seems to be surrounding me of late.

"Ok, think it's time us two skivers go back to work," Ted says.

"Yeah, I feel I've taken the piss big time of late."

"No darling, the day you came in dressed like a leprechaun is the day you took the piss," he says with a peal of laughter.

"Feck off! You know I have a lack of natural lighting in the flat,' I say, laughing. "I'll never live that one down, will I?" I ask.

"Not a chance my lovely! Not a chance! But at least you take it all with a pinch of salt. I only take the pee out of you because you never get offended. That's why I love you so much," he says.

"Ahhhhh, Ted, you're like my little knight in shining armour. Come on, before Joe sends out a search party for us," I say as I get up from my seat and hold my hand out to grab his. Instead, he just pulls me closer and walks with his arm around me down the corridor. *Ted, I love you, you're the best friend anyone could ask for.*

We wander into the office and of course as we do, shouts of "Skivers, where the hell 'ave you been?" come from across the office. "Piss off twat," Ted says with a laugh.

I feel lucky as while I never felt I fitted in at the beginning, the banter in the office seems far better than what it used to be before I went on maternity leave. For the first time in days, or even weeks, I suddenly sense that a burden or pain has been lifted from my shoulders. While I feel that I've lost something great in Enrico, I feel relieved to have spoken to someone about it and Ted has made me realise that I might just have done the right thing. The relief is massive and one thing is for sure, time will tell if I have done the right thing or not. I also know now, that Ted will always be there for me, and he is someone I should have had more contact with throughout my whole pregnancy. He is a solid friend to have. *I need to appreciate my friends more.*

41

$\mathcal{I}$t's two months later. I've had what can only be described as spo-
radic contact from Sarah lately. She calls when she can, and I
understand she doesn't have the coverage she'd like to. However,
part of me feels that maybe she's using that as an excuse as she's obviously
very loved up with this new guy of hers. I'm happy for her, but I'd love to
hear or see her again soon.

It's a Friday morning and I'm glad it's the weekend at last. I arrive at
work and Ted is sitting at his desk and laughing to himself. I walk towards him.

"What are you giggling at?" I ask and can't help but laugh myself as
Ted's laugh is very infectious.

"Oh I'm just watching some YouTube videos here and they are hilarious. Watch this!" he says as he turns the screen towards me.

I see his point, I can't stop laughing and what's worse is that he points
out someone who looks like Tony Winters in the background. "So that's
what he does in his spare time!" I say.

"Oh God, I'll get fired. I know it's Friday, but I have that Friday feeling at such an early hour. Funny how the mood changes so easily when
you know it's the weekend and party time. I'd better do some work," he
says.

I smile at him and shake my head. He's such a fun person. I'd love to join him in his fun after work, but I can't. I'll need to get home and let the child minder free for her weekend fun. I can't complain, I've had enough years of going out after work, and on the odd occasion not remembering things the next day... it was embarrassing to say the least especially when I started getting flashbacks to the events of the night before.

I sit at my desk, and when I switch on my computer all I can see as the screensaver is a photo of a beach. I don't know where it is, but it looks divine and somewhere I'd like to be. *Maybe I should go visit Sarah? Eva is old enough to travel now, not a bad idea at all.* I, like Ted, haven't much interest in work this morning so I open up Google and do a search for flights to Italy just to see what it would cost.

That's a bit expensive right now — three hundred and fifty pounds for the flights alone. Accommodation on top would be expensive too, especially if I'm thinking of going within the next few weeks. Nah, I'll leave it. No point in spending money I could spend on Eva. She's too young to enjoy a holiday anyway and I suppose it might be a bit warm for her there at the moment. My thoughts go from a holiday in Italy to wondering how Enrico is and if he's still in the UK. I heard from him after that night he left, he was staying at a work mate's house, but I haven't heard anything since. *Maybe I'll call him later to see how he is.*

The day drags on very, very slowly. I'm delighted when my phone rings as I'm hoping it might be someone who will distract me for a bit and help the time to move on.

"Hello?" I say, but there's silence from the other side.

"Hello," I say again. Nothing. I hang up. For some odd reason, I think of Pete again and wonder if it could be him. It rings again. I'm a bit apprehensive about answering and then the thought strikes me. *It could be Sarah. Stupid idiot Katie, why on earth would you think it was Pete, you know it was Sarah who called the last time.*

I answer, "Hello?"

"Doll face, it's me, Sarah! How are you?" she says.

I smile. "Hey lady, what the hell have you been up to? You've been very silent!"

"I know and I'm so sorry Katie. I've been meaning to call you, but you know how things are here with trying to get coverage and also, well, I've been a bit forgetful as I get otherwise occupied sometimes," she says with a giggle.

"Oh, I can imagine. I was actually just looking at flights to Italy for myself and Eva. I was thinking it would be nice to make a trip over to see you, but it's a bit pricey and I can't really justify paying that right now, especially when Eva can't even appreciate it all," I say.

"No, no, don't come over now, because I'm coming to see you, my lovely!"

"Oh, really? That's great, when are you coming?" I ask.

"It'll be four weeks time, so get Eva ready for an onslaught of hugs and cuddles as I am dying to see her again," she says.

I can feel the smile creep across my face, this is exactly what I need and want. To have Sarah around again, even for a few days, would be wonderful. I've missed her greatly, especially as she's gone well over her three month stint away now. I have a strange feeling she may think about staying in Italy.

"Fantastic! She'll be delighted to receive them. You won't recognise her she's grown so much, Sarah. I'm worried I'm over feeding her. She's not fat, but she's a big baby. She's such a cutie though, full of smiles, gurgles, and little stories now. You'll be shocked at how much she's changed," I say with pride. "I tried a few times to send some photos to your phone but they won't send. When are you going to move to a place with proper coverage, lady?" I ask.

"I've no plans to move Katie. It's one of the things I love about where I am. I was so reliant on a phone in London, and now I just realise how amazing and simple life is again without one. Besides, I really don't need a phone when everything is a stone's throw from me. Well, apart from staying in contact with you of course! I feel bad in that respect and I can only imagine how much Eva has grown. That's the downside of this whole trip. How are you and Enrico doing?" she asks.

"Ah, well that's a story I need to tell you over a glass of wine. Enrico is gone, Sarah," I say with sadness.

"Oh fuck! What? Why? Tell me briefly now!" she demands.

"Look, he's lovely, and he's wonderful. Some girl out there really deserves the love he's got to give, but I love Pete, and I always will. I can't believe he's gone. I have this weird feeling he's coming back to me one day. I know the chances are slim, but I have this hope inside of me that just doesn't fade ever. Until I get an answer as to what happened to him or where he is, I will always believe he is still alive and just living his life, not knowing he has a little girl, and me here in London," I utter.

"Katie, I'm so sorry to hear that. I think, though, to be fair, you gave it a good chance and you'll never give up on Pete as you'll always believe he's somewhere out there until you're proven otherwise. I think it was the right thing to do — assuming you did the breaking?"

"Yeah, yeah, it was all me. He sensed it was coming. He said he knew I was still in love with Pete. He was just hoping that one day, I might realise that Pete wasn't coming back and that I'd fall for him. But I can't give up hope. My gut instinct says he's still alive. I can't live a lie and pretend that I love Enrico, it would be wrong for everyone and very unfair," I say.

"You're right girl. Good on you as it must have been difficult considering how great he's been with Eva. You know what, you're a very brave woman, and I'm not sure what I'd do if I was in your shoes. You're so strong all the time and no matter what you never forget that you have a little baby to look after. Be proud of yourself girl, you're a great mother," Sarah says.

"Thanks, girl. So, moving on from that as I've been feeling like crap over it for the past while and it's happy Friday today! So, what's the plan? Are you going to stay with me when you're here?" I ask.

"Emm, no actually I'm not. I'm bringing lover boy with me so we've booked a hotel," she says.

"Oh wow! That's a big deal, must be very serious?" I ask.

"Yeah, it's free flowing, but becoming more serious definitely. He's great. I know you'll love him. He's quite cheeky and fun. I haven't met anyone like him before. He's different for me, and he has a beard! You know me, I don't go for guys with beards normally, but I like it on him.

He's sexy and cool and I don't know. You'll see what I mean when you meet him," she says.

"Oooohh, someone's in lurve. He sounds great. So, what's his name? You got cut off the last time I wanted to ask you about him," I say.

"Drifter, he is affectionately known as! He's very chilled and relaxed and funny and sexy and oh I have to say I am loving this guy big time. He's just perfect in every way, shape and form. No bullshit, just straight up honesty and just fun, you know?" she says.

"I know what you mean. He sounds great! I can't wait to meet him. Bit of a strange name though. What's his real name?" I ask.

"He doesn't use his old name any more. He didn't tell me what it is. I think there's a bit of history there which he'd like to forget about so I don't pry too much. Yeah, I know, it is strange, but he is a bit of a drifter so it's just stuck," she says.

"So, why is he there, what does he do there?" I ask.

"He works with the local fisherman and leads a simple life, which I really like. As I said, he doesn't want to talk about his life before he met me too much. I'm his new start and that's fair enough to be honest, as I don't really want to have to talk about Jarvis to him either. Drifter is my fresh start too. Listen, I have to go again. You'll be around I assume then?" she asks.

"Most definitely! Sure, where will I be going with a baby? I'll definitely put that holiday on hold now," I say with a laugh. "You go chicken, and I'll talk to you soon. Just, just call more often please? Every time I try to contact you, I get one of those Italian voice messages," I say.

"I know and I'm sorry, that message says that I have my unit powered off or am out of coverage...funny that! I'll definitely call, at least once a week if not more from here on in. I'd love to Facetime but I'd say I'll be pushing my luck with that," she says.

I laugh heartily. "True, but just call some evening so I can put the phone to Eva's ear, she might not understand, but at least she might recognise your voice when you do come to visit," I say.

"You're right and I'm sorry for being a rubbish friend. I'll call again during the week if I can, ok?" she says.

"Sure, that sounds good. You go now and thanks for calling," I say.

"Bye, speak soon... Ok Drifter, I'll be with you now," I hear her shout to him in the background.

"Bye, talk soon. Bye, bye, bye, bye," I say in my usual Irish habit.

I hang up. *And I was just thinking about you this morning, how strange that you rang me now. Jesus though, Drifter? I hope he's not a member of the Mafia or a big drug lord or something. He sounds a bit dodgy to me. She could do without getting into any trouble. She's had enough to deal with this year.*

I smile to myself. "Ted, Ted," I shout across the room as I get up from my seat. "Guess who just called me!" I say.

"No idea, do tell," he says.

"That was Sarah!" I say with glee.

"You haven't heard from that chica in a long time. Where is she these days? Travelling still or sitting pretty in the mountains or hills or wherever she is, with no coverage?" he asks.

"Yeah, she's still there, but the great thing is, she's coming to visit in four weeks time!" I say with a little squeal of excitement.

"That's so cute. I haven't seen you this excited in a long time. I'm glad. This is going to give you a massive boost, and it's just what you need," he says. "Plenty of girlie nights out and who knows, you might meet a nice beau while you're on the town. Oh Katie, it's all going to happen for you now," he says.

I smile. "No it's not, I can hardly go on the town with a baby in tow."

"Baby in tow? My girl, Uncle Ted will be looking after baby so mummy can go and have a yummy mummy time, because that's just what she is!"

"Ted, really? You'd want to look after Eva for me, while I hit the town? You do know she could start crying profusely, and drive you slightly crazy, as you have little or no experience with babies?" I ask.

"Oh Katie, come on. I'll be fine with her. I've got two nephews and I've been trusted with them plenty of times before. She's loved me anytime she's met me. I might not have masses of experience with babies, but any I've come in contact with adore me. They sleep the night away or even if they wake they just ooh, ahh and smile at me. I've just got one of those faces that they adore," he says with a laugh.

"You know what, you'd better be careful or you'll walk yourself into a permanent babysitting slot," I say with laughter. "Thanks, Ted, I might just take you up on that. I could do with a night out, it's been a long time since I've had one," I say feeling pleased. "Now it's almost time for elevenses, and I haven't done a tap all morning, I better skip coffee and get on with things," I say.

"Oh, for God's sake woman, it's Friday. Look around you, there are five people in the office. Your own boss isn't even here. Let's just take it easy and go for coffee, sister," he says as he grabs his wallet from his jacket. "Coffee and scones on me today, it's payday," he says with a grin as we walk towards the canteen.

42

The weeks are passing quickly and I've managed to catch up with quite a lot of people who I haven't seen in a while. Eva was with me each time. She's as good as gold, and not a peep from her most of the time. She's becoming more responsive by the day, and it's incredibly satisfying to see her grow and learn. I'm getting very excited now as Sarah is due to visit in a week, and true to her word she's called as many times as possible since her grand announcement.

I'm in the kitchen pottering about when I realise I really need to give the place a good scrub. If I don't do it now, I won't have time later, and I want the place to look clean and tidy when Sarah gets here. I head out to the shops and call to Edith and Eddie on my way. They are so good to Eva, they spoil her rotten. They've been an amazing support to me and very encouraging through this whole business of Pete disappearing.

"Edith, how are you? Some small lady wanted to call to see you today. She's in great form and wanted to give you all her smiles and hugs," I say with a smile.

"Oh that little beauty, she's such a mix of both you and Pete, it's just beautiful to see. She's growing up so fast. Before you know it, she'll be toddling, then school. Then she'll be working 'ere to look after the shop for us and wanting money to save for CD's or whatever it is they listen to these days," she says.

"It's more Spotify and iTunes these days. All downloads I'm afraid. I'm sure it'll be far more advanced again by then," I say.

"I just don't know about all this modern technology stuff. All I can say is bring back days where a child would bounce a tennis ball off a wall and make a game from it or play board games. Or simply kick a ball around the street. It's just gone too far these days. They'll all have glasses before they're even six. I just don't understand it. Oh here, let me have a squeeze from her, she's just a little doll," she says.

"She loves your hugs. You're like a pacifier. Although saying that, she's so good anyway, never any trouble at all," I say.

"Have you heard from Enrico at all? He's not gone back to Italy 'as he?" she asks.

"No, I heard from him a couple of days later. Think he felt bad and contacted me as I had left numerous messages wanting to know if he was ok. You know how it is, when you break up with someone, it can be devastating, and I know he was really upset. So was I, but I know he was heartbroken. I was really worried about him. So, I must have left around ten messages on his phone over the first three days. I was probably like a stalker, but I needed to know he was ok. Being a typical male he ignored them and made me sweat. Then he called me letting me know he was at a workmate's house I was relieved, but I haven't heard anything since," I say with sadness.

"Oh love, he is heartbroken. I think he thought you two would marry one day. I do think you did the right thing though as if you let it go on any longer, who knows how horrible an ending it would have been. You did well love and don't ever think otherwise. I'm sure you must miss him a little, though?" she asks.

"Yeah, of course I do. And I feel bad for Eva as she's used to seeing him, then suddenly two months ago he was gone. Who knows what she's thinking. She might not care, but she loved when he used to pick her up and cuddle her or make stupid faces at her, especially as she started to become more aware of everything around her. But, as you said, I think I made the right decision. I did say he can visit when he wants to see her. I can understand though, if he doesn't want to. I mean, why would he want to see Eva, especially when I don't feel the same way about him, as he does about me? It doesn't make any sense whatsoever," I say.

"Hmm, that's true love, very true. So where you off to today?" she asks.

"Oh just some shopping, thought it would be nice to call and see you on the way as I know you like to see the little princess as often as possible. Listen, you know you can call by whenever. I'd love to see you. Actually, where's Eddie?" I ask.

"He's a bit sick love. He's in the hospital at the moment, but should be home within the next few days I hope," she says.

"Oh no! You can't keep these things to yourself! Make sure you let me know if this happens again. How long is he in?" I ask.

"'Bout two weeks now, but he's good. I'll be 'appy to have him home," she says.

"Listen, I'm so sorry. It's only at times like this I realise how time consuming a little child can be. But if you need help in any way at all, let me know please?" I ask. "I'll bring Eva with me to mind the shop if I have to, I don't care. What have you been doing? Have you had someone to mind the shop?" I ask.

"Yes, yes, our kids have been down. Don't you worry at all, you've got yourself a little one to look after, and I've got my little ones looking after us, so don't you worry chuck. It's all fine and I will say, he'll be looking forward to seeing you and little Eva when he's home," she says as she tickles Eva under the chin.

I'm a bad neighbour. I need to get a more structured life. It's only now I realise they could be dead, and I wouldn't know it. Is it really that long since I've called to see her? Right that's it. No more pining for Pete, no more feeling bad over Enrico. I need to sort myself out and that's it.

"Here love, you head off for your walk and shopping," she says as she hands Eva to me. "You'll need to get going as the shops close soon enough and I don't want my gabbing on to stop you from getting what you need," she says.

"Ok, thanks. I'll pop by another day this week ok? I'm so sorry for not being around as much. I feel really bad," I say.

"Oh stop it! Silly girl. You have a great responsibility in your life now and you need to remember that. Now go, go, go, shoo, go on shoo," she says with a cackle.

I do love Edith, she's such a strong character and I've always get the impression that she's been through a great deal in life that no one knows about. I place Eva back in her stroller and wander out towards London Bridge tube station. I like this station as it's easy enough to access with the stroller, and I want to make it to Waitrose on Oxford Street if possible as they have a lot of the things I want and need for Eva which I can't get in the other shops. We stop at Bond Street tube station. I exit and head towards John Lewis. Eva is gurgling away and laughing to herself. I'm glad she's such a happy little one.

I have no idea why, but as I look at her, I think to my dream again of Pete returning. I don't know, these thoughts and dreams are becoming more frequent each day, and I can't help but feel there's something more to it.

I gather my shopping which turns out to be far more than I planned on buying and decide to hail a taxi to head back home. There's no way I could manage all of the bags and a baby, so it makes sense. When I reach the flat as I enter the lift, I have this odd feeling like someone is outside or nearby watching me, and I can't understand why I feel so uneasy. I continue to make my way to the first floor in the lift to deliver most of the shopping, and Eva, inside the door. I rush out again to grab the last three bags downstairs. As I glance towards the gates, I see Enrico standing there pacing up and down.

"Enrico, Enrico," I shout. He glances up and sees me.

I beckon to him to come in. "Come in, say hi to Eva?" I ask.

He nods and makes his way through the gate slowly. I feel relieved to see him and he looks good.

"Hey," I say as he walks towards me. I open my arms to hug him and give him a kiss on the cheek. "You look great," I say.

"Thanks, Katie, it's great to see you," he says. "I'd really like to say hello to Eva. I think she must have grown lots since I saw her?" he asks.

"Yes, she has and I know she'll be very happy to see you. Come on up," I say.

"Oh, go! I take these for you," he says.

I run up the stairs this time as I'm literally only twenty seconds, not even, from my doorway. Eva is happy chatting away to herself. Enrico is behind me with my extra bags in tow. *You're such a great guy.*

"Oh let me see my little beautiful princess," he says as he takes her from the stroller. Eva bursts into laughter the minute she sees him. I can see tears forming in his eyes. "I've missed you so much my little angel," he says as he hugs her tightly.

I can feel the tears welling up inside of me. *Enrico, why did we end up in this situation? You're such a great guy and I feel I've messed you about. Why does it have to be like this? When I see you with Eva, I feel you're exactly what she needs and I wish I could give you the love you deserve.*

I walk into the other room to hide my tears and start to unpack the shopping.

"She's a grown so much," he says with a laugh. I keep my back turned to him and I keep unpacking the bags as I don't want him to see my tear filled eyes.

"You know Katie, I understand why you did what you did. It's fine and I think I can be friends with you now," he says. "It make a lot of sense, and while I will always probably have the stronger feelings for you, than you will have for me, I know that I can see you as just a friend. And I want to see Eva and have her in my life. It's good?" he asks.

I turn to face him. For the first time in months, I feel proper relief. I still want him in my life, but I can't handle the idea of me pretending to be in love with him just to have him there. I'm glad that I have been honest and open with him and I'm glad that he still wants to be around, and be there for Eva.

"That's the best news I've heard in months," I say with a smile.

We sit and chat for a few hours. I make dinner and he eats it heartily. It feels good that we can sit and talk like that again. I'm feeling good and from what I can tell, Enrico is too. I feel we are finally heading in the right direction and things might get back on track after a few months of upheaval.

43

My phone rings. "I'm here, I'm in Heathrow Airport. Aghhhh, can you hear me clearly now?" says the voice on the phone.

"Ha ha ha, Sarah ya loon, I can hear you loud and clear. Is lover boy with you?" I ask.

"Yes, Drifter is here. He's excited to meet you. Ok, bags are on the carousel, just going to collect them and we'll make our way then. We'll probably just stop to change at the hotel first and call over then. I can't wait to see you and Eva!" she says.

"Me too lovely, me too. Take your time, you have two weeks at least here, there's no rush," I say. Myself and Eva aren't going anywhere fast.

I decide to give the flat one last tidy up. My OCD is ridiculous of late and there's not really a great deal to tidy, but I plump the cushions again. I check that the food I've prepared is ok and hasn't gone too soggy or gone the opposite way, and dried out. Eva is sound asleep and so I take a few minutes to relax on the couch. Before I know it, my phone is ringing, and I jump with fright.

"Hello, Miss. Are you there? We're outside at the gate, but didn't want to ring the bell in case we'd wake herself," Sarah says.

"What time is it? I nodded off on the couch. I must check on Eva, I'll let you in then," I say.

I look at my watch. *Feck! I've been asleep for over an hour. Still no noise from Eva, she's sleeping well lately.* I peek into the cot. She's snoring soundly, and I leave her be. I know her good sturdy lungs will let us know shortly that she's awake and ready for attention. I look in the mirror and fix my hair as I know Sarah and her new man will take their time coming in knowing that I nodded off. I put on a little lipstick, and wipe the sleep from my eyes. *I can't believe I nodded off and into such a deep sleep.*

I fix my skirt and head towards the door. I open it thinking they'll be standing outside, but there's no sign of them. I leave the door ajar as I know they will probably be observing the new rockery which was built outside. It's quite impressive the way they've landscaped it all. The plants and shrubs are beautiful. It's something Pete would have loved as he liked plants, and had many of them in his flat. I wander in to Eva again and I can see she's getting a little restless, but I don't want to wake her up yet, just to say hello. They will be here for a few hours and that will give them plenty of time to give her cuddles and kisses. I hear a shuffling noise as I wander towards the hallway.

"Helloooooooo!" the voice says.

"Woo hoooo come in girlie, how are you?" I ask. "Where's himself?" I enquire with a smile. *I can't seem to bring myself to call him Drifter without wanting to laugh. I'm hoping he hasn't got a stash of drugs in his pockets.*

"Oh, he's outside observing the plants and the landscaping. He'll be up shortly. Is that new?" she says.

"Yeah, they completed it around two weeks ago. It looks really good, certainly brightens the place up. Anyway, enough about that, how are you. Give me a hug," I say.

"How are you? You look amazing, got your old figure back, and you just look fantastic," she says.

"Well so do you, got the old love glow going on there Sarah," I say with a laugh.

"I know, he's great, just wait! You're going to love him, you are going to love him," she says with great aplomb.

I turn to make my way to the sitting room and she follows me.

"Sarah, darlin', where are you?" says the voice from the hallway.

"Shhhhh, we're in here. Eva is asleep so keep the voice down please?" she says.

I stop myself from sitting down as the footsteps get nearer, and he walks in.

"I closed the front door, I assume you'd want that?" he whispers with a smile. "I'm Drifter, pleased to meet you darlin', I've heard a bit about you, but not enough. This one tells me you have quite a story to tell?" he says as he shakes my hand.

I can hardly move as I look into his eyes and as the tears well up I say, "It's, it's lovely to meet you too Pe...." I stop myself just in time. "Drifter...it's nice to meet you too," I say as the tears stream down my face.

I glance at Sarah whose face drops. She runs from the room screaming in hysterics "NOOOOOO! NOOOO! This can't be happening!! It's not fair!! Just NO!!!!"

The noise has woken Eva. I don't know where to look. I cannot move. I feel paralysed, apart from the tears that trickle down my face. *I don't understand this. Why have you been brought back to me in this way? Sarah's right – it's just not fair!!*

Pete just stands there, looking lost, not understanding what's happening.

The End

Elaine Cremin is a native of Cork, Ireland. She lives in London and makes a living working as a PA. *Somewhere Out There* is her second novel. She has yet to challenge herself with the screenplay she'd like to pen one day, but would like to write more novels before getting to that stage. If you enjoyed this book, Elaine's debut novel *Waiting for a Star to Fall* is also available in paperback and on kindle.

    Connect with Elaine at:

    www.facebook.com/Elaine-Cremin-395650717281865/ or

    www.twitter.com/ElaineCremin

www.ingramcontent.com/pod-product-compliance
Lightning Source LLC
Chambersburg PA
CBHW051420170626
46809CB00006B/2250